SPY

MELISSA K. MORGAN

DEDICATION
For Jeff, I love you.

CHAPTER ONE
STEVEN

The stench of motor oil haunted me in my dreams and the heat of the C4 explosion against my back made me sweat.

Months later, I still found myself going back to the night Randall Hawks died. I'd been a part of his crew for several years, trailing him at first, then getting on his good side to become his right hand man. Every single aspect of my job centered around gaining as much information as I could to report to the boss. Not Hawks. Sure, he was the leader of his crew and I was on his payroll, but he wasn't my boss.

I belonged to another group, a much more powerful one that made what Randall Hawks and the Silvers do look like a children's theater group. No offense to Mickey Silver, of course. He was a fucking badass and stopped at nothing to get his girl back. But my uncle, Roman Cuccione, was the Don of the Mafia on the East Coast.

Dragging a hand through my hair, I inhaled a deep breath before letting it out slowly. I was no longer in California. I was back on my own turf in New York, which was a completely different animal compared to the laid-back lifestyle out west.

Tossing the sheets I'd been tangled up in aside, I got out of bed. It was barely dawn, but there was no way I'd be able to fall back asleep. I'd been sleeping like shit the last few weeks since coming back. Maybe it was due to the fact that I wasn't allowed much downtime.

I walked out into the small main area of my one bedroom apartment. It wasn't much, but it had a great view of Central Park and was quiet. I'd leased the place when I was twenty, before leaving for a job that took far longer than expected. Thankfully, my uncle kept the rent paid for me so I could come right back after everything ended.

My last mission had become far more involved than I originally expected. When I took the job initially, I'd expected to be in and out within a year. Over five years later, I was a grown man as well as a different person. It wasn't the senseless violence that broke me or the copious amount of illegal activity I'd seen. It was the people I met that had suffered the consequences of another man's actions. The innocents forced into a lifestyle they hadn't asked for. One of those people was a woman who is still like a sister to me.

Cynthia was my brother's fiancée. They'd just gotten engaged when Randall Hawks murdered him in cold blood and kidnapped her. She was the main mission from day one. My uncle ordered me to Washington to retrieve her, but when I got there, I found so much more.

Randall had quite the evolving business, including trafficking women and selling narcotics. I couldn't simply kill him and take her back without first discovering exactly what he was up to. So I sat back and waited, gaining what information I could while kissing his ass to earn trust. I hated pretending to be his yes man, loathed acting like I had little intelligence in his endeavors.

Every ounce of intel I had I reported to my uncle and the others. Then the Silver crew was introduced and a cut and dry mission became more intensive than we could ever imagine. Jack Silver was just as corrupt as Hawks and much more established. He single handedly controlled the sale and use of drugs up and down the Washington border through Oregon. When Hawks was brought on to work with them by

Jack's son Mickey, I was forced to wait even longer in hopes of taking down both crews.

Little did I know that Mickey Silver no longer wanted to be involved in the business and was eager to see both his father and Randall Hawks burn as much as we did. I made the executive decision to help him out. Okay, maybe it wasn't quite my decision. One of his men had a gun to my head and it wouldn't have ended well for me so I had no choice but to blow my cover. Which wasn't something I made a habit of doing. The vow I made to my uncle years ago was etched into my skin.

I spent the last year in Northern California at Hawks' estate before we ended him. After that, I helped with clean up and setting up a group of men on the West Coast.

Randall was dead. However, in my nightmares, he was still very much alive. I was haunted by the memories of my time with him, the way he'd intimidate and abuse those around him. The way he'd intimidate and abuse *me*. I took one for the team, so to speak.

But I'd take my secrets to the grave and tamp down the feelings of anxiety and fear that plagued me. I had to because it was already time to start my next mission. Work would keep me occupied and eventually the memories would disappear. At least, that's what I kept telling myself. The job never got easier, no matter how much violence I saw or was involved in.

As a kid, I had a knack for smooth talking and moving around undetected. I'd always been sly and determined. My aunt Betty said I got that personality trait from my mother. She was always quick on her feet and everyone that knew her fell in love with her.

I would have to take her word for that. Both my parents were killed when I was five years old. They'd died in a car accident during a really harsh winter, so my siblings and I were raised by our aunt and uncle. It's why I held tight as much as I could to Celeste, my sister and only immediate family left.

Roman didn't balk at my demands to ensure her safety and promised a guard was always appointed to her. Now that she was in college, I worried about her ability to keep her wits about her, but she lived off campus in a secure building and knew extensive self-defense.

I grabbed a bottle of water from the refrigerator and swallowed it all in one long tug. I had a few hours to kill before meeting Giovanni Daleo, my uncle's capo and the one that supervised my missions and placed me where I needed to be, so I decided to go for a run. Putting on a t-shirt and hoodie with a pair of sweats and my running sneakers, even though the cold of the late February air was physically painful, I kept my head down with ear buds in my ears, letting the upbeat music drown out the constant sounds of the city while I ran through Central Park.

Physical exertion helped me a lot. I found exercise useful in reducing my anxiety and helping to sort my thoughts. I was both metaphorically and physically moving forward while running from the past I desperately wanted to leave behind.

I'd never known a life outside the Mafia. Before they passed away, my parents were just as involved as my aunt and uncle, so it wasn't new for me. There was a rumor that we were distant relatives of Al Capone and my fascination with the old gangsters in history only amplified my pride in the work I did.

I wasn't interested in switching professions but being gone as long as I had made me certain that New York was where I belonged. Maybe I was a little homesick, too. I was grateful my next job would keep me here for the time being.

After my run, I went home to shower and change before my meeting with Gio. We were scheduled to meet at Moonlight Tavern, a local bar that Grim's grandfather owned.

Elliot "Grim" Hargraves was one of our resident hitmen. At only twenty-seven, he was one of the best and well on his way to a lucrative career. I'd grown up with him and even worked with him a few times when we were both soldiers starting out.

Typically, the bar wasn't open on Sunday mornings, which was why we'd always meet up here. Grim let me in the door, slapping me on the back.

"Good to see you, man. How are you acclimating to being back home?"

I walked to an empty bar stool, taking a seat. "I'm slowly adjusting." Everyone knew I wasn't the same since being back, but I didn't like to go into detail about the reasons why.

He sat next to me, clasping his hands together and leaning his elbows on the countertop.

"You know I would have been there if I could. They had me catching cartel scum over in Buffalo."

I nodded. He'd been eager to be a part of the takedown of Randall Hawks, but between me, Mickey Silver, and some other guys on my uncle's crew, we were able to handle it. That's just how Grim was though, always ready for action.

He'd earned his nickname for his clean shots that killed instantly. He was like a machine. It was almost as if he had no conscience, or maybe it'd been buried deep. I wondered if he felt anything at all. His laid-back attitude given the work he did always confused me.

"We handled it. In fact, the last captive was the one to pull the trigger. She'd been more than willing after what she went through."

"No doubt. I heard Hawks was a real piece of shit."

I snorted. "That's putting it lightly."

Gio appeared from a door behind the bar. Wearing a charcoal gray suit and black tie, the man was always dressed to the nines, which made me and Grim, both in jeans and jackets, look like peasants before him.

"Fab, you made it," he said, offering a quick smile.

I flinched. I still wasn't used to being called my real name after years of going by my alias. It was as if that genuine part of me was lost now. I had a very typical Italian name and was given the first name Fabiano after my father. But I couldn't tell everyone my name was Fabiano Cuccione. That'd draw too much attention. My middle name was Stephano after my grandfather, which I adopted as Steven. While on the job, I used my mother's last name, Cline.

"I'm here," I said.

"Good. I know you've only been back for a short time, but I've had my eyes on a few gangs in town and it's time we infiltrate and see what more they're hiding," Gio said.

I nodded. This was usually how it worked. Gio would put a man or two staking out suspicious activity. Once he gained enough evidence and feared they were working against us, he'd send me in to get information.

"There was a shootout down by the docks a couple of weeks ago. We know that Sebastian Gallo was involved. He's protecting something in a warehouse there that's locked up tight. Word on the street is a few cops are on his payroll helping hide whatever is in there."

"Drugs or weapons?" I asked. It didn't take a leap of logic to realize whatever he was hiding was illegal. Those were always the two main choices because they made the most money.

A small smile formed on Gio's face like he was proud of me for having that knowledge. "We have reason to believe they're hiding weapons. Not just hand guns and silencers, either." His gaze shifted to Grim and I followed it.

Grim turned toward me, his vivid green eyes lighting up. "I was on the roof of an adjacent warehouse, casing the place. Low and behold, out walks a guy with an open crate. We're talking high powered assault rifles, automatic machine guns, and grenades."

My brows inched up. "No shit?"

He nodded, grinning.

Gio spoke again. "That kind of arsenal is something we don't want on the streets here or anywhere. Someone is buying or selling the weapons for the Gallos. I placed a few soldiers around the city to follow their men and they ended up at one place in Manhattan."

"Who's in Manhattan?" I asked.

"Albert Ricci."

Ricci was a well-known man in New York City. His father had taken up residence in the city decades before I was born. At one time, he and Uncle Roman's father were friends. That was until Vincenzo Ricci tried to kill my grandfather.

Albert typically made his money in real estate but dabbled in illegal gambling groups underground. As long as the Riccis didn't infringe on our own business endeavors, we left them alone. However, we still kept an eye on them since their track record wasn't good for staying out of trouble. Meanwhile, the Gallo family was known for testing their limits many times but followed the rules for the most part. If they were providing weapons of that caliber to known enemies, we had a massive problem.

"You think he's selling the weapons for Gallo?" I asked.

Gio shrugged. "Could be, we're not sure why else one of Gallo's men would pay him a visit. He might also be buying them and that makes Roman nervous. Albert Ricci has threatened before to take down the Mafia."

My uncle didn't like things chaotic. He was incredibly level headed and preferred structure and routine. Confronting the Gallos and potentially starting a war wasn't a choice. We had to be precise, do things carefully.

"So, what's the job?"

"The Gallos are locked up tight. They never recruit outside sources. However, Albert Ricci needs a few new guards. Particularly one for his daughter."

I raised a brow at him. "You want me to be some girl's bodyguard?" The last thing I wanted to do was stand around while some teenager went shopping and called her friends.

"She's not just *some* girl," Gio said, his eyes narrowing slightly. "She's Aida Ricci, princess to Albert's throne. She's twenty-two and deadly as hell, wrapped up in a pristine package."

"She works for him," Grim added. "She knows the ins and outs of his business, handles a few jobs here and there when needed, and is our best shot at gaining information."

Well damn, that would be incredibly helpful. "What's the protocol?"

"I've got a contact who knows his requirements for the position. You'll meet with Albert in two days for an interview."

I nodded. An interview was more than just meeting in some high-rise office and talking about my strengths and weaknesses. I'd have to prove my worth, my strength, and skill as a soldier. That shouldn't be too difficult considering I'd done that and then some in my previous jobs.

"You think he'll let just anyone guard her? Hell, her father won't want some random guy protecting an asset like her."

"You're not a random guy. Remember when we sent you to Hawks?" Just hearing that name made my skin crawl. "I'll have a resume forged up for you. It's our best option."

Working with the enemy wasn't new to me. It was the smoothest way to gain intel when we needed to act quickly. But I wasn't sure I was up for another round of being a boss man's bitch. I certainly wasn't prepared to be cut to pieces by some woman who thought the world revolved around her.

Loosening a breath, I dragged a hand through my hair. "How much?" Gio shot me a questioning look. "Celeste has tuition due for Spring Quarter. What's the pay?"

He smiled briefly. "I'll talk to Roman. You were put through hell over on the West Coast and it hasn't even been a month since you got back. What's your price?"

I felt I was worth more than my uncle could pay at this point. But I needed the money to ensure my sister received the best education possible and would be set for a few years until she found the right job after graduation. If I could pad her trust a little more and make enough to ease up on the jobs in the next few years, I'd be happy.

"Half a million," I said. "If it gets sketchy like the last job, I'm pulling out. I won't go through that again."

"What exactly happened to you the last five years?" He was merely curious, which was understandable. But that wasn't a road I was going down any time soon.

"Talk to Roman." I got up from my chair. "Tell him my terms and have him call me if he's got a problem with it."

I didn't stick around for a response.

AIDA

My father thought it best if I had a bodyguard. Like some sort of modern day princess in his little kingdom, I needed protection at all times. The fact there might be threats on my life didn't bother me as much as it should. But then again, my lifestyle is and always has been … unique.

I knew the only reason for the new guard was due to my father's latest business venture. I was well aware of the facets of his job and what it entailed. Real estate investment? Yeah, right. I'd learned the truth years ago when I was thirteen and walked into his home office to find Marcus, his right hand, and another guy, cleaning their guns while covered in what looked like soil and blood.

Instead of being terrified and running in the other direction, I'd been curious and started spouting off as many questions as I could about what they'd done until my father grabbed my arm and ordered me out while reminding me to knock first.

I've always been inquisitive and probably less cautious than the average person, but I was still alive so I didn't see it as a problem.

Obviously, I knew right from wrong and when to fight or flee. I wasn't stupid. It's just that the line of business my family was a part of seemed so thrilling and exciting to me. It was like a real life movie or TV show playing out in front of me. There was drama like a modern soap opera thanks to my stepmother and her taste for the finer things and there was chaos when my father would declare war on a person or group of people who'd done him wrong.

We always had soldiers and guards around the house and accompanying us if we took trips to other cities or states. I'd been monitored and tailed my whole life. So having an appointed bodyguard wouldn't be all that different. Although, they'd be all up in my business constantly. That is, if they were anything like Marcus.

My father's go to guy, Marcus Pelossi, was groomed to be the perfect second in command. He'd never been married, liked women younger than his forty, and creeped me out with his longing looks and comments. Those didn't start until a few years ago, after I turned twenty. Now, he was my personal guard until the man my father wanted to hire could start.

The last few weeks had been awful. Marcus posted outside my apartment, walking just behind me everywhere I went, and waiting like a glorified stalker outside the door of my office when it was time to go home for the night. People definitely noticed, and I thought it careless of him to be so blatant about my safety.

If I had a target on my back, his behavior would only lead the enemy toward me. Maybe with a specifically appointed guard I could gain more of a social life. My father has always controlled where I go and what I do. He didn't want me interacting with people he hadn't approved first. I was barely allowed to go shopping, let alone take a vacation by myself. It made me feel like he didn't trust me or think I can handle myself even though I've proven, time and again, just how strong I am.

I was twenty-two after all. I deserved to start living a normal life despite my father's occupation. Especially since his latest endeavor didn't sit right with me. I didn't agree with his business arrangement with the Gallo family. He was becoming too bold in his ultimate goal of taking over New York and eradicating the Cuccione Mafia.

It's not like I could disagree and call him out on making a mistake by working with the Gallo family though. He'd probably threaten to end me himself if I impeded on his plans or questioned him. He might even cut me off which meant goodbye job or any chance at ever having one again.

I worked for him as a liaison when needed and as his accountant. The last one he had was caught embezzling and that mistake led to his execution. My father trusted me not to take what wasn't mine and offered to pay me a steady wage.

To say my father was protective would be an understatement. He didn't have a son to pass the business down to and hoped that I'd step up to be his rightful heir when the time came. They were big shoes to fill and I wasn't looking forward to it, but again, I had little choice in the matter.

It was difficult not to be involved when my very future depended on the knowledge of who my father was and where he came from. It was important to me to know as much as I could because a day would come when I would take over and I wanted to be on the living side. It's why I was thoroughly trained to fight physically and knew everything there was to know about firearms since the tender age of fifteen.

As I waited for my father to arrive at my apartment, I curled up in my favorite reading chair in my living room and picked up the romance novel I'd started yesterday. This one was about a young girl who'd fallen in love with a man older than her. I loved romance novels and wasn't terribly picky on tropes or triggers. It simply depended on my mood.

I was caught up in a summer camp and horseback riding scene when my doorbell rang. It had to be my father. The apartment building was so secure that they wouldn't let just anyone up to the seventh floor to wander the halls. Sighing, I set the paperback down on my ottoman and went to the door.

My father stood in the center of the doorframe in a suit and tie, overwhelming my threshold with his typical scowl. "Are you ready to pick your new employee?"

"Sure," I said, grabbing my jacket from the back of the couch. "Although it would have been nice to narrow down the prospects from the beginning."

He frowned at me, stepping back into the hall. "I needed to ensure each candidate was who they said they were. It's politics, paperwork. Nothing you need to worry about."

I quelled the urge to roll my eyes as I locked my door and followed him down the hall to the elevator. How my father expected me to run his business once he was gone without knowing *everything* was beyond me.

It wasn't unusual for him to keep me in the dark about certain business practices. He either saw me as a threat for some unknown reason or thought that little of me because of my sex. I was aiming more toward the latter. My father only ever hired men, viewing them as more level headed and capable. Even though I knew just as much as his soldiers, and trained like one, he couldn't fathom any other woman working with or for him.

Once we stepped off the elevator and out the secured doors of my apartment building, we were met by Demetri, another man of my father's, standing outside a black town car with the door open.

He smiled at me as I slid into the back seat, followed by my father. Demetri was older than Marcus, closer to my dad's age, and the kindest of all his men. I'd known him my whole life and considered him more of an uncle than an employee.

Demetri got into the driver's seat and merged out into traffic, heading for the warehouse outside the city where I would be hand selecting my new guard. The applicants would be instructed to complete simple tactical tasks against each other and be rated based on skill. That was probably already happening with Marcus overseeing the operation. I'd be focused on their ability to look me in the eyes. The last thing I wanted was some guy that gave off creep vibes like Marcus did. I wanted someone who would do their job well and leave their personal life out of it. Someone who was capable and intelligent, who wouldn't hover.

The fact my father was allowing me to choose surprised me. When he'd come to me a few weeks ago and insisted I have an appointed guard, I'd thrown a temper tantrum the size of Texas. I eventually caved when I demanded I choose the candidate and he agreed to it.

The drive to the warehouse was short despite the late afternoon traffic. As I got out of the car and headed inside, I caught sight of a man standing to the left of me with his arms crossed over his broad chest, head tilted in the direction of a group of men sparring with each other.

His hazel eyes met mine, narrowing slightly. I gave him a quick once over before continuing to the middle of the large room. The men sparring froze when they noticed me and my father just a few steps behind.

"Good afternoon," I said with a slight smile.

Each of the men stepped back, forming a line from left to right. The man I'd seen when walking in joined the rest. He was tall with broad shoulders, powerful yet graceful in his movements, wearing a pair of black cargo pants and a fitted gray t-shirt. Some of the others dressed similarly and a few wore their street clothes.

"You're here because you were chosen for a job that's highly important," my father began, perusing the seven men. "I've gone through your resumes, your backgrounds, and all other important information. This job is not only critical, but also classified and confidential. Ultimately, one of you will be selected to work as a personal bodyguard for my daughter."

Each of the men seemed to go wide-eyed at that, blinking at me with mixed looks of awe and curiosity. Except for the hazel eyed man. He barely spared me a glance, keeping his gaze fixed on my father who continued speaking.

I liked that he didn't seem affected by me, that he was willing to listen and pay attention.

Marcus appeared from the shadows with a gun in his left hand. He smirked at me before settling on the recruits and handing the gun to the first man in line, one who looked younger than me.

"Next, I'm going to have you take turns shooting a target. It is imperative that you aim to the best of your ability. This position may require you to use a weapon in order to protect her. We need to know you're capable of making a clean shot."

"You're going to aim there," Marcus added, pointing toward the far wall. A red circle was painted on a pallet leaning against it. "Hit the bullseye, if you can."

Marcus came over to stand on the empty side of me. "How are they fairing so far?" I asked.

"A few of them are doing very well."

I stepped back and watched as one by one, each man fired a shot at the target. Three of them were close to the bullseye, one hit it dead on.

"Incredible," my father murmured beside me as the man with hazel eyes handed the gun back to Marcus. "What's your name?"

"Cline, sir," the man responded, placing his hands behind his back.

"Cline. You're a great shot. What formal training do you have?"

"Military, sir," he replied. "Marines."

My father turned to look at me with a wide smile. "He's quite capable."

"Quite," I muttered, glancing at Cline. "How old are you?"

"Nearly twenty-six," he replied.

I nodded. "You're young. Are you fresh out of the military then?"

"I've been working as a personal guard the last few years."

"For whom?" I asked.

"A congressman in Chicago. Roberts was his name. He no longer needed my services."

"You have no other obligations? Nothing that would keep you from diving in to do the job?"

He shook his head, shifting his gaze to my father before landing back on me. "Nothing." He was a great shot and carried himself well. Out of all the men, he seemed to be one of the few who didn't check out my body.

"He's been top of the class during the training so far," Marcus added.

I gave Cline a genuine smile, holding my hand out in front of me. He glanced at it, raised a brow, then took my hand. "Congratulations, Cline," I said.

He gave my hand a slight squeeze before releasing. "Thank you, Ms. Ricci."

"Aida, you can call me Aida."

His hazel eyes sparkled at me. "It's a pleasure, Aida." He turned away from me then, going back to stand against the wall.

I drew my eyes away from Cline, scanning the other men and taking note of the way they watched me. "Thank you for your time. You are dismissed," I said as Demetri escorted the men away. "Welcome to the team," I told Cline before heading for the exit.

I'd done my job and there was no need for more pleasantries. Besides, I was sure I'd learn enough about him once he started working for me.

My father left with me, allowing Marcus to deal with the new employee. He'd be given just enough information to allow him to do the job, no more and no less. We were always careful with just how much we shared, especially with new people.

"That was quick and painless," I said as Demetri weaved through the early evening traffic.

"Yes, you did well. Now we can move on to bigger things."

I rolled my eyes as I stared out my window, watching a man in a taxi head bang and smack his steering wheel. I wondered what he was listening to and wished I could listen to music in the car, but my father didn't like background noise.

"Bigger things?" I asked, even though I really didn't care.

I loved my father because I had to, but that didn't mean I respected him. Albert Ricci was a violent man with a wicked temper, and I'd seen that side of him more times than I could count. You might think I'm heartless, but you don't know what I've been through. What I've sworn to keep secret in order to stay alive. I've been used and abused the better part of the last ten years.

The moment I hit puberty, everything changed. Maybe if I'd had a mother growing up things would be different, but she died when I was young, killed by the man my father loathed more than anyone, Don Roman Cuccione. The man he was trying to take down even if it ended in his own demise.

To be honest, I wouldn't be sad to see my father go. It was a guaranteed death sentence no matter what weapons or connections he had. I didn't agree with it, but I couldn't change his mind. Even if the Don did kill my mother, there was nothing I could do to change the fact she was gone and my father wanted revenge.

"If we can get Gallo on board to hand over his weapons, we'll be ready to fight for control of the city."

"Does the Gallo family know you plan to use the weapons to overthrow the current order?" I asked.

"It's none of their concern what I do with them. I simply need to acquire the arsenal."

"And how do you plan to do that with no money?" It was a dig at him that earned me a vicious snarl.

It wasn't my fault he'd gone into debt with another gang a few months back and lost the ability to purchase the weapons outright. Maybe if he didn't try and swindle every damn person he came into contact with he'd actually get something right for once.

All my father cared about was power and control. He didn't care who he hurt or stepped on to get there, including his own blood.

"Mind your tongue, daughter," he snapped.

I picked at my chipped nail polish. "Is there anything else you need me for? I'd like to go home."

He shook his head, his eyes slightly softer than before. "You'll be needed tomorrow night for a gathering of colleagues."

I stiffened. "What? Why?"

"Because in order to get what I want from Gallo, I had to cut a deal. You will still work for me, while also becoming Mrs. Sebastian Gallo."

Surely, I hadn't heard him correctly? He was pawning me off on a man twice my age as collateral? "That's not fair!" I shouted.

"Do not raise your voice at me," my father warned in a low growl. I huffed out a breath. "Do you want fair or do you want this business to keep running? You can't have both."

I wanted a completely different life. One that didn't involve having to choose between happiness and surviving. But I wasn't dealt such a fate so I kept my mouth shut. I didn't even know what I could say at the moment.

"Thank you, and remember, it will be worth it. This business is your legacy, don't forget that."

How could I forget when he'd been beating that into my brain since I was old enough to understand words? Everything Albert Ricci did claimed to be for the greater good, but it was growing more and more difficult to believe that when he stepped on everyone, including me, to try and better himself.

CHAPTER TWO
STEVEN

"You're already back to work?" my sister asked before taking a sip of her coffee.

She'd been thriving at school, had a ton of friends and a social life that made me twitchy. I couldn't keep track of the number of people that said hi to her in the last half hour while we sat at a café on campus.

"I don't have much of a choice," I said. "Roman needs as much information as possible before going after Ricci. If he acts now, he'll start a war and that's the last thing we need." I didn't expect Celeste to understand the semantics of it all. In fact, I wanted her to know as little as possible. It was my goal to protect her and allow her to live in the real world free from unending violence and fear.

She nodded, trailing a finger over the lid of her coffee. "You'll be careful, right? I can't stand the thought of you leaving again." There was a sadness in her eyes that made my heart squeeze.

I had little communication with her over the course of the last five years because I didn't want her implicated if shit went south. She was the first person I saw when I got back and she cried in my arms for hours. I didn't want to put her through that again. Hell, I didn't want to put myself through it.

I reached across the small table, covering her hand. When her eyes met mine, they were laced with tears. "I won't leave you like that again. I promise. I'm staying in New York for this job."

"Is it safer than the last one? I know you went through a lot there." I opened my mouth to object and she shot me a knowing look. "Don't tell me you're fine. You're different, Fab. Darker and more closed off."

I released a heavy breath. "I'm not going to lie to you. The things I went through were … rough." Memories of a night a few years back flashed in my mind. *A man with a hunger for control who enjoyed punishing his subordinates.* There were scars on my body from what he'd done. However, it was the invisible ones that haunted me more. "It doesn't matter though. I'll be careful. Don't worry about me, okay?"

"I'm your sister and I love you. It's in my DNA to worry," she argued.

"I know, but I'm older. It's my job to take care of you, not the other way around. It's a bodyguard job, that's all."

She snorted. "Yeah, guarding a woman who's probably just as lethal as her father. Who knows what her motives are? What if she catches on to you and tells her father? They won't keep you breathing once they know who you really are."

I was well aware of the risks. It's not like this was my first time walking into the lion's den. "Don't worry about that," I said. "Roman agreed to my payment, so you'll be set for your final year of school. I can do this, Celeste."

She squeezed my hand before sliding hers away. "Just promise me you'll be careful."

"Always."

I changed the subject after that to something more casual, asking her about her classes. She began speaking excitedly about a design course she was taking that was overseen by a woman who worked for a major fashion company. Happiness for my sister filled me as she spoke about her passion.

After hugging her goodbye, I headed back to my apartment in the West End to prepare for my first night of work. As I stepped off the elevator on my floor, my phone started ringing in my pocket.

"Hey," I said as I unlocked my apartment and stepped in.

"You've got a meeting setup with Albert Ricci this afternoon?" Gio asked.

"Yeah, I start tonight. The second in command wants me working Aida and Gallo's engagement event." I wandered into my bedroom, sitting down at the edge of the bed.

Before I left the initiation at the warehouse yesterday, Marcus told me that we were debriefing later in the afternoon so I could get my gear before officially guarding Aida.

"You sure you're ready for this?"

"As ready as I'll ever be."

Gio grunted. "Good. All we need is to know exactly what Albert's doing with Octavio and Sebastian Gallo. It'd also be nice to have solid information on why he's interested in the weapons."

I bent to unlace my boots before kicking them off. "Got it."

"I'm emailing you more information on Aida Ricci that I got from my contact. Good luck tonight. Be sure to touch base when you can."

"Thanks,"

"Yep." He disconnected the call and I tossed my phone on the bed.

I needed a shower to clear my fucking head. I'd already been preparing myself for the job. It was increasingly easy as time went on to withdraw from my surroundings and simply observe. I wasn't sure if that was a good thing or a bad thing. I tried to keep my mind blank, to not allow any emotions to seep in whenever I was working. I'd gotten so good at it over the last few years that I wondered if I even knew how to tap into real feelings anymore.

Sometimes I toyed with the idea of quitting, if only to gain back the part of me I lost with Hawks. But then I didn't know what the hell else to do with my life. Besides, I enjoyed my line of work. I felt useful, fulfilled. Actively doing things helped distract me from the shit I'd been through and if I were forced to dwell on my past, I'd probably go insane.

I took a long shower, letting the water run cold, numbing my body. It wasn't until I was shivering that I turned off the faucet and toweled off. I got dressed and grabbed my laptop from the shelf next to my dresser before traipsing to the kitchen and grabbing a beer to calm my nerves.

Settling on the couch, I took a long tug while my laptop booted up. True to his word, Gio sent an email with information on my new target. I clicked on the attachment and began reading.

Name: Aida Rosemary Ricci
Birthday: August 22nd, twenty-two years old
Occupation: MBA in Finance – Accountant at Ricci Real Estate
Interests: Reading, shopping, animals, hiking
Aida Ricci was born in Albany, New York at St. Peter's Hospital. She's always been a curious girl full of questions and adventure. As a child, she enjoyed traveling with her parents to their estate in the Hamptons and spending time at the beach there. Her mother, Alana Ricci died when Aida was young. An unknown assailant murdered her. Aida is a quiet girl with an interest in literature and math. She graduated high school with a 4.0 GPA and valedictorian of her class.

Aida knows self-defense, taekwondo, and can hit a moving target with a 9mm pistol.

Damn. They weren't kidding about her being able to defend herself.

The bio was typed up and perfectly formatted. Gio had a contact that worked in a local government office. He knew everything about everyone and had been gathering information on various people for the Mafia the last twenty years.

But none of this information mattered to me to be honest. I'd do my job of keeping her safe, but I didn't give a shit about her high school career and interests.

I took another drink of my beer and rubbed my forehead with my index finger.

This was just another job. One that would be nothing like the last. I could do this.

Albert Ricci wasn't Randall Hawks, and Hawks was dead and gone. I screwed my eyes shut, shaking my head as another memory popped up. *Hands around my throat from behind, the sound of a blade being sharpened and a low growl in my ear as I was pressed against a concrete wall.*

My hands began to shake as I drained the last of my beer. I stood up, marching to the window and staring down at the people coming and going in the park. He couldn't hurt me anymore, couldn't take anything away from me. Not that I had much left to give anyway.

I remember Claire, Mickey Silver's girl, asking me once why Hawks threatened and gawked at her but never acted on it. I lied and told her he was all bark and no bite. It was his thing. Little did she know that every ounce of frustration he had was taken out on me instead because I put myself between him and the women intentionally.

I was beat up, stabbed, and broken down mentally. I was countless shades of fucked up thanks to that son of a bitch.

Yet the worst was over now. In time, the memories would fade. They had to.

AIDA

I'd been a prisoner in my own home the last day, literally trapped within the walls of my apartment. Demetri was posted outside my door in case I tried to make a break for it. My father had told the door attendant and front desk of my building to contact him immediately if I was seen outside. It was such crap.

The only silver lining was being able to get out tonight for the first time in what felt like forever. Even if it was more of a business event for my father. Not much better, in the grand scheme of things, but at least I would get to be in a different location. However, I wasn't happy about the reason for this party. Being expected to marry Sebastian Gallo made me nauseous.

I'd met him a handful of times over the last few months after my father decided to work with the Gallo family, and he made me uncomfortable. He was always watching me with this gleam in his eyes, like he knew something I didn't. I wondered if it was his idea for us to marry, or my father's way of solidifying his plans.

I was dressed in a beautiful evening gown that was a deep blue color, which accentuated my eyes. My hair was done up in a high bun. A flashy diamond choker wrapped around my neck, feeling exactly like a collar. Maybe my father and Sebastian would have a matching leash for me once I arrived.

I tapped one of my silver pumps against the marble floor impatiently. Apparently, my new guard would be escorting me to the party and I was to wait for his arrival. He wasn't off to a good start being late. The anticipation of what tonight would bring weighed heavily on me. I didn't want to be Sebastian's arm candy. I didn't want to be a wife.

Ten minutes later, there was a knock on my door. I glanced at the clock, rolling my eyes. The party was to start at six and it was already quarter to. We were running late and that soured my mood further. I was ready to make a passive aggressive comment upon opening the door, but instead, my breath caught in my throat.

I gaped at the man before me, dressed in a black tux with a matching tie. My eyes shifted from Cline's perfectly disheveled hair to his feet, which were clad in cleaned up leather boots. His lips tipped up in the corners, hazel eyes sparkling in the golden light of the hallway.

"Hello, Aida." His voice was deep, yet smooth. My muscles clenched low in my belly.

He certainly cleaned up well. "Hi," I said, suddenly feeling flush.

His eyes trailed over me like a soft caress. Sticking his hand out, he said, "We weren't properly introduced before. I'm Steven Cline."

I glanced at his hand, noting his long fingers and the small tattoo at the base of his thumb. Was that a heart? When I looked up at him again, his smile had faded.

"We're running late," I blurted. "Forgive me, *Steven*, but I'm not in the mood for pleasantries." I didn't like that my heart rate increased under his perusal. I hated that I liked it.

He dropped his hand and shrugged. "Suit yourself."

Huffing out a breath, I snatched my clutch from the table near the door and stepped out into the hall. Steven waved a hand in front of him, allowing me to lead the way. Rolling my eyes, I headed for the elevator, catching a whiff of his scent. He smelled like leather and rain. My stomach dipped further.

"You look nice," he said as we rode the elevator down to the lobby.

"Thanks, so do you," I mumbled, staring at the closed doors.

"Are you looking forward to your party?"

Rolling my eyes, I shook my head. "Not exactly. Did they tell you this engagement was without my consent?"

He frowned at me. "I'm sorry."

I nodded. "Yeah, me too."

We spent the rest of the ride in silence. I wasn't in the mood for small talk with this man I'd only met once before and knew nothing about. His job wasn't to be my friend, and I couldn't risk voicing my true feelings with my anxiety at an all-time high. The last thing I wanted to do was confide in an employee.

Steven stepped closer to the elevator doors at the sound of our arrival to the main floor. They slid open and he stepped out, placing a hand out to me. "Let's go."

Ignoring his hand once again, I walked by him toward the entrance. A black town car was waiting for us; Demetri seated in the driver's seat as usual. He was the one that typically drove me where I needed to go. Steven opened the back door for me, closing it soundly the second I got in, then slid into the passenger seat easily despite his height.

The journey through traffic was quiet, which I was grateful for. I stared out the window as we passed crowded sidewalks and flashing lights. It wasn't until we were on the freeway that Steven turned around in his seat, glancing at me.

"Mr. Gallo is expected to announce your engagement tonight and your father would like you to meet them both in his office when we arrive."

"Fine," I replied, going back to staring out the window.

It wasn't uncommon for my father to throw a party to celebrate new beginnings. He'd done it with the O'Hares last year before screwing them over and not paying them back fully. Yet another reason I didn't respect the man who raised me. Once I took over the business, I'd pay back every debt he owed, even if it meant saying goodbye to his too large house and front company.

When we arrived at the sprawling mansion tucked back away from the city, my stomach turned. I attempted a few cleansing breaths to calm my nerves but it didn't help much. I should have eaten before. I was hungry and that only made my mood worse.

There were already a lot of people at Sebastian's house based on the number of cars coming and going in the half-circle driveway. I took a deep, cleansing breath again as Demetri parked in front of the entrance. Steven got out and opened my door for me.

I stepped out onto the gravel drive, nearly rolling my ankle on the rocks. He caught me by the elbow, steadying me. *Damn these spiked heels.*

"Thanks," I muttered, pulling away from him. My legs were trembling like crazy as we made our way into the house.

My guard stuck close to me as we navigated through people I didn't recognize toward the back of the house. I followed him down a hallway off the foyer to a door that was partially closed. I recognized my father's voice and Sebastian's coming from inside as Steven gave two solid knocks on the door, waiting for a reply.

"Come in, please," Sebastian said. His voice was gravelly and rough. Like sandpaper.

I absolutely could not be stuck with him. I was living the worst nightmare imaginable.

Pushing the door open, Steven waved me in. He looked at my father. "She's here, sir."

My father smiled at him. "Thank you. Please, wait outside."

Once the door was closed, my father's calm demeanor changed. His angry eyes focused on me. "I expect you to be on your best behavior this evening."

Sebastian raised a brow at him, his lips curving up. "She'll be fine, Albert." He shifted his gaze to me. "Won't you, Aida?"

"Sure," I said with a slight shrug. *As long as I can have a glass or five of wine.*

As if able to read my mind, my father said, "You're allowed two glasses of wine. No more than that. I wouldn't want you acting foolishly in front of these people. This is business."

"Ye of little faith," I muttered with an eye roll. "I'll be on my best behavior, *Father*," I added snidely. That earned a look of contempt but I didn't care. I was a show pony, nothing more.

Sebastian cleared his throat. "I'll be giving a speech, thanking everyone for coming to celebrate us." He stepped closer to me, placing his finger under my chin, forcing me to meet his gaze. His eyes looked a dull brown, lifeless. "I'm the luckiest man."

My blood went cold. How could he want me when he didn't even know me? Bile rose in my throat. I glanced back and forth from him to my father who stood from a chair in front of Sebastian's desk.

"She'll be a great wife to you. Aida is incredibly loyal and obedient," my father said, narrowing his eyes at me.

Sebastian's gaze lowered to the front of my dress, lingering on my cleavage. I wanted to vomit. How was I going to get out of this?

Sebastian released me and took a sip from a small glass he had on his desk. "Your new guard has been given strict orders to keep an eye on you. While we don't expect any enemies tonight, we can't be too careful. You will not so much as use the bathroom without him knowing. Understand?"

The look on his face reminded me so much like my father's that a shudder ran through me. There was no way in hell I could pretend to love Sebastian Gallo, let alone *like* him. My heart kicked up.

"I'm not marrying him!" I choked out. "I … can't. I don't want this." I shot my father a pleading look, hoping to find any sense of remorse in his hollow gaze. Of course, there was nothing but irritation with me for speaking my true feelings.

"You'll do as you're told," my father said, his face coloring red.

It felt like I'd been kicked in the chest. I couldn't get enough air into my lungs as both men stared at me. Sebastian's eyes scanned the length of me again, amplifying the fear coursing through me.

"I like you, Aida. You're a beautiful young woman, the perfect pet for me." He purred.

"And you're a Ricci," my father added. "A *noble* woman with class and kindness. Don't forget your role here."

The ever-humble servant forced into a life I didn't ask for. How could I ever forget that? I quelled the urge to be a smartass. "Father, you can't be serious. Why should I have to marry a man I don't know?" I could feel tears pooling in my eyes and tried to fight them back. Crying was a weakness and I couldn't appear vulnerable to them right now.

"This ensures our agreement is solid and binding," he replied.

"It's my life," I argued, lifting a hand to my heart. "You're promising my life to a man for a business dealing!"

Sebastian cleared his throat and I gazed at him. "It will be a good life, Aida. I'll take care of you. You'll want for nothing."

Shaking my head, I sniffled as a tear escaped, rolling down my cheek. "This isn't what I want," I said in a broken whisper. Everything felt so much more real right now. The mere thought of him touching me again broke my heart.

"Sometimes we have to do things we don't want to for the greater good. You know that. Our families will be merged, what's theirs is ours now and vice versa," my father said.

I narrowed my eyes at him. This was all a ploy for Gallo weapons and his ridiculous vendetta against Don Roman. I was merely a pawn in my father's twisted game of control. A game he would surely lose if the Mafia knew what he was trying to do.

I wished that I could say something, turn him in. It wasn't that easy though. He didn't care who he hurt in the process, and if he found out I was willing to rat him out to his number one enemy, he'd probably kill me. Just because I was blood didn't mean I wouldn't have consequences.

"I'll come find you when it's time for the announcement," Sebastian said. "For now, you can mingle. Enjoy some food, though pace yourself. Can't have you gaining any weight." Sebastian eyed my hips, his brow creasing slightly.

I didn't care for the look of disdain on his face and if I were any less of the lady they claimed me to be, I'd happily punch that self-righteous smirk. I was curvy. It was in my DNA and I couldn't change it. Not that I wanted to anyway. So my hips were a little wider, big fucking deal.

"May I be excused?" I asked in an overly polite tone.

"There's a lot riding on tonight. Remember that" my father reminded me.

I only nodded before turning for the door again. When I opened it, Steven was planted to the right, leaning against the wall of the hallway like a loyal sentry.

Ignoring him, I continued down the hall toward the main living area where the party was being held in search of a glass of wine. *Only two glasses? We'd see about that.*

A man dressed in a white collared shirt and black slacks appeared with a tray of white wine. I snatched one up, continuing toward a table with a variety of appetizers laid out.

I popped a mini crab cake in my mouth and then another. Steven stood beside me, silent. "If I had the choice, I'd marry a man who genuinely loved me. I wouldn't care about his station in life or what he could do for me," I said quietly.

I risked a glance at him and found him eyeing me curiously.

"And I'd eat whatever the fuck I wanted whenever I wanted and he'd let me." I devoured another crab cake then went for a handful of blueberries. "There's worse things in life than having a little meat on your bones." Not that he would know. He was tall and built like a Greek God.

His shoulder lifted in a slight shrug. "Like a man who forces his daughter to marry someone she doesn't want to."

I smiled tightly. "Yes, that's way worse." I took a healthy sip of my wine, scanning the room.

I didn't know any of these people. They probably didn't even care that Sebastian and I were betrothed. This was a show put on to benefit my father.

I really wished I had someone in my corner right now. I had no one to talk to, no one to listen to me vent. I wanted to upturn this damn snack table, wanted to scream and storm out. Releasing a heavy sigh, I took another sip of wine.

When were they planning to have us get married? The food I'd just eaten turned sour in my stomach as I realized I could have mere days, months at most, to be single. Sebastian would take my virginity. He'd be the only man I would ever be with.

Panic filled me and I closed my eyes, trying to regulate my breathing. When I opened them, I searched the room again. A few people glanced at me between conversations, offering short smiles. I caught sight of Marcus who was speaking with my father while surveying the crowd for any ne'er-do-wells.

I finished off my glass of wine and snagged another before heading toward my father, who shot me a look, reminding me to behave. I plastered a fake smile on my face, ignoring my new guard who stood against a far wall while I was paraded around and introduced.

After an hour of introductions to people I didn't care about, I felt the urge to fake sick and leave. Every once in a while, I'd glance over at Steven, noting how he watched the room carefully. It seemed that he took his job more seriously than I'd anticipated. He was moving around the room slowly, as if trying to listen in on the many conversations.

His face was stoic and slightly menacing despite the boyish quality of it. I wondered if he ever relaxed, ever had any fun. I couldn't picture him out at a nightclub dancing the night away or simply lounging on the couch in front of the television. He probably did nothing but work out in his free time.

Suddenly, my father gripped my arm. "We're getting ready for the announcement. Do not mess this up for me," he growled low.

Releasing a sigh, I gazed up at him. "I can't believe you're letting this happen."

"It's the only way, Aida."

That couldn't possibly be true. In fact, if he'd paid his debt to the O'Hare family and let go of the past, we wouldn't even be here in the first place.

"One day, everything's going to blow up in your face," I whispered harshly as I moved closer to where Sebastian was waiting. I hoped to be the one to light the fuse.

CHAPTER THREE
STEVEN

Aida wasn't what I expected. So far, she'd spent more time alone, hiding against the wall, instead of engaging with people. I thought she'd be more outgoing based on her demeanor the other day at the initiation. I also expected her to be okay with the engagement to Gallo.

She was definitely rattled from being forced into marriage to a man she barely knew. The fact that she'd voiced her irritation had me wondering if she liked her father at all. If that were the case, I'd hopefully be done with this job sooner than I initially thought.

In between watching out for Aida like the job entailed, I spent my time checking out the other guests at the party. Sebastian Gallo dominated the room in his three-piece black suit. He had this air about him as if he were God's gift to the world. Every single person, including Albert Ricci, kissed his ass and sung his praises while giving him their undivided attention.

Octavio Gallo, his father, was the same. I had yet to hear anything incriminating against them, but I doubted they'd talk a lot of their supposed weapons in this setting.

Albert's right hand, Marcus Pelossi, stood by while stalking Aida most of the evening. He seemed incredibly interested in every movement, which at first I thought was due to a fear that she'd flee. After a while, it was clear he didn't like the attention she was getting.

I was studying the way he tracked her steps toward Sebastian. His jaw muscle clenched. Was he not happy about this engagement, either? He turned toward me and I looked away quickly, toward where Aida and Albert were. She looked visibly upset as he whispered something to her.

Marcus stretched his hand out, grasping my shoulder. My heart rate spiked and I stiffened. He released me with a crooked smile. "Why don't you get yourself some food or a drink. You must be bored, standing here all night."

I met his eyes. "I'm working."

He grinned, nodding. "Your dedication is appreciated. Albert made the right decision in hiring you." He clapped my shoulder again before heading toward some men near the back of the room.

I didn't trust Marcus. A second in command was the liaison between the boss and everyone else. His interests were for the betterment of the boss only. He should be content with being number two. This guy struck me as more of an opportunist, and the more he looked at Ricci's daughter, the more I wondered if he felt something for her.

At our meeting this afternoon, he'd given me a run down on what I needed to know, which wasn't much. Aida didn't have a life outside the business. At all. The woman spent most of her time in her apartment, locked in a tower like some sort of medieval princess.

I got the feeling she was only kept around for the sole purpose of how they could utilize her for leverage or payment. It seemed clear that's how she was being used with Gallo.

Gallo placed an arm around her waist and she winced as he pulled her into his side. He left his hand rested on her hip while his father clinked a knife on his crystal glass, signaling the imminent speech.

Once the room quieted down, Sebastian spoke. "I'd like to thank you all for coming this evening. It is with great pleasure that I announce Aida and I will be getting married at the beginning of the summer."

People applauded the news and murmured amongst themselves. I watched as Aida's eyes widened slightly before falling to the marble floor beneath her.

"It may seem unexpected, but her father and I are developing a lucrative business relationship and that includes getting to see this beauty often." He drew her closer to his side, and I didn't miss the way she cringed. "I had to have her." He chuckled and winked as the crowd laughed in blind happiness.

Aida's blue eyes lifted to mine. There was a sad desperation in her gaze, as if she were willing me to save her.

Even if I wanted to, which I didn't, I couldn't save her from whatever fate her father planned for her. I was here for the information my uncle needed to take down her father and also the man she was set to marry. What she did with her life, if she still had one once we were done, wasn't my problem.

I shifted my attention to Albert who gave a slight wave when Sebastian mentioned him. The entire party seemed more like a way to solidify a deal than anything else. It was a way for Albert to publicly kneel to Gallo's mercy. I needed to figure out what their intentions were.

When Sebastian was finished rambling about how much he was looking forward to Aida making an honest man out of him, and the relationship he'd develop with her father, he lightly shoved her away and mingled with the crowd some more.

She looked relieved to be away from him. I made the decision to play off her frustration and hopefully gain some trust.

Grabbing a glass of sparkling wine, I made my way to her as she seemed to numbly walk toward the edge of the room, near a hallway. Now that the announcement was over, it seemed no one cared about her attendance any longer. When I stopped in front of her, she glanced up at me with tears in her eyes. I frowned.

I was used to seeing women cry in my line of work, but for some reason, her tear-laced eyes affected me differently. A twinge of concern mixed with pity as I noticed the look of confusion and sadness on her face.

"Follow me," I said quietly as I brushed by her down the hall.

She did as I said, glancing toward her father and Marcus who weren't paying any attention to us. I pushed open a closed door, finding a bathroom, and reached for her hand. My palm warmed against her soft skin as I guided her into the small room and flicked on the light. I kept my back to the hall, leaving the door open so as not to raise any suspicion should anyone come our way. The last thing I needed was to be caught behind a closed door with this woman.

I held out the glass of wine to her.

Her lips parted and she blinked up at me. "Thank you."

"You looked like you could use another drink," I said, giving her a short smile.

She took the glass, immediately bringing it to her lips and taking a healthy sip. "Oh my god." She moaned and the sound was like a jolt of lightening rushing through me. "This is so good."

I chuckled in spite of my present station. It was kind of adorable how much she revered food and drinks. I wondered if she was often limited in her enjoyment by the men who controlled her. Maybe she wasn't as independent as I'd originally perceived her.

"I don't want to marry him, even if he can help my father." She bit down on her bottom lip, shaking her head. "It's a fruitless attempt anyway."

I didn't speak, didn't move as she let out a heavy sigh. I wanted to ask why they were working together and what Albert's intentions were, but it wasn't the right time.

She frowned at the wine and then looked up at me again. "Why are you working for us?"

I wasn't expecting her to ask me that. "You hired me," I said with a shrug of my shoulder.

She gave me a tight smile. "Yes, but why did you apply?"

"I need the money," I said simply. It wasn't technically a lie.

"For what?" she asked and there was nothing but curiosity in her gaze.

I decided to be as forthcoming as I could in an attempt to work toward gaining her trust. "My sister."

She smiled again. "That's sweet." She finished off her wine, handing me back the glass. "I should probably make my presence known again before my father realizes I'm missing."

She headed back out to the main room while I covertly set the glass on a table nearby.

I hung back from her, staying close to the far wall while I watched her approach her father. He put an arm around her briefly, whispering something in her ear. Her body seemed to stiffen at whatever he said and I scowled at Albert Ricci's back.

How could he pawn off his own child like this and why did Aida put up with it instead of standing up to him? I felt sorry for her.

Her life was at risk once the Mafia found out exactly what his business with Gallo entailed. He was a known enemy to us and this deal with Gallo, trading his daughter, put her in a dangerous situation. Did he think about what consequences might arise for her should he be caught? Did he care at all if she ended up in the crossfire?

Thankfully, the party began to fizzle out after another hour. I needed to write down all I'd discovered about these groups so far and was more than ready to get out of here. Demetri texted me on the cell phone I'd been given to let me know he had arrived to take Aida home. Albert thanked me for watching out for her before I escorted her to the awaiting car.

The ride back was quiet and I found myself wishing I was seated in the back with Aida to see her face. I heard her sniffle a few times and knew she was trying desperately to hold it together. The poor woman was stuck between a rock and a hard place, being forced to marry a man she didn't love or run the risk of disappointing her father.

I wondered how Albert would react if she stood up to him and told him no.

Once we were back at her building, I followed her up to her floor to make sure she was safely tucked back inside. One of the requirements of my new job was to move into the building as well, which I'd spent my morning accomplishing. They wanted me close in the event the building security was breached. My new apartment was down the hall from hers.

Aida pulled a key from her small purse before unlocking the door and turning around to face me. "Thanks again for the extra wine," she said with a sad smile.

My chest tightened when I noticed the red around her eyes. She'd definitely been crying in the back seat. I stuck my hands in my pockets as the sudden urge to comfort her sprang to life. "No problem."

Her head tilted slightly as she studied my face. "You should quit."

My brows raised. "Excuse me?"

Shrugging, she said, "I'm willing to bet that your experience would be better served elsewhere. You shouldn't get wrapped up in my father's business."

"I can handle myself," I said.

Was she seriously worried about me? I didn't understand her sudden concern for my wellbeing.

Her eyes scanned over me from head to toe as if sizing me up. "I'm sure you can but trust me, you don't want to get tangled up in this lifestyle."

I frowned. "What's wrong with this lifestyle?"

She seemed to think of a response for a few moments, chewing on her plump bottom lip. When she spoke again, she gazed at the wall behind me. "It can be brutal, dangerous. My father is a selfish man and he doesn't care who he hurts to get what he ultimately wants."

I nodded. That didn't surprise me. She was being forthcoming right now, and since we were alone, I took the opportunity to pry a little.

"Why does he want you to marry Sebastian Gallo?"

Her eyes flicked to mine again. "It's a business transaction," she stated matter of fact. "He needs me to secure favor with them." The rejection in her gaze was evident.

A pang of regret shot through my chest. She was being used and she knew it. She'd accepted her fate without putting much fight into it. That bothered me. Aida didn't deserve to be treated like an object. No one deserved that.

"Why does he need favor with the Gallo family?" I
asked and immediately regretted it. I bit back on my molars.
That was a loaded question and the hesitation in her gaze let me
know I was crossing a line. A guard wouldn't need to know the
answer and shouldn't be asking.

"I … can't." She hung her head. "Goodnight, Steven."

She turned away then, leaving me staring at the gold
numbers on her apartment door as it closed behind her. I
muttered a curse as I dragged my hand through my hair.

Aida Ricci was more than just a pretty face with a
legacy to uphold. She was intelligent, she was loyal. It was also
evident that she seemed to have a heart. She cared about others,
unlike her father. I was using her to get to him and she'd
thanked me, told me to get out while I could.

Little did she know I was in this life deeper than she
realized. I was destined to remain in the Mafia forever. It was
my duty, my birthright. I couldn't save her. Just like with
Claire and Cynthia, I'd have to hang back, let whatever was
happening unfold while trying to gain information. Once the
job was done, I'd walk away again. I'd move on to the next one
while the parts of my soul that I'd been born with shattered
away from me, leaving nothing but an empty man.

After the party, I didn't feel much like doing anything the rest of the week. I ended up staying in, binge reading the series I'd started earlier in the week. Staying tucked into my apartment had its benefits. I didn't have to deal with Marcus or my father.

By Sunday afternoon, it finally sunk in that I was truly engaged to Sebastian Gallo, a man I didn't know and didn't like. My life as I knew it was over. I spent the rest of the day in bed, crying and drowning my sorrows in a pint of chocolate truffle ice cream and a bottle of rosé.

I went to work like normal on Monday morning, only this time Steven escorted me. I was surprised to see him when he knocked on my door as I was getting ready to leave. Apparently, since the announcement of my betrothal, my father wanted to ensure I was watched at all times. I wouldn't be surprised if that was more likely him thinking I'd run away, or if he truly feared I'd become more of a target to our enemies now.

I managed to spend the entire week avoiding my father and that suited me fine. I didn't want to speak with him because I was afraid of what I might say. I hated him for his actions. Instead of throwing a pity party and crying over what he expected of me, I chose anger toward him. It made me feel better.

Friday afternoon, just as I was getting ready to leave for the day, my father called me into his office. Steven had arrived to escort me back home and hung back in the lobby to wait for me. He was quiet and didn't hover. I liked that about him and was grateful that at least I had a decent guard despite the reasons for hiring him.

My father sat behind his large oak desk when I entered. His arms were crossed and he tracked my every step as I sat in the chair across from him.

"How are the books looking?" he asked.

"They're fine, everything's in order. We'd be better off with an extra hundred thousand though."

He grunted. "We'll get there soon enough. With the engagement officially announced, we can start taking inventory from Gallo and selling part of the stock they received."

"Who are you selling those weapons to?" I asked out of mere curiosity. I'd heard it wasn't regular guns and ammo, but larger contraband like automatic assault rifles and machine guns. I overheard Marcus mention explosives as well at one point.

"That's none of your concern," he replied calmly.

Scoffing, I shook my head. "Of course it isn't. I don't need to know anything because Sebastian will take over instead of me, right? Once we're married, what's mine is his."

He squinted his eyes and leaned forward over his desk. "You're extremely disrespectful for someone who will be set for life."

"A life I don't want!" I shouted. "You're marrying me off like an archaic tyrant. This is bullshit!"

He pounded a meaty fist on his desk, startling me. "Keep your voice down," he warned in a low growl. "You will not speak to me that way."

"I'd rather not speak to you at all," I sneered.

His face reddened in anger. "Your marriage to Sebastian ensures immunity for you. They can offer safety should the Mafia come sniffing around."

"If they're not already," I mumbled.

He glowered at me. "They're not, I would know. With my resources, I can sell off a few of the weapons to pay our debt to the O'Hares. Once that's done, I'll implement my plan to take over the city. The Cuccione family will be nothing."

Despite the loyalty forced upon me by my father, I knew better than to openly mess with the Mafia. Especially when they'd spent a great deal of time and energy on keeping a well-oiled machine like New York City running smoothly. Even the drug dealers were on their payroll. No job was too small, no person unimportant.

They had eyes on *everyone* and it would only be a matter of time before my father was implicated and disposed of. This new relationship with the Gallo family would raise concerns for sure. I truly wouldn't be surprised if they weren't already looking into this sudden business arrangement.

"Does Octavio Gallo know what your intentions are?" I asked, my voice smoother than before. "Does Sebastian?" Most people were smart enough not to pick a fight with Don Roman. If my father wasn't clear on his plan to the men he was getting those weapons from, they might cut him down before the Mafia ever got the chance.

He uncrossed his arms, resting his elbows on the top of his desk. "I want to be out of debt and I will do whatever it takes to make that happen. Besides, I'm not getting any younger, Aida. If I don't act now, there will be nothing to leave behind for you."

"You don't think I can run things on my own? That I'm not capable without Sebastian Gallo?"

He quirked a brow, a slow grin spreading across his face. "It's a man's world. You'd be strung up and robbed blind if I left you everything." His lips curled up in a sneer. "You're too careful and kind, like your mother was. People take advantage of that."

Indignation filled me and I glared at my father. "I don't want to marry Sebastian."

"My hands are tied." He lifted his hands. "It's done, and I can't go back on my word. Not if we want to do business with them."

I stood slowly, crossing my arms. "Fine," I said. "I'm going home for the night."

"Goodnight, Aida. Take the weekend to blow off some steam. We'll begin wedding preparations in the next couple of weeks." Dread filled my stomach like a lead balloon. "Also, I'll need you Monday evening for a job."

"What job?" I asked, trying not to panic over the fact that I was about to be involved in planning a wedding. My wedding.

"I need eyes on Jonathan Thompson."

I blinked at him. "The bank investor you just sold a condo to?"

He shrugged. "He owns a night club downtown and knows someone interested in buying some of the Gallo armory. I want you to talk with him, discuss a deal."

"Marcus can't do it?"

"He's needed for something more pressing." *Of course he was.*

"Fine," I said again before leaving.

I grabbed my jacket and purse from my office before meeting Steven in the lobby.

"You heading home?" he asked, tossing a magazine he was flipping through back down on a side table.

"Like I have a choice," I muttered, pushing open the glass door of the entrance.

*

The intrusive thoughts of my imminent doom started to get to me. I began to wonder what my life would be like once I was married to Sebastian and no outcome made me feel better. An overwhelming sense of defeat pushed me further and further into depression. I couldn't shut my brain off, couldn't stop worrying about the future my father mapped out for me without my consent.

Would I be a prisoner in Sebastian's home, only allowed out when it suited him? Would he demand that I attend events with him and share his bed whenever *he* felt like it? What was to become of me once I said, "I do"?

I felt trapped. There was no way to get out of this unless I ran straight to Don Roman and told him what was going on. Although, that might not end well for me. If the man murdered my mother as my father claimed, he might kill me, too. There was a deep hatred between our two families that I never fully understood.

I couldn't just disappear, either. Even though the thought of hopping an international flight seemed more and more appealing, I knew I'd eventually be found by my father. He was persistent. He'd surely enlist the help of my fiancé and I'd be captured and dragged back here. I'd also likely be punished for trying to flee. I didn't want that.

My only other option was the one that led to my death. It seemed morbid, but I was quickly growing tired of having zero options. It was either end it all now or continue suffering under the thumb of my terrible father.

He'd spent my whole life training me to be an accessory, his tool for business. I felt used, stupid. The only ounce of freedom I ever had was when he allowed me to take care of dirty jobs for him. The best years of my life to date were when I was training with the other soldiers and out on the streets, catching snitches and making them pay. How sad was that?

I feared that I wouldn't be able to do any of those things once I became Sebastian's wife. That word make my stomach hurt. *Wife*.

There was no way out unless I did the unthinkable and at the moment, with a heavy heart and busy mind, I just wanted it all to stop. I wanted to disappear for good.

There's a lot that can happen to a person by just taking one step. You might enter a room either empty or full of people. Maybe you'll meet the love of your life across the threshold of a coffee shop or bookstore. Maybe you'll take a left instead of a right and alter the path of your life entirely.

Nothing would ever be the same once I took my next step. No, my very existence would be ended. I was one step away from losing everything, and while the prospect of that might scare others, I wasn't afraid. For the first time in a long time, I was alone with my thoughts and looking forward to the nothingness I'd feel.

The sun began to sink beyond the tall skyscrapers as I stood on the edge of life and death, contemplating my final moments. I could turn around, hop down from the ledge and go back to my too large apartment that my father paid for, or I could move in the direction I was currently facing and land on the sidewalk below.

My mother would greet me in the afterlife; I was sure of it. My father wouldn't miss me. Neither would my stepmother who was rarely around. She happily stayed out of the business, reaping the benefits of the illegal activities my father engaged in.

Closing my eyes, I tilted my head to the darkening sky above, allowing the crisp, early spring air to dry my tears. I inhaled a deep breath, savoring the burn of my lungs as I continued holding it until my ears rang. Try as I might, the tears wouldn't stop flowing and my cheeks felt sticky from the mix of warm liquid and cool wind.

I opened my eyes, daring a glimpse of the world below. I'd never really been afraid of heights. My apartment complex wasn't as tall as some of the other buildings in the city, but it was high enough. I inhaled a shaky breath, running a hand through my long hair.

Just one more step. All I needed to do was take that final step.

"If you're gauging your descent, don't bother. You'll be too dead to care," a deep voice said from directly behind me.

I whirled around quickly, letting out a yelp as my foot slipped. A strong hand grabbed my forearm, yanking me forward. I was tugged off the ledge and he kept his hand locked around my arm tightly. I caught the familiar scent of leather and rain before lifting my head to see Steven.

I could just make out his face in the glowing light from inside the access door that was propped open. He didn't look happy. His smooth, almost boyish face was harsher than normal. He glowered down at me as I tilted my head back to meet his eyes.

"I wouldn't be doing my job if I hadn't stopped you," he said in a husky tone. "What the fuck were you thinking?"

"Let go of me!" I pulled my arm, trying to free myself from his grasp. He didn't release me.

"You're a risk to yourself. There's no way in hell I'm letting you go," he growled.

"What are you doing up here?" I glared up at him, still trying to escape his hold.

"That's not important, Aida."

I swung my free arm back before cocking my fist and propelling forward. The punch connected to his cheek with a loud thwack. He released me then and I nearly fell to the ground as I scrambled away from him. His hand flew to his face, rubbing at the faint red mark that was already forming, his nostrils flaring in anger.

Smiling, I crossed my arms. "Didn't think Albert Ricci's daughter could fight back? Well you're wrong." I gave him a once over as he continued staring at me, bracing his hands on his hips now.

He was wearing a pair of light colored jeans, his feet bare, and no shirt. I zeroed in on the well-maintained set of ab muscles and the chiseled chest. I was right about what he looked like underneath his clothes. There was a tattoo on his left pec with some sort of script, yet in the growing twilight, it was difficult to read.

When my gaze finally lifted to his, he was smirking at me again and my cheeks heated.

Damn it. I'd been caught staring.

"Why aren't you dressed?" I asked. My throat was suddenly incredibly dry.

His shoulders lifted in a lazy shrug. "I came out here to get some fresh air for a minute."

"Half naked?" I raised a brow at him.

He chuckled and the sound caused butterflies to spring to life in my stomach. He risked a step closer to me and I immediately took two steps back. He scowled, his thick, dark brows furrowing as he stilled.

"I wasn't sure what you were doing at first, but then I heard you crying and you spread your arms as if you could fly."

"You had no business spying on me!"

"Spying on you?" he asked in disbelief. "I live in the building, Aida. I didn't expect to come out here and catch you in the act of attempting suicide. That wasn't in the manual for guarding you."

There probably was an actual manual knowing my father. I wasn't happy to learn Steven lived in my building now. Although, it was probably more convenient than commuting every day to babysit me.

Scoffing, I said, "You should have just let me jump."

"And be responsible for your death? You clearly aren't capable of being left alone." He ran a hand through his hair, shaking his head. "Not that it's any of your business, but I was supposed to have the night off. Where the fuck is Patrick?" He gazed around the rooftop as if expecting him to appear.

I wasn't aware he was supposed to be guarding me, but then I didn't leave the building, so how would anyone have known to watch out for me here? Patrick was a guard for Marcus typically.

"No one was in the hall when I left my apartment," I said.

"You're supposed to call one of us if you're leaving."

"But I didn't go anywhere," I said with a shrug. "What would you have liked me to do, call you up and tell you I wanted to spend some alone time on the roof?"

His jaw muscle clenched as he studied me carefully. "Clearly you need a babysitter all the time." He pulled a cell phone from his pocket, swiping across the screen before placing it to his ear. "Patrick? Aida is up on the rooftop."

"Snitch," I muttered.

He ignored me, listening for a moment. "Yeah, I thought you'd like to know." His eyes pinned mine again. "Move an inch and I'll tackle you. Got it?"

I didn't respond. Instead, I lifted my middle finger in his direction while shooting him a glare. Screw him for tattling on me.

"Yep, will do." He slid the phone back in his pocket. "Let's go." He jerked his head toward the access door that led back into the building.

"I'm not going back in there." I clenched my hands into fists, planting my feet as he stalked toward me.

"Would you prefer it if I throw you over my shoulder? Don't think I won't do it."

I huffed out a breath. Honestly, I believed he *would* do that.

"Fine," I bit out before marching toward the door. Damn him for coming up to the roof and snitching on me to another guard.

Sure enough, when I entered the hall on my floor, Patrick was standing outside my door. He gazed at Steven with a tight smile on his face.

"Didn't expect her to go up instead of down," Patrick said as we approached. "I was in the lobby."

"That mistake could have cost her life!" Steven roared. I froze a few feet from my door as he marched around me, getting in Patrick's face. "I'll be sure to let Albert know you weren't on task tonight."

The other guard swallowed roughly, placing his arms up in front of him. "Take it easy, Cline. She's fine."

Steven's jaw ticked as he glowered at him, his hands balled into fists at his side. While I hated that he'd caught me on the roof, I couldn't help but be stunned by his protective behavior. He genuinely seemed to care that I'd put myself in danger. It may have only been because he'd lose his job and probably be killed by my father, but still.

He backed off Patrick, pushing open the door to my apartment. His furious eyes met mine. "Get inside. Now."

I decided not to talk back this time. With a quick nod, I slid by him. He closed the door soundly behind me, leaving me alone.

I scrubbed my hands over my face and through my hair. So much for getting out of this. A mixture of irritation and relief swept over me as I sank onto my couch, pulling my knees to my chest. What would happen once my father found out?

Steven saved me tonight. I wasn't entirely sure it was worth the effort yet, but he'd done something no other person had ever done for me. He was worried about me. Whether it was simply due to his job to protect me or something else, it didn't matter. He'd taken initiative, ensured I was safe.

In all the years I'd gone on jobs for my father and worked with other men on his team, no one had taken cover for me, let alone stopped me from doing whatever I chose to do.

Even that one time I'd been in a stake out a few years ago with two other soldiers. We'd been watching a dealer who owed my father money and it was time to collect. I'd waltzed right up to him while the other's stayed behind. I'd been the one to strong arm him into paying up.

I was never afraid to get my hands dirty, which was a benefit in my father's eyes, but he'd had no one watching my back. If things had gone south, I seriously doubted either of the guys I was with would have defended me. They were there to do the job and go home after getting paid.

Did my father ever genuinely care about me or love me at all? In a matter of minutes, Steven had shown more toward me than my own father. That brought on a whole other level of sorrow.

I'd been competing for his attention my whole life and just when I thought he viewed me as an equal partner, I found he was only using me to gain favor with Octavio and Sebastian Gallo. Just like he'd been using me to do jobs no one else wanted to do. Once he found out I'd tried to jump from the roof, what would his reaction be?

Would he be glad I lived or sorry I hadn't gone through with it?

My mind drifted to Steven up on the roof and in the hall when he'd torn apart Patrick for not watching me. Thinking of my guard wasn't much better than whatever future my father planned, but it was a lot more appealing.

He'd been basically naked apart from the jeans hanging low on his hips. The memory of his body in all its muscular glory sent a flood of warmth through me that settled between my legs. It was dangerous territory to be attracted to him, but I couldn't help it. Especially after his concern for my safety.

Letting out a sigh, I shook my head. Sure, he was hot, but he was off limits. Besides, I wouldn't know what to do with a man like him even if I had the chance. I'd barely even kissed a guy and had little experience when it came to men. Not because I didn't want to. That wasn't my decision at all, it was one of my father's strict rules. I wasn't to be touched.

I'd be willing to bet a million dollars that was one of his selling points when offering me up to Sebastian Gallo. He'd probably always planned to trade me for his benefit at some point.

It occurred to me that maybe if I slept with someone, my father would have no choice but to break the contract of me marrying Sebastian. Perhaps Sebastian wouldn't want used merchandise. The thought of how I might be punished for trying something like that stopped me from acting on it.

I didn't want the wrath of Albert Ricci to come down on me. Father or not, he'd had no issue reprimanding me in the past both verbally and physically. Not knowing how he might react to my incident tonight terrified me as it was.

The sound of my front door opening startled me and the air got caught in my throat as Steven waltzed in, now clad in a white t-shirt and boots. He closed the door and crossed his arms, glowering down at me.

He was still upset with me and instead of fear, I felt that attraction to him amplify. It was difficult not to get lost in the intensity of those hazel eyes.

CHAPTER FOUR
STEVEN

After dismissing Patrick and convincing him to keep quiet about Aida's little act, I went back to my apartment to get dressed. I hadn't expected to see her on the roof when I went up to make a call to Gio. I also didn't expect her to inspect my body so thoroughly. The way she looked at me once she noticed I was only in jeans, sent a spark of awareness through me. That was a major problem considering our positions.

Albert had given me the night off and told Patrick to monitor the perimeter and keep an eye out at the complex since Aida seemed to be staying in for the weekend. I'd just woken up from a nap when I saw that I missed Gio's call. It's why I wasn't fully dressed, and the second I saw the way she was devouring me with that stare of hers, like a lioness at a feast, I knew I couldn't make that mistake again.

Aida was undeniably beautiful with her bright blue eyes and long hair that looked silky to the touch. Her curves were on full display tonight since she was wearing a crop top and leggings that fit like a second skin. If she were any other woman and the situation wasn't so serious, I'd probably make a move. But she was my responsibility and the only option I had right now to gain intel on Albert Ricci. Fucking that up because of my selfish desires would be the dumbest thing I could ever do.

Once I was properly dressed, I went back to her apartment to check on her. Seeing her standing on that ledge and hearing the pain and desperation in her sobs shook me to my core. I understood her desire to get out of the mess her father made, but there were much healthier ways to accomplish that. If I had to chain her to a damn chair to make sure she stayed in her apartment the rest of the night, I would.

I didn't knock before entering, startling her. Good. She felt something. Maybe she'd second guess standing on ledges from now on.

I crossed my arms, studying her carefully. The tears on her face had dried, her blue eyes sparkled up at me and I noticed a faint blush on her naturally tanned cheeks. What had she been thinking about before I walked in?

My curiosity took hold and some of the anger I felt toward her deflated. "Who else does your father have on guard for you?" I asked.

"Um … I don't know. I thought it was just you." Her brow crumpled in thought.

I nodded and moved further into her open living room, standing near the arm of the couch where she sat at the other end.

"Patrick won't talk if he knows what's good for him." That earned a gasp and I shrugged. "Figured you wouldn't want your father knowing about what happened."

"You didn't tell him?"

"No. I probably should since I'm his employee, not yours, but I won't breathe a word." I uncrossed my arms. "Why'd you do it?"

Aida opened her mouth to speak but no words came out. Her eyes pooled with tears and I frowned. I'd seen her cry more than smile since I met her. I wondered if she was this miserable all the time and those feelings of sympathy for her grew.

Dragging a hand through my hair, I took a seat on the opposite end of the couch. "Hey, it's okay," I began and she shook her head, swiping at her cheeks.

"It's not," she cried. "Nothing about my life is *okay*. I'm little more than a form of currency to my own father. He doesn't give a damn about me."

The urge to comfort her was so strong that my hands spasmed, yearning to pull her into my arms. As tough as I was when it came to my jobs, a crying woman always cut straight to my heart. It's why I helped Claire all those months ago when she was grieving what she thought was the loss of Mickey Silver. It's why I accepted whatever Hawks did to me in order to protect both her and Cynthia. It was the reason I refused to let my own sister get involved in this world.

"Did he always plan for you to marry Sebastian?" I asked, trying to gain some more insight into their little deal.

She hugged her knees tighter against her chest. "If it weren't him, it probably would have been someone else. He's in debt with a group and can't afford to pay them back. He's desperate to take care of it and the Gallo family can help."

"How?" I was hoping she'd tell me about the weapons. I needed to know if Albert was buying them for his own personal use or selling them for Gallo.

Her eyes met mine. "They have a particular supply that's incredibly valuable."

Albert was in debt to the O'Hare clan according to what Gio learned from his contact. Maybe he was selling their supply for them and making a profit to settle the balance.

"What kind of supply is it?" I needed to tread lightly here in case she caught on to my intense curiosity. However, I also needed confirmation that it was the weapons Grim thought it was.

She dropped her legs, her bare feet slapping against the marble floor. "It doesn't matter. All Albert Ricci cares about is being on top. He'll do whatever it takes, including selling his only daughter off like a piece of livestock." She got up then, heading toward the kitchen. "You want something to drink?" she asked as she opened the refrigerator.

"No, I'm good," I said, turning to face her.

She unscrewed the cap of a bottled water, leaning against the edge of the small island. I watched as she took a long drink, her slender throat rolling in a swallow. I bet the skin there was soft and would break between my teeth. I bit down on my bottom lip, stifling a groan.

Jesus, what the hell was I doing? A woman like her would be reduced to nothing under a man like me. Besides, she was off limits and an enemy to boot.

My head throbbed. I needed more fucking sleep. I shouldn't be here, trying to interrogate her for information when I wasn't able to think clearly.

I stood up, smoothing my hands over the thighs of my jeans. "I should get going," I began. She nodded, but her lips turned down as if disappointed.

Foolish girl. You don't want me near you.

"Can I trust that you won't pull the same shit you did earlier?" I asked in a stern voice.

Setting the bottled water on the countertop, she nodded slowly. "I won't go back to the roof."

"Or out a window." I arched a brow at her.

She huffed out a laugh. "I hadn't even thought of that."

My chest rumbled. "Aida …"

"I won't, I swear," she said. "I don't want to die. Truly. It's just that I feel so alone, more so than usual." I frowned at that. "I also don't want to marry Sebastian, but I can't run because they'll find me. I know they will and it feels like the only option is to end it all." She sniffed. "But I won't try that again. I'm sorry for making you work on your night off."

"You're my responsibility now. I'm only glad I caught you in time," I said.

She blinked at me as if I'd just told her the sky was yellow. "You're different than anyone I've ever met."

I shrugged, wishing I hadn't let my personal emotions get the best of me. I put my weakness on display and that was dangerous when I still needed to figure out what Albert was planning. It was also stupid because it's not like her and I would ever be friends. I silently reminded myself that she was an enemy's daughter.

"The more I know, the easier it is to do my job. If you're feeling cagey again, you can contact me. I'm just down the hall, number seven twenty-two."

She nodded. "Thank you." She tucked her hair behind her ear, turning away from me. "Have a good night, Steven."

Unsure of what to say further, I headed for the door, leaving her alone for the night. Once I was back in my new apartment, I called Gio.

"It's about time you called me back," he snapped.

"Listen, she almost killed herself. I was a little busy."

I heard him rumble out a growl on the other end. "What the fuck?"

"I went to the roof to call you in case they bugged my apartment or something. She was standing on the damn ledge, ready to jump." The image of her still seared in my brain. Five more minutes alone and she'd be splattered on the sidewalk below.

"Damn."

"Yeah." I'd made sure to check every inch of the apartment before getting dressed earlier and didn't find any suspicious devices. Still, I made my way to the bathroom and started the shower to drown out my voice before leaning against the bathroom counter. "She confirmed Albert's debt."

"What kind of business deal does he have with Gallo?"

"All she said was that Gallo has a valuable supply. She didn't confirm the weapons, but I'm not sure what else they would have. My guess is you and Grim weren't far off in your assumptions."

"That supply is likely military grade and foreign. Is Ricci selling it for them?"

"I don't know. She didn't give me anything further other than mentioning that Albert only cares about making it out on top."

"He might be planning an ambush on us then."

It would make sense for him to sell the weapons to cover his debt, and it would also make sense for him to keep them to try and take on the Mafia. For all we knew, he was planning both, but we needed irrefutable proof of that before confronting him.

"Are they starting business before the wedding?" Gio asked.

"From what I've gathered, they're in the beginning stages now. Albert's second in command went with Sebastian to some location outside Albany this morning. I'm sure it had something to do with the supply."

"See what information you can get over the next few days. Gallo has always worked in petty crimes and dealings, so with access to weapons, they're more dangerous than we thought. If we've got two groups against us, that's cause for quick action."

"Will do," I said before hanging up.

I shut off the shower and made my way back to the living room. This apartment was way too fancy for me. With marble floors and state of the art appliances and furnishings, I felt out of place. I was used to upscale, but I much preferred the simplicity of a well-worn couch and a comfortable bed. My mattress was one of those elite pillow top types and still I couldn't sleep well.

I grabbed a glass from the kitchen, filling it up with water from the sink before popping a couple of sleeping pills I'd bought from a drugstore and knocked them back.

As I lay in bed in the darkness, my thoughts wandered to the way Aida had looked tonight. The cool skin of her arm when I'd grabbed her was soft and she smelled like roses. Even broken and on the verge of taking her life, she was beautiful.

She seemed genuinely confused that I'd been willing to protect her. The fact she wasn't used to being treated well bothered me. She'd said I was different than anyone she'd ever met. Had she honestly spent the last twenty-two years being treated like nothing by her father?

I tucked my hands behind my head and closed my eyes. I needed to steer clear of any thoughts of her. Feelings for her of any kind, including sympathy, could potentially blow my cover. It wasn't my job to worry about her outside of the assignment.

I had this deep desire to help her regardless of who she was and what my goal entailed. Something about her crawled

beneath my skin, leaving me wanting to explore every inch of
her mind and body.

I wanted to believe that Steven hadn't said anything to my father about what had happened on the roof the night before, but I spent all day Sunday in fear that he'd call me or haul me back to live in his home. Even if Steven hadn't said anything, Patrick might.

By the evening, I finally began to relax. Although, I was still left curious as to why my new guard kept something so important to himself. I also wasn't sure how he'd convince Patrick to remain quiet.

Being left alone with my mind racing in a million different directions was driving me crazy, so I decided to go for a walk. However, that wasn't something I could just lace up my shoes for and go.

I had to contact Steven and he'd have to escort me.

I couldn't stop thinking about him the last few days. Something about him was different. He didn't seem eager to kiss my father's ass like everyone else. He didn't hover over me, either, despite the fact we now lived in the same building. It was nice to feel a small sense of freedom, having him look after me instead of Marcus or my father.

I threw on some sneakers and a jacket, tucking my keys inside the pocket. I wasn't sure if Steven would be up for walking with me, but I was desperate to get out for a while. I made my way down the hall toward his apartment, trying to ignore the ridiculous fluttering in my chest. I didn't like how excited I was at the prospect of seeing him again.

Releasing a breath, I knocked on his door and waited for him to answer. I counted to twenty and there was no response. Frowning at the door, I knocked again. Was he not home right now? I waited another solid minute before I heard the lock click.

The door swung open and Steven stood there, the lids of his eyes low and his hair completely disheveled. He was dressed, but his black, long-sleeved shirt looked wrinkled like he'd been sleeping in it.

"Um … hi," I said, lifting my hand in a small wave.

He yawned. "Hey, Aida. What's wrong?"

"Were you sleeping?" I asked, feeling like an idiot. It wasn't even six o'clock yet, but maybe he'd had a long day. I felt bad for knocking on his door.

He ran a hand through his hair. "Yeah, but it's okay. What's going on?"

I chewed on my bottom lip, fidgeting with a silver ring on my thumb. "I wanted to go for a walk. But I feel terrible now because you were sleeping and it's late. I should go," I rambled, starting to turn away.

"No, it's cool." His brow crumpled, his eyes, now more alert, scanned up and down the hall. "Wait here, I'll just grab my jacket." He closed the door and I leaned against the opposite wall to wait for him.

A few minutes later he appeared again, looking slightly more awake with his hair fixed to a more styled chaos. We headed for the elevators and waited for it to arrive on our floor.

"You sure I'm not troubling you? I feel bad …" I started to say.

"It's fine." He shot me a quick smile. "I don't sleep well, so I try to catch a nap when I can."

The doors slid open and he let me step in before him. "Why do you have trouble sleeping?" I asked as the elevator descended to the lobby.

He stuck his hands into the pockets of his leather jacket. "Occupational hazard from my previous employer."

"The congressman?"

"Yeah, he kept odd hours."

The elevator doors slid open and we wandered toward the exit. Steven gave a quick nod to the door attendant who let us out. Honestly, I half expected him to ask us where we were going. Did Steven have to report my whereabouts?

It was still partially light out thanks to daylight savings time and my mood instantly lifted. It felt good to be outdoors, to be away from everyone for a while.

"So, why the walk?" Steven asked as we headed south.

"I just wanted to get out. Being stuck in my apartment more often than not really kills the serotonin."

He nodded. "That it does.

We walked next to each other, me on the inside, furthest from the busy street. Even on a Sunday evening, the sidewalks were crowded in places. Steven's arm brushed my shoulder a few times. I tried to pretend that he wasn't my guard, that I was simply taking a leisurely stroll with a friend.

"Did you like your job before this?" I asked, trying to fill the silence with the thousands of questions I had.

He was silent for a few beats and I glanced up at him, noting the way his lips thinned. "No. I'm glad to be back in New York."

"Have you lived here your whole life?"

"Yeah, there's nowhere else I'd rather be."

I nodded. "Do you have a girlfriend?"

His lips tilted up one side and he gave me a sidelong glance. "No. It's not easy to be in the line of work I'm in and maintain a relationship."

That wasn't really a shocker. A guy like him could probably have any woman at his fingertips anyway. Why get tied down? My father had many women at his disposal, until my stepmom came around a few years ago.

"Do you only work?" I asked, curious if he ever had any fun. "Do you have any hobbies?"

He chuckled. "Damn, they weren't lying."

I frowned. "Who?"

"Marcus and Demetri. They mentioned you like to ask a lot of questions."

"Oh." I folded my arms as we stood at an intersection, waiting to be able to cross. "I guess I just like to figure people out. You know, understand them. In case you haven't noticed, I don't get out much or meet new people."

Steven's gaze fluttered around us, scoping for any threats I assumed. He scratched at the back of his neck, meeting my eyes. "I haven't had time for a lot of hobbies. My last job was pretty enthralling." He grabbed my upper arm, pulling me slightly closer to him as a man on his cell phone brushed by me, nearly taking me out.

"Thanks," I muttered.

He released me before walking again and I followed. "What are your hobbies?" he asked once we crossed the street.

I shrugged. "I like reading. Anything that's a form of escape from reality really."

"So you were locked in your tower before I was hired, too?"

"Basically," I sighed. "I've always only done whatever it was my father wanted. I've never had a choice."

"Why is that?" he asked as we crossed another intersection.

"Honestly, I don't know. I don't think he trusts me or maybe it's other people he doesn't trust. Either way, I'm left only spending time with him and other people in the business. Even when I was in college, I lived in my apartment and wasn't allowed to really attend any social events."

I risked a glance up at him and caught him frowning. "That's fucked up." It was, but there was nothing I could do about it. "Where do you want to go?" Steven asked, stopping in the middle of the sidewalk. A woman swore at him before breezing by us.

Shaking my head, I ran a hand through my hair. "I don't know. Just … anywhere. Not home." I wasn't sure if I had a destination in mind, but the park seemed like a good idea.

He gazed down at me, his hazel eyes searching my face. My heart beat faster under his scrutiny, making me shift my gaze to the sidewalk, chewing on my bottom lip. Why did he affect me like this?

His lips tilted up on one side. "Come on." He pulled his cell phone from his jeans pocket and began texting someone.

"Alerting my father of our whereabouts?" I asked as he slid his phone back in his pocket.

"I was letting Marcus know we're going to take a walk in the park."

I rose a brow as irritation surfaced. "Does he really need to know that?"

He offered an apologetic smile. "Albert's concerned for your safety. Do you know how many enemies the Gallos have? How many your father has?" he asked as we entered the park under the nearly bare branches of trees.

I tucked my hands into the pockets of my coat, relishing the fresh spring air in my lungs. "As many as anyone, I guess," I said bitterly. "Maybe if he tried talking to Roman Cuccione, we wouldn't be in this mess." Steven stopped walking abruptly and I spun around to look at him. "What is it?"

He blinked at me. "The Mafia?"

"Yeah …" *Shit.* I probably shouldn't have mentioned them. What did he know about Don Roman?

He nodded slowly, continuing our walk. "I've heard the name before."

"My father thinks he'll be bigger than them one day," I said with an eye roll.

He cocked his head to the side, glancing down at me. "Is that why he secured you to Sebastian Gallo?"

I grimaced at his choice of words. Secured me? Did Steven only see me as collateral, too?

It was strange that Steven seemed so curious about my father's motives. He was probably caught off guard by learning who he was working for. The Mafia was a scary entity to those who didn't understand them. Hell, I feared them because I was a Ricci and right now, we were playing with fire by working with the Gallo family.

"I told you; you should get out while you can," I said and that earned a look of confusion from him. "It's dangerous, Steven. Whatever plan my father has won't end well if he's truly going after the Cuccione family."

"I'll be fine, Aida. Don't worry about me. So, he is planning to take out the Mafia?"

"Do you have any idea what they do to those that cross them? If they find out what he's planning, they'll kill us all," I said in a hushed voice as we passed by a woman walking her dog.

He shrugged. "They might kill *him* for being a traitor," he said. "I think we'll be fine."

A humorless laugh escaped and he narrowed his eyes at me. "You've got a lot to learn," I said. "I'm the daughter of a man who wants to overthrow them. I'm marrying a man who is operating outside their rules. I'll be guilty by association and you'd die trying to protect me."

His jaw muscle clenched tight, ticking several times before he spoke again. "If I die saving someone innocent, then it's worth it. I doubt it will come to that."

"How can you be so sure?" I was the one to stop now and he continued walking a few feet before noticing.

He turned around, frowning at me. "You're safe. You'll be safe."

"Then why do I need you?"

Shaking his head, he said, "You don't. They just think you do and I'm here to give them peace of mind." He walked toward me then, not stopping until we were toe to toe. I had to tilt my head back to look at him.

The air in my lungs ceased as he peered down at me with sparkling eyes and a slow grin. His voice was low when he spoke again. "You're stronger than they know. And if you have to fight, you will. Don't ever let anyone tell you otherwise."

I was left blinking after him as he turned on his heel and continued on. A kernel of hope sprouted deep within me, a sense of control I'd never felt. Did he really believe that I was strong? How had he seen that in me after only knowing me for just over a week?

I *was* strong and capable. I'd proved myself time and time again. Steven's words lit a fire inside me, a burning for something forgotten. I didn't need him to babysit me, but maybe I needed him as an ally. What if he was brought into my life to help me, not my father?

CHAPTER FIVE
STEVEN

Aida needed to realize that she was more than what her father wanted. It made me sick to know that he'd reduced her down to nothing but a mindless pet for him when he needed. She was smarter than he gave her credit for.

I was shocked when she mentioned my uncle's name. I hadn't expected her to know that much about the Mafia and I wanted to figure out if she'd simply heard her father's conversations in passing or was told specifically about us. She'd grown up in this world, so our name dropping wasn't uncommon.

I saw the look of panic and depression in Aida's eyes when she said she didn't want to be home. I couldn't blame her. It was bad enough working for Albert and having to spend most of the last week sitting around on my ass, waiting for my shifts to guard Aida. She was my only source of information.

I tried to get some intel at the real estate business when she was working but found nothing. I doubted the other employees even knew about Albert's nefarious endeavors.

We stopped walking after a while and sat down on a bench. I stuffed my hands into the pockets of my jacket and stretched my legs out, crossing my ankles. Aida watched the few people that walked by. Her hair blew softly in the breeze as she tucked a strand of hair behind her ear.

I was hoping she would talk to me a little more, share some more of her father's secrets. This was the most we'd really talked since meeting and she seemed open to sharing details that I needed.

Aida turned to look at me with apprehension. "Is this breaking the rules?" she asked. I didn't miss the irritation in her voice.

"It doesn't count if we don't get caught," I said, shooting her a wink. "You're free to do what you want. Marcus just likes to know your location."

She rolled her eyes. "You know, it makes sense now that they wanted to hire an appointed guard. At first, I thought it was just because we were working with another group, but I think my father wants to ensure I don't get into trouble before I marry Sebastian."

"What kind of trouble?" I asked.

"Anything that might make me less desirable. I have no real friends, no social life."

It wasn't fair the way she was being treated. I wished I could help her out, but my hands were tied. "What would you be doing if your father hadn't promised you to Gallo?"

"I'd probably be doing the same thing. I'm not just his accountant. I also handle odd jobs for him. Do you know about the one tomorrow night?"

I knew I was to escort Aida to a club so that she could meet with someone. Marcus had given me the orders and told me to watch her. I had no doubt this kind of work was common for her. They truly used her as bait to gain business and that pissed me off.

I cleared my throat. "Yeah. Do you do a lot of street work for Albert?"

She licked her lips, distracting me. Why was I completely obsessed with them all of a sudden? I shifted my gaze to the trees ahead, tamping down the errant feelings of attraction.

"I've helped with a lot of stuff he didn't want to deal with directly. Tomorrow night is just a meeting, but I've done some takedowns before, too." Her brow crumpled. "That's when you go after a narc or spy and capture them." I knew what a takedown was. I'd nearly had it happen to me a few times in the past. "Shot a man in the leg once." She shrugged.

My brows inched up my forehead. "No shit?"

She giggled at my surprised reaction. "Yeah."

"That's badass," I said, shaking my head. She utterly dumbfounded me. "And incredibly dangerous."

"You were right earlier about me being stronger than people think. If it were anyone else telling me how to live my life, I'd have more resistance. But my father is powerful. He's brutal and heartless. I can't go up against him."

"Would you, if you knew you could come out unscathed?" If she didn't care about her father, I could possibly turn her. I could make her one of us as long as Uncle Roman agreed. I could flip the entire Ricci and Gallo clans on their heads by bringing her to our side.

"I don't think that'd ever be possible," she said quietly.

It was totally possible. I was Fabiano Cuccione. My connections and power trumped her father's any day. "Why not?"

She looked at me as if I were speaking another language. "Because I'm a woman and that automatically disqualifies me from positions of power. Don Roman wouldn't listen to me anyway."

My jaw hardened in irritation. "Who the fuck told you that?"

"My father only hires men, including at his real estate company. 'Women are little more than trophies and play things,' he says." Her nose crinkled in disgust. "Unless he needs someone for bitch work. Then I'm suddenly an asset."

Jesus, this woman was being completely discounted and disrespected. Albert Ricci was a piece of shit and not just because he was an enemy. Aida needed to know that what he'd told her wasn't true. Not at all.

Against my better judgement, I reacted without thinking. I reached out, twisting a strand of her hair between my finger and thumb. It was softer than I imagined. Leaning in close, I heard her breath catch. My heart hammered in my chest as I placed my lips close to her ear, inhaling her sweet scent. Roses.

"Women are far more powerful than men. A man who doesn't agree is weak, flawed, and incredibly stupid." I sat back, releasing her hair.

Her body visibly trembled and I wasn't sure if it was from me or the cold weather. Her cheeks glowed a faint pink color as she stared ahead at the frosted lawn in front of us.

"You're beautiful," I murmured. Her head slowly turned and she met my eyes. "And you're smart. Probably more so than the men you've been raised by. What do you intend to do once you're married to Sebastian Gallo?"

I felt compelled to drive the point home that she was so much more than an accessory. It was partly instinct and partly because I wanted her to trust me. She was giving me a lot of great information right now.

"I haven't really thought about it. I keep hoping I can get out of marrying him somehow. It's why I went to the roof the other night. I'm out of options."

"Would you really be willing to go to the Mafia for help?"

She snorted. "You don't just confront the Mafia, Steven. I have to request a meeting with Don Roman himself and that's not easy to do. Like I said before, he wouldn't agree to meet with me."

"Why not?" I asked.

I couldn't understand her hesitation in asking my uncle for help. It wasn't that hard to gain an audience with him. If she were seriously looking for a way out, I could organize the meeting myself. This could be simpler than we originally planned.

We could move her to a new state, give her anonymity.

She shook her head. "My father would kill me for ratting him out. And if he didn't, then Sebastian would." She closed her eyes briefly and when they opened, there was a flash of sorrow before her brow creased. "My mother was murdered when I was young."

I swallowed. I knew this already based on the information from Gio. "I'm sorry."

She smiled tightly. "Her murder is the reason I can't go to the Don."

"Why?"

"He's the one that killed her."

I opened my mouth to argue that she was wrong, but I wasn't sure if she was. No wonder she didn't want to turn over her father. She was probably afraid that she'd be killed, too.

"How do you know that?" I asked, trying to keep my voice even. I didn't want her to think I was second guessing what she'd said.

She shook her head. "My father told me. It's why he wants to disband the Mafia entirely. He wants Don Roman to pay for taking my mother's life."

That changed things. A lot. If what she was saying was true, she'd never trust me. She'd never come with me and rat out her father. I needed to figure out what really happened to her mother.

"Are you certain he's telling you the truth?" I shouldn't have asked that question. It was evident I'd fucked up by the look on Aida's face. Her head cocked to the side and she narrowed her eyes at me.

"Why would he lie about *that*?"

"I don't know," I said quietly. "I'm sorry, I shouldn't have said that."

"You don't know Albert Ricci like I do. He's a bad man, I'll agree with that, but he didn't kill my mother."

"I didn't mean to imply that he did," I said. "I just … I think it might be beneficial for you to talk to the Don—"

"The Mafia is serious business, Steven," she said, cutting me off. "They wouldn't hesitate to use me the same way my father does or worse. I could be killed as a way to send a message to my father or Sebastian Gallo. Maybe that's why they killed my mother." She blew out an exasperated breath. "Just a few months ago, there was talk of one of their spies taking down a group on the West Coast. They killed over forty men in a matter of days."

Throughout the time I was with Hawks, it was well over that number, but I wasn't counting. She'd heard about me and I wasn't sure how to feel about that. Would she fear me if she knew who I really was then? Did she think of me as a cold-blooded killer?

It was true that we didn't hesitate to kill an enemy, but I would never harm an innocent person. Especially a woman who was being used and abused like her. My uncle wouldn't harm her, either, even if he was responsible for her mother's death. He would protect her as much as I would. Despite what we wanted the city and other groups to think, we weren't monsters. Not completely. There had to be a reasonable explanation for what happened to her mother.

"Don Roman isn't going to care about what I have to say anyway," she said. "He needs evidence, proof that my father's working against him. I don't have anything other than my word."

We were slowly getting that proof now that she'd all but confessed to why he was working with Gallo and what his intentions were. I needed to talk to Gio.

"I want to help you," I said quietly.

Aida studied me carefully, her eyes searching my own. It felt like she was looking directly through me in that moment, as if she could see the truth written on me and peer into my shattered soul.

I shifted under her scrutiny, bending my legs as I sat up straighter.

Her head slowly began to shake. "You work for my father. Even just talking about going against him could put you in a body bag."

She had a point. What if Marcus found out Aida and I weren't just taking a leisurely stroll in the park, but talking as friends? What if she confronted her father about what happened to her mother because I'd planted a seed of doubt? I had to end this conversation and save it for another time.

I stood up, rubbing my hands together in front of me. "We should probably get back to your place."

She stood reluctantly. "Yeah, okay."

Our walk back to the complex was quiet. I was trying to think of a way to relay everything I'd just learned to Gio. I needed to get away and meet with him. I might also need to confront my uncle on the murder of Helena Ricci.

Once I dropped Aida off at her place, I went to my own apartment and texted Gio from the burner phone I'd brought with me. I was issued one specifically from Albert Ricci, but I wasn't stupid enough to use that to communicate with my crew.

He agreed to meet me this evening. I compiled every ounce of intel I had so far into a notebook. Now, I just needed to find a way to sneak out for a while and pray I wasn't being followed.

*

It wasn't difficult to get out of the building. I simply lied and told the door attendant that I had a few personal errands and told him to call me if Aida left her room. I met with Gio a few blocks from my old apartment at a sushi restaurant owned by a good friend of my uncle's.

He was already waiting for me in a booth, devouring salmon spring rolls.

"Hey," I said, sliding into the seat across from him.

He took a sip of the beer he was drinking. "I like having you back, Fab. It's nice meeting face to face instead of coded phone calls."

A server stopped by to hand me a bottle of beer with a wink. I mumbled thanks and took a long tug before speaking again.

"Yeah, it's great," I said. "Sure would have been nice to drive though, but I wouldn't be surprised if they've got GPS trackers in the cars we're allowed to use."

Gio nodded. "So, what do you have for me?"

I pulled the small notebook from an inside pocket in my jacket, sliding it across the table to him. He picked it up and began reading through all my notes while I drank more of my beer. After about five minutes, he set the notebook down and slid it back to me.

"We could turn her if you trust her enough," he said before popping another sushi roll into his mouth.

70

Shaking my head, I said, "I can't say I trust her, yet. She's venting without realizing what information she's sharing. She's also incredibly apprehensive about confronting her father. He's done a good job belittling her. I think she's afraid of him."

Gio raised a brow. "You think he beats her?"

A kernel of pure rage sprouted. "I don't know. Maybe." I wouldn't be surprised if he'd trained her harder than the other soldiers. She was definitely brainwashed into thinking we were the enemy over her waste of life father.

"It sounds like he's planning to use Gallo or at the very least, his weapons, to take us on."

I nodded. "Aida's meeting with someone tomorrow night. I don't know who it is. Maybe a buyer?"

"If you can get a name, I can run research on him. The girl didn't say what the meeting was about?"

I shook my head. "That question didn't come up organically," I replied.

"I don't like that the prick thinks he has a chance at taking over New York. Octavio Gallo is as good as dead in my opinion unless he chooses to betray Ricci. I'd also like to know where he got that stash of weapons."

I played with the label on my beer bottle. "If he's being supplied from overseas, we might have to do recon abroad."

"You volunteering?"

Scoffing, I said, "Fuck no. I like it here."

His face turned serious and he searched my face. "How you holding up otherwise? Grim said you're on a sleep aid."

I bit back on my molars. I really wish he wouldn't open his mouth sometimes. "Yeah, I'm good."

Gio's eyes narrowed slightly. "We'll get this job done quick, Fab. Then you should take some time off. Whatever Hawks put you through will eat you up inside if you don't face it."

I knew my uncle's capo meant well and had seen and been through plenty of his own shit, but I didn't want anyone feeling sorry for me. I'd already spent the last five years grieving the loss of my brother and the distraction of what I went through helped. I just needed to keep looking forward and I'd be fine.

"I might do that," I said, offering a tight smile.

He nodded. "I'll look into the death of Helena Ricci. I don't think Roman was responsible for that."

"Any idea on who might have done it?" I asked.

He shrugged before taking a swig of his own beer. "My bet would be on her husband. If we can prove it and you can put that in front of Aida, maybe she'll be swayed."

I wasn't a fan of adding any more to Aida's plate, but I needed her trust. Without proof that we wouldn't harm her; she wouldn't give up her father willingly.

I finished debriefing with Gio and scheduled to meet with him later on in the week if he found proof on Helena's murder. I left feeling a sense of hope that this job would soon be over. Perhaps I'd take some time off. Take a real vacation or something and try to work my shit out.

"I want you to do whatever it takes with Jonathan Thompson. If you can get him to commit, even better," my father said.

He was pacing in front of his desk, hands behind his back, his light gray suit freshly pressed. I could tell he was anxious to secure a buyer for the weapons the Gallos had ready to sell. It was probably due to the fact that the O'Hare clan was breathing down his neck.

I had to get Jonathan Thompson to commit to helping us by any means necessary. I was prepared to sweet talk him if I had to and hoped he wouldn't rat me out to the Mafia or the local police. Although, I seriously doubted a man like him was the snitching kind.

"You're sure he can be trusted?" I asked.

He stopped pacing. "Of course, I am. We've already spoken briefly about how he earns his money during the purchase of his condo." I nodded. "He's a friend of a local organization that specializes in unique weapons."

"Which club will he be at?"

"The Den. He's part owner and is eager to meet with you."

He knew I was coming, that would make things easier. Although, I can't say I was nearly as eager as he was. "What will I say about my guard?"

"Cline will go in with you, however, he is ordered to hang back."

Knowing that I'd have backup should things take a turn helped ease my nerves slightly. I was used to meeting potential allies and had done it before, but with all the new attention from working with Octavio Gallo and his son, I feared there was an even bigger target on my back now. My conversation with Steven yesterday regarding the Mafia made me all the more paranoid. Would he rat us out?

After leaving my father's office, Steven escorted me home to get ready for the meeting. I put on a newer dress, turning in my full-length mirror to make sure it fit well.

The dress was short, falling to the middle of my thighs, and fit me like a second skin. It was a deep purple color with shimmery sequin that glinted off the light in my bedroom. I paired the strapless dress with a light denim jacket for warmth. The jacket did little to hide my pronounced cleavage and full hips, and I smirked as I looked at myself.

I was confident enough in my body to embrace my curves and this is exactly something I'd wear if I had the opportunity to go to a club for pleasure instead of business. I tousled my dark hair to help add volume to the loose waves and painted on some pale lip gloss. I looked good enough to maintain the attention of our potential new business partner.

Steven drove me to the club, walking alongside me from the parking garage to the surprisingly busy entrance. I hadn't expected a line outside the door on a Monday night.

I flashed the bouncer a smile and he waved me in ahead of the others, which earned me a few glares and nasty comments. I didn't care. I was used to getting what I wanted when it came to working.

The inside of the club was quieter than I expected. Soft music played through the speakers in the dimly lit space as people sat at booths and small tables, talking and drinking cocktails. I stood at the edge of the bar counter, scanning the room.

Steven looked good in a pair of dark jeans and a fitted sweater as he navigated through people to find a table. His hair was slicked back instead of disheveled tonight. He looked casual and sexy.

I winced at that thought. I shouldn't be thinking of him that way. Not only because he was an employee of my fathers and my guard, but because I was a betrothed woman. A woman who even if she wanted to let loose, couldn't. Fraternizing with anyone, let alone *him*, would get me in all kinds of trouble.

I spotted Jonathan sitting at a booth kitty corner from where Steven ended up. He locked eyes with me and smiled, raising his glass. I sauntered over to him, shifting my gaze to my guard who was watching me intently. I slid into the seat across from Jonathan.

"Hello, Mr. Thompson."

"Ms. Ricci, you look lovely this evening."

"Thank you," I replied with a smile. "How are you?" I didn't miss the way his eyes roamed over me, focusing a little too long on my chest.

"Better now," he mused.

I resisted the urge to roll my eyes. If he thought he'd be able to hit on me, he was in for a rude awakening. I'd play nice for now, act like the dumb bimbo most of my father's associates thought I was.

"I'm glad to hear that," I said, turning my attention to a server who stopped at our table. I ordered a merlot and focused back on Jonathan. "How are you enjoying your new condo?"

"Oh, it's great," he replied, swirling the glass of amber liquid in his hand before taking a sip. "Albert did a great job getting me the place. I owe him."

I lifted a brow. "Hence the reason for our meeting."

He chuckled and nodded. "Yes, I hear he's in possession of a special arsenal." His voice dropped lower. "I know a group who would love to get their hands on the product."

The server came back with my glass of wine and I took a drink before setting the glass down, stroking my finger along the rim.

"We need to sell the product quickly," I said. "If you could have it sold before the end of the week, we'd love to work with you." I scanned his face, batting my eyelashes at him. "It could be the beginning of a great relationship," I added in a sultry whisper.

That seemed to get his attention and his gray eyes darkened as he adjusted his tie. "That sounds wonderful."

"I trust you'd maintain strict discretion should we choose to work with you?"

He gave a slight nod. "Of course. I can speak with my associate to set up a time for us to meet and take a look at the product. Would that be possible?"

"I'll have to ask my father about that. His supplier would like to maintain anonymity." I was told not to mention the Gallo family. They didn't earn their business by being flashy.

"I look forward to hearing from him." He raised a brow. "Or is it you I'll be working with?" There was a hopeful gleam in his eye and I cringed inwardly.

I definitely wouldn't be working with him further than this meeting. Not if I could help it. My father used me as a lure, nothing more. Entice the men to gain favor and make myself scarce. That was my job.

I shot him a coy smile, draining the rest of my wine. "I'm sure I'll see you around." I stood from the booth and extended my hand to his. "I'll have my father call you the day after tomorrow."

He grabbed my hand, squeezing tightly as he stood as well. He leaned in real close, placing his lips to my ear. "Why don't we celebrate our new venture together?" He ran a hand down to my waist, pulling me into him, and I gasped.

"I'm engaged," I bit out, struggling to free myself from his hold. He held my hand tighter, not allowing me to tug away.

"What a lucky man he is."

"Thank you," I said, slipping my hand from his.

He winked and bile rose in my throat. I rubbed my skin, praying a bruise wouldn't form. Bastard.

"My office is in the back, if you'd like to join me for a celebratory drink."

My eyes narrowed at him. "I need to be going. My fiancé would be *murderous* if I were late in getting back home."

That seemed to drive the point home. Jonathan nodded, retreating toward the back of the club, down a narrow hallway.

I loosened a breath, shaking my head. "Jesus, that hurt." I glanced down at my wrist. It was a faint pink color.

Suddenly, Steven was beside me. I knew it was him by his familiar scent. He gingerly grasped my forearm, lifting my wrist to inspect it closely. He ran his index finger over the area and a shiver ran through me.

"He hurt you," he mumbled, frowning at the pink skin.

"I'm fine," I assured him. Butterflies swirled beneath my ribcage as I watched him study my wrist. His hazel eyes lifted to mine.

"Would you like me to remind him why we don't touch things that don't belong to us?" His eyes darkened and there was an angry bite to his tone.

I sucked in a sharp breath at the menacing look on his face and immediately began shaking my head. "No, he left. The last thing I want is for him to second guess working for my father."

His jaw muscle ticked as he stared into my eyes. Slowly, the anger he'd exuded began to dissipate. "Let's get you home."

Steven held my hand, leading me out of the club. He didn't let go of me as we walked toward the parking garage. I found myself distracted by the warmth of his palm against mine, the feel of his thumb sliding along my skin absently.

Once we were at the car, he released me and crossed his arms. "Are you okay?"

My brow crumpled. "Yes, I told you I'm fine. That was nothing." Why was he acting so protective of me? I'd been in worse situations before.

His eyes shifted, taking in my appearance. I felt my cheeks heat under his scrutiny. When his gaze lifted back to mine, there was a predatory look on his face that sent a flood of warmth between my legs.

Holy shit, was he checking me out? Did he find me attractive? I swallowed the lump forming in my throat as we continued staring at each other. The air thickened between us and I sucked in an unsteady breath as Steven uncrossed his arms and moved closer to me. He bent his head as I tilted mine up, our lips hovering dangerously close. His hand brushed my waist and my eyes closed as I wondered if he was going to kiss me.

The click of the passenger door opening forced my eyes open. Our gazes locked on to each other's, neither of us moving. I could feel my heart pounding against my chest.

"Aida, get in the car." His voice was low, urgent.

Before I could respond, he stepped away from me and made his way to the driver's side. I sunk into the passenger seat and tilted my head back. What the hell just transpired between us? Why was my heart racing like I'd just ran a marathon?

*

The next week flew by and while I saw Steven nearly every day, we didn't speak much. He spent most of the days staked out near my office door while I did my best to ignore him. Although I couldn't help studying him occasionally.

The deal was set, the ink not yet dry on a contract for the purchase of Gallo weapons to whatever crew Jonathan was involved in. It seemed my father was able to convince him he had an ample supply without involving Octavio or Sebastian.

Because the exchange would be happening soon, Steven was told to stick close to me. Marcus had a number of guards throughout the building should an enemy catch wind of the weapons being sold.

Luckily, it all went off without a hitch. However, by the end of the following week, I was feeling even more restless and cagey. Part of that had to do with the fact that I'd been given information about my wedding to Sebastian. Apparently, we were to be wed at his private home in the Hamptons. Knowing there was now a venue in place added to my feelings of being trapped.

This weekend things were back to normal. Or as normal as it had been before the weapons deal. The O'Hares received their money and my father was finally debt free with them. It was one thing taken care of which should have made me feel better. It didn't.

Now, my father wanted me to meet with Jonathan Thompson again to ensure his buyer was happy with the purchase he'd made. The last thing I wanted to do was see that man again, but as usual, I was not offered a choice in the matter.

I wasn't looking forward to being alone with Steven again after what happened the last time he'd taken me to The Den. I'd been paying more attention to him unconsciously and even fantasized about what it'd be like to curl my fingers in his hair or feel his lips against my own.

It was a stupid crush, and if I didn't get a handle on my body soon, I'd end up embarrassing myself for sure.

Instead of wearing a dress tonight, I went with a pair of black jeans and a fitted white tank top under my favorite leather jacket. The boots I wore had spiked heels that added a few inches to my height. Yet even in the boots, Steven was taller than me by several inches.

He picked me up clad in jeans and a t-shirt with a leather jacket, as well. We didn't speak much on the drive to the club. It wasn't until after he parked the car and cut the engine that he turned to me.

"What's the goal tonight?" he asked.

"I'm supposed to bump into Jonathan casually. Strike up a bland conversation and ensure he isn't saying anything about his buyer's purchase to the wrong people. Basically, I have to let him know that we're watching him." I rolled my eyes.

Steven nodded. "I want you to stay close to me tonight. If he touches you at all like last time, I'll break his hand."

My eyes widened slightly as warmth flooded my belly. Something was wrong with me for being turned on by his protectiveness. "Okay," I said.

"Okay." He nodded before opening his door. I exited the car as well and he met me at the back of it. "Are you sure he's here tonight?" he asked as we began walking toward the club.

"Yeah, he's part owner. I think he likes to party a lot." I shrugged.

The bouncer recognized me from the other night and let us pass just as easily. The music was louder since it was the weekend and I felt Steven's chest press against my back.

"Let's grab a drink and get a table," he said in my ear.

My heart hammered in my chest at his proximity and I nodded lamely, heading in the direction of the bar.

Steven ordered a beer and a cocktail for me, carrying them as I followed him to a small table away from the dance floor. As I sat down, I caught sight of Jonathan dancing with a blond woman.

"There he is," I said, angling my head in his direction. Steven followed my gaze, taking a swig from his beer.

Jonathan looked up, catching me watching him. I offered a small wave and smiled. His eyes widened slightly. He wasn't expecting to see me here, that much I was sure of. He excused himself from the woman he'd been dancing with and approached our table.

His eyes slid between me and Steven, settling on my guard. He glared at him momentarily before looking back to me.

"Aida, I didn't expect to see you here," Jonathan greeted, shouting over the upbeat music.

"I needed a night out," I said. "This is my friend, Steven Cline." Jonathan blinked at Steven who shot me a questioning look before forcing a smile.

"Nice to meet you," Steven said, sticking his hand out to Jonathan's.

They shook quickly. Jonathan forced a smile. "You as well. Miss Ricci here is a business associate of mine and I must say, one of the best." He winked at me and I ignored it.

"Yes, she's definitely the best." Steven gazed at me as he spoke and I felt my cheeks heat. He was looking at me the same way he had the other night, as if he were committing my face to memory.

Jonathan cleared his throat and I turned my attention back to him. "I heard the trade went well," I said casually.

"Yes, quite. My buyers are incredibly pleased with their new arsenal. In fact, they're hoping to continue business with your father for some time."

I nodded. "Wonderful. I'll be sure to let him know that."

"Please, do."

I should have just let it go at that, not questioned him any further or let my curiosity get the better of me. I wasn't sure if it was the desperation to find another way out of my engagement to Sebastian Gallo, or the fact that I'd been thinking more and more about what Steven and I discussed in the park.

I couldn't help but wonder what might happen if I went to Don Roman for help. Yes, he may have killed my mother and he may kill me for whatever past him and my father had, but what if I had leverage to keep myself safe? Perhaps I could get the Don to trust me and keep me alive.

He'd want to know about these weapons; I was certain of it. I couldn't risk turning in my father or the Gallos, but what about Jonathan Thompson or whoever it was that purchased the weapons?

"I'm curious as to who would need so many weapons of that grade," I said. Jonathan's gaze shifted to Steven. I waved a hand in front of me. "Oh, he's aware of our business. Don't worry."

He smiled. "Perhaps we could speak somewhere more private."

"Sure." I stood from the table, grabbing my glass. Steven stood as well, picking up his beer and eyeing me cautiously. Maybe I should have talked this over with him first.

As we walked down the dark hall toward what I assumed was Jonathan's office, I felt Steven place his hand at the small of my back. He shifted closer to me. I know he was just protecting me, just doing his job, but I liked the contact.

There was a look of familiarity in Jonathan Thompson's eyes as he'd approached our table. My hair was longer since the last time I was in town and I'd aged a bit in my face, though not enough to be unrecognizable to those that may have known my family.

I knew him. Not directly, but I'd seen him around town in the past when working street jobs. He wasn't an enemy of the Mafia or a friend, either. He was simply there. I was worried he'd place me and my cover would be blown, but the look of surprise when Aida said I was her friend had me wondering if he simply stared me down as an opponent.

Not that either of us had a chance with her in reality. Not only was she betrothed to Sebastian Gallo, but I couldn't touch her. It wasn't about the fact she was an enemy's daughter anymore. It was the fact that I'd already spent too much time thinking about her and it was becoming a distraction. I couldn't act on the feelings she elicited and I desperately wanted to. The way she was dressed the other night sparked a deep-rooted need within me and I almost messed everything up by giving in to temptation.

I didn't know who Thompson was and Gio had been unable to get much dirt on him when I gave him the name. We were close to being done with this job and the only thing stopping us now was to figure out who was behind the purchase of these weapons.

Aida didn't realize she just helped me out by asking the question directly. I had no idea what her angle was at the moment, but I'd let it play out for now. The way she carried herself and her ability to stay calm in the midst of danger sent a wave of desire through me. She knew how to use her body, her sex appeal to her advantage. She was fucking dangerous.

I kept my hand on the small of her back as we followed Thompson into his well-lit office. He leaned against his desk, placing his hands on either side atop the wood. Aida took a seat near him, crossing one leg over the other as she took a healthy sip of her cocktail.

I stood slightly behind her, ready to grab her and run if this bastard tried anything. He stared at me again, his head cocking to the side. I kept my face blank of any emotion, trying to remain calm under his scrutiny.

"You know there's a lot of people in this city who refuse to be told how to live their lives," he said.

"I'm sure there are. It's hard to make everyone happy all the time," Aida replied.

He smiled down at her. "Your father is a smart man to provide for our organization. That'll be a benefit in the near future. We have a lot of plans."

"War?" Aida asked and my shoulders tightened.

What the fuck was she doing? Her boldness was going to get our throats slit if she wasn't careful. I didn't trust Thompson and when he smirked at me, I was almost certain I saw that look of familiarity again.

He chuckled. "Not quite war. However, there's a lot of families that have been running things for too long. Groups that advocate for order yet pick off other crews that are smaller than them."

I clutched my bottle of beer tightly, biting back on my molars. Maybe this motherfucker *was* an enemy.

Aida cocked her head to the side, acting as if she didn't understand what he meant. Something told me she was playing dumb. "Who?"

"The Mafia, for one. They infiltrated the western part of the country, expanded their territory by means of force."

"I was under the impression the company that they eradicated was worse than them," Aida said. "Didn't the man they go after kill Dante Cuccione? The Don's nephew."

I swallowed. She knew about that?

Thompson shrugged. "I've heard many different rumors. It doesn't matter anyway; they're trying to overtake the entire country. We have to stop that from happening."

He moved behind his desk, pulling out a bottle of whisky from a drawer along with a glass. He poured the amber liquid and took a sip.

"What do you do for work, Steven?" he asked, flicking his gaze to me.

"I'm a personal guard."

"For Ricci?"

"Yes," I replied.

His lips tilted up in a slight smile. "I'm sure Albert is pleased to know his daughter is protected by such a trusted man."

"Who did you sell the weapons to?" Aida asked, turning his attention from me.

Thompson shook his head. "Let's just say that the weapons your father managed to provide are now closer than ever to being used for their purpose." He took another sip of his whiskey. "Taking out the Cuccione family."

Aida gasped and I had to restrain myself from not shooting this guy where he stood. I had my gun tucked in the back of my jeans, so I could do it. His bouncer did him a disservice by not patting me down as he should have.

"This group wants to take out the Mafia?" she asked.

"Has your father explained what he wanted to use the weapons for?"

Aida's brow crumpled. "I wasn't aware that he'd be using the weapons. I only know he's seeking to control New York."

If Albert were working with Gallo and Thompson to try and take over the city and providing guns to someone else who was doing the same, we'd be seriously fucked. It didn't make sense that Gallo would be selling the weapons to Albert and paying him for it though. Something wasn't right.

"I'm sure my father would love to know who he's providing an arsenal of weapons to since they share a similar interest."

Thompson finished off his whisky, sucking his teeth. He narrowed his eyes at her. "He already does."

His eyes darkened in a way that had me feeling all kinds of territorial and murderous. He gave her a thorough once over and I instinctively placed a hand on Aida's shoulder. He caught the movement and looked at me with a smile.

"Such a shame you got to her first." I refused to speak on that. He gazed back to Aida. "Perhaps your father and I can discuss matters further soon. I'm sure he'd love to know you stopped by for a visit."

"I'm sure he would," Aida said, standing. "We should be going though. We have a dinner reservation."

"Of course." He stepped around his desk and approached her, extending his hand. He lifted hers, placing a kiss upon her wrist, the same one he'd grabbed the other night. "It's always a pleasure seeing you, Aida. Be cautious of the company you keep."

I grasped her forearm, stealing her hand from his. "It was nice to meet you," I bit out.

Thompson straightened. "Likewise," he murmured as I interlaced my fingers with Aida's and guided her out of his office.

This was bad. I needed to make sure Thompson didn't blow my cover to Ricci. It was clear they were working together and he knew exactly who I was. I pulled my burner phone from my pocket and dialed Grim's number.

"Hey man, what's—"

"Straight shot. The Den. Immediately," I rumbled into the phone.

"On it," he replied before disconnecting the call.

Thank fuck I'd decided to alert him of our whereabouts tonight. I wasn't sure who we could run into at the club so I'd put him on standby. New York was full of a lot of people, which made it difficult to remain inconspicuous.

Thompson was a dead man. It was the only way to ensure he didn't tell Albert Ricci who I really was. I couldn't risk being caught and when a choice has to be made between me and them, it will be them every time. The problem now was figuring out where those weapons were and hopefully Albert would give a location, or maybe his second in command would.

I needed to know where they were so that we could get rid of them before Albert tried to take us down. After tonight, that may just happen sooner than any of us expected.

Once we were outside the club, I released Aida's hand and turned on her. She blinked up at me, her eyes wide in shock.

"What the fuck were you thinking?" I growled.

Her ice blue eyes narrowed to slits. "I had it handled."

I scoffed. "Oh, you had it handled, did you? You realize outright asking someone who they're working with is improper spy etiquette 101?"

She stepped closer to me, tilting her head back to look me square in the eye. "Are you telling me how to do my job?"

"Did you enjoy making me risk *mine*?" I glowered down at her.

Her brow crumpled. "How were you at risk?"

My brows inched up my forehead. "You said I was your *friend*, Aida. You gave him my fucking name."

Her mouth opened as if she were about to say something but closed as she thought better of it.

"He knows I'm your father's guard which means if he speaks with him again, he'll ask about me."

"I'm well aware of that fact!" she shouted and a passerby stopped for a moment, staring at us.

Huffing out a breath, I grasped her hand again. "Let's go," I said, dragging her along toward the parking garage. I waited until we were both in the car before speaking again.

"I have a job to do. One fucking job that if I don't do properly will get me fired or worse. Do you understand what will happen to me if your father finds out about you telling someone we have a non-professional relationship?" I tried really hard to reel in my frustration, but it was difficult.

She could ruin everything if I got let go by Albert, or worse, ended up having my cover blown. The job for my uncle would be dead in the water, and I'd likely be taken captive or killed on the spot.

"I'm sorry," she muttered quietly, keeping her eyes focused on the dash. "I didn't think it was a big deal."

"There are secrets your father maintains from even his associates and they probably do the same. It's pretty clear he sold those weapons to Thompson so they could both use them to take out the Mafia. I don't think Gallo knows that. This is dangerous territory, Aida. You can't take it upon yourself to investigate your father's business. This isn't a fucking Scooby Doo mystery."

Her head snapped up and she glared at me with such a fierce intensity in her eyes that I froze.

Fuck.

"Because I'm just a measly woman who can't handle the truth?" She shook her head. "Fuck you, Steven! I'm just as capable of running the business as my damn father! In fact, if I *did* have a say, I'd do things completely differently and we wouldn't have ever been in this mess in the first place."

I blew out a heavy breath. I wasn't trying to hurt her. "I'm sorry, I didn't mean—"

"To belittle me because of my sex?"

"I didn't mean it like that," I argued. "What I meant is you could get yourself killed. If they think you're sniffing around for information, they might harm you, torture you for what you know or worse."

She snorted and rolled her eyes. "Like you care if they kill me."

Before I realized what I was doing, I reacted. Hearing her speak as if I couldn't possibly care about her had me desperate to prove her wrong. Yes, she was part of the assignment. Yes, she was the enemy's daughter. Yes, I had no fucking business getting mixed up with her. That didn't mean I'd let her play some twisted martyr for her father's sake. It sure as hell didn't mean I'd let her think no one gave a shit about her.

I took hold of her chin, drawing her face close to mine. I inhaled her sweet scent and swallowed roughly. She stared at me with a look of shock and the faintest hint of lust. Damn it, I didn't like knowing she wanted me the same way I wanted her. That made everything more difficult.

"Listen to me," I spoke slowly, quietly. "If you die, I lose everything." Her breath hitched and I closed my eyes, shaking my head. She probably thought I meant something else. I opened my eyes again. "I need to work for Albert Ricci. Do you understand? I can't have your blood on my hands."

I sat back and inhaled a deep breath before releasing it as I dragged my hand through my hair. We were both silent for several minutes. When Aida spoke, her voice was soft.

"How have I never met anyone like you before?"

She'd be better off not knowing me at all.

"Despite the world we're in, I still like to think there's good people," I said, looking at her. "You're one of them, Aida. Maybe it's because I have a sister, and I've met other women in my life who were … tormented. I just want to look out for you."

"You shouldn't waste your time on this, on me. Why do you care?" She studied me carefully. "How do you know so much about the underground businesses?"

I stared out the windshield at the darkness around us. It almost felt like we were in a different world in here. I wished things were different for a while. That it was just me and her talking without my secret between us. That I could act on what I felt for her even if it scared the shit out of me.

"I've just heard things in the different jobs I've had." I shrugged. "I'm pretty observant." I risked a glance at her again.

She was facing me, inspecting me carefully. "You know about Roman Cuccione. Not a lot of people know the Don's name unless they've got ties to the Mafia itself or their enemies. No one has ever asked me so many questions about my father's business before." She let out a low chuckle. "If I didn't know any better, I'd think you were a spy or something."

I smirked at her. Damn, she was smart. "You think I'm a spy?"

She bit down on her bottom lip, her eyes lowering. "I hope not."

My attention shifted to her mouth. "Why is that?"

She swallowed roughly. "Because I like you and that would mean … you're only using me."

I looked into her eyes again. I *was* using her, but that didn't mean I didn't like her, too. The air grew heavy between us and my blood warmed as we stared at each other, just like the other night in this same parking garage.

I wanted so fucking badly to taste those cherry lips of hers, to hold her hand again. Somehow, she'd leaned closer to me or maybe I'd moved toward her. If I dipped my chin, my forehead would rest against hers. Her scent invaded me and I felt the slow ache in my lower stomach as a dangerous desire took hold.

I bet she tasted sweet, that she'd moan in my mouth if I ran my fingers over her thigh, parting her legs to feel the heat between her legs.

"I like you, too," I murmured.

My lips brushed against hers when I spoke and my body trembled as I attempted to hold back. God, I wanted to claim her. No, scratch that. I wanted to *own* her. Jesus, I was spinning out of control.

The shrill sound of my phone ringing startled us both and I straightened. Aida exhaled a shaky breath as I pulled my phone from my pocket. I frowned as I saw Marcus' name flash across the screen.

"Marcus?"

"Where's Aida?" he demanded.

"With me," I said. "She's safe."

"You need to get her home," he said in a clipped voice. "We've got a problem."

"What happened?" I asked, glancing at Aida who was looking at me in confusion.

"Jonathan Thompson is dead."

*

After dropping Aida off back at her apartment, I met Marcus, Patrick, and a few of the other guys at a warehouse near the docks. Octavio Gallo was there, along with Albert.

On the way, I'd contacted Gio to get confirmation that Grim was the one to end Thompson. He had, which was good for us and bad for them.

Aida didn't know what was going on yet because I didn't want to freak her out. We'd just been with Thompson before he was killed and I was afraid her brilliant mind would discover that I was somehow behind it.

Before leaving her, I told her to sit tight for a while and there may have been a possible threat. She'd seemed to believe me that it wasn't a big deal.

"All we have is the call that came in an hour ago. It was a clean headshot from above," Marcus said, pacing along the dirty concrete floor. "No one saw who it was." He glanced around the room, stopping on me. "You'd just seen him, hadn't you?"

"Yeah," I said. "He was in his office, drinking whiskey when we left him."

"It had to have been Cuccione," Octavio snarled. He glared at Albert who stood with his arm's crossed, looking bored.

"I've got eyes on Roman," he said and my spine stiffened. "They're too wrapped up in expanding out west."

That was partially true, but we weren't turning a blind eye to our home turf. He was dumber than I thought if he'd think we'd become so easily distracted by new territory. I wondered who he had watching us.

"I've got men casing the scene," Albert said.

"*Your* men," Octavio scoffed. "Maybe you were the one to do it! It seems suspect that your buyer liaison would end up dead. Was it one of our weapons that was used?"

91

"Easy," Marcus warned with a pointed glare at the Gallo leader. "We have just as much at stake here as you. It was a standard sniper rifle, not one from your arsenal."

"That bitch could have done it for him," Octavio said, still shooting a death glare at Albert.

My hands clenched into fists at my side at the mention of Aida. "I was with her and we didn't kill him. If she'd been planning something, I would have known. If she'd tried something, I would have stopped her."

"Octavio, I gave you my word. I'm completely invested in this. We will figure out the killer and we will ensure the weapons aren't tracked to you."

The Gallo leader shook his head. "You're the only one with connections to distribute." He looked at Albert. "The girl will be married to Sebastian still, correct?"

Albert nodded. "I told you I would sell the shipments and I've delivered on that promise. I have connections to more buyers as well, and yes, Aida will marry your son. She's looking forward to it."

It became increasingly clear that Gallo was being misled. I needed to let my own men know and figure out how we might be able to use this to our advantage. Albert Ricci was desperate to prove himself to Octavio Gallo even if he already had the weapons he needed. He didn't care who he hurt in the process and that was evident in the fact that he still planned to marry Aida off.

Jonathan Thompson was dead. He'd been killed by a random hitman minutes after we'd left him the other night.

A new fear took root as I wondered what might happen now. My father called me to tell me the news and assured me that everything would be okay. He wouldn't give me any more information than that.

That was three days ago.

Patrick arrived this morning, taking guard outside my front door. Steven was on his way over now with my father and I had no idea why. If my father was paying me a visit in person, it couldn't be good. Although, seeing Steven wouldn't be so bad.

I couldn't get over Steven's concern for me or the way he'd admitted he liked me, too, and almost kissed me. In the moment, I thought I'd combust, that I'd die if he didn't kiss me. If we hadn't been interrupted by the call from Marcus, I wondered if it would have happened.

There was this mutual attraction we shared and even if it wasn't right, even if he worked for my father, I wanted him. I wanted the freedom he ignited in me without realizing it. I wanted the courage I felt when he was near. Maybe I should take his advice and tell the Don my father's plans. It might be worth the risk even without the information I tried to gain from Jonathan Thompson.

I sat in one of the stools at the island in my open kitchen, peeling the label off my bottled water, anxiously awaiting their arrival.

What if the Mafia was already on to us and they're the ones that killed Thompson? The thought crossed my mind again that Steven knew more than he was telling me. I'd been joking the other night when I accused him of being a spy, but somehow I felt like I wasn't too off base.

He'd called someone as we were leaving Jonathan's office that night. What was it that he'd said? I shook my head, trying to recall what it was that he'd told the person on the other end.

There was a brief knock on my front door before it opened. I glanced over to see my father stride in, followed by Steven. He looked good in a pair of black jeans and a long sleeved t-shirt with the sleeves rolled up to his elbow.

His hazel eyes were narrowed, concentrated on my father's back as they approached. My father crossed his arms, leaning against the counter beside me. Steven kept his distance, staying closer to the living room.

When his gaze shifted to mine, he smiled tightly. I got the feeling he wasn't happy about whatever my father had to say to me.

"There have been some new developments in the last few days," my father said without so much as a hello.

I frowned at him. "What kind of developments?"

"The person or people that took out Thompson have claimed they're coming for you next."

Ice flooded through my veins. I swallowed roughly, dropping my hands to my lap. "Someone wants to kill me?"

My father nodded, maintaining the same composure he would in a business meeting. Clearly, he wasn't too upset about my life being in danger.

"Yes. It could be Roman Cuccione; it could be another group entirely."

"Well, what are you going to do?" I asked as panic overtook the fear.

"We're currently working on a way to put you front and center with any potential threats." My mouth popped open in shock. My focus shifted to Steven who looked like he wanted to kill my father.

My voice broke as I asked, "Why?"

"There are too many potential suspects. If we can coordinate an event of some kind, or find another way to draw out the perpetrator, we can end them quickly and get back to work."

I sprung from the stool, causing it to clatter against the floor. There was no way in hell I'd jeopardize my life for *him*. Maybe it was the newfound strength from knowing Steven was in my corner, or maybe I'd simply had enough.

"You're going to use me as bait?!" I shrieked. "You want me to parade around in front of potential enemies in hopes that they act?"

My father's face turned red and his jaw clenched several times. "Watch your tone when you speak to me," he spoke in a low, warning voice.

I didn't care anymore. I wasn't going to let him use me this way. It was a death trap. "I'm not going to do that."

"You will do as I tell you," he bit out through clenched teeth. "If you don't, you'll be punished."

I closed my eyes, inhaling a deep breath through my nose to try and calm down. His punishments ranged from a simple slap across the face, to a twenty-four hour stint in one of the personal cells in the basement of his business.

One time, when I was seventeen and ditched my duties to go out with a few of the other soldiers, he'd locked me up for three days.

This was why I feared him. It's why I didn't call him out, didn't refuse to marry Sebastian, and why I hadn't turned him in. He treated me no better than the men who worked for him. Sometimes worse than that.

I took a deep breath, releasing it slowly as I opened my eyes. "Fine," I seethed.

His shoulders relaxed and he shifted his gaze to Steven who stood there, staring at me. "We're not leaving you without some sort of protection. Steven or Patrick will be with you at all times. Patrick is posted outside your door currently. Steven will relieve him of his shift once I leave."

"They have to be posted outside my door? Really?" I lifted a brow.

"Since we have no leads, we have to assume everyone is a suspect apart from those immediately employed by me," my father explained.

Did that mean he suspected Octavio or Sebastian Gallo as well? If someone had a hit out on me and wanted me gone, that meant my guards could potentially be caught in the crossfire. I didn't want that for them. They'd been put through so much already in just the last few weeks.

"I'd rather Marcus stand guard," I said.

My father scowled at me. "Marcus will be canvasing the exterior. These men," he hitched his thumb behind him in Steven's direction, "have made the vow to protect you at all costs."

I scoffed. "Like the men supposed to be protecting Sebastian? Are you certain he's not the one behind this?" I shouldn't have said that, but I was fed up.

What if my father was using Gallo like Steven had suggested the other night? He could have played him for the weapons and used Jonathan's money. Or whoever else he was connected to.

"*We* want to guard you and will do whatever it takes to keep you safe." It was the first time Steven had spoken. His voice came out in a low growl that made my stomach coil and tighten. I snapped my gaze to him, ready to argue. "It's not a negotiation," he added.

Shaking my head, I threw my hands up before letting them fall to slap against my thighs. "Whatever. What happens if it's an inside job? For all we know, someone could be inside the building already, ready to take out whoever is at the door and break in here."

"We've interviewed the staff as well as the other tenants. Most people in this building have no idea about our business dealings," my father said.

"That doesn't mean they won't slit my throat and leave me here for you to find tomorrow morning."

Steven snorted. "That's colorful."

"*Someone* has to make sure all bases are covered," I bit out, glaring at him.

I couldn't believe he was agreeing with my father. I thought I could trust him, and while I appreciated his concern and ability to do his job, I didn't want him harmed.

"They've been covered!" my father snapped. "The sooner we can put Octavio Gallo's mind at ease, the sooner we can begin conducting business again. You'll still be marrying his son. We still need to make sacrifices for the greater good."

Scoffing, I said, "The greater good for who?"

"All of us!" my father roared. "Do you want a legacy left for you or do you want everything I've worked hard for annihilated by Roman Cuccione and the God damn Mafia? Because if they get a hold of you …" he trailed off, looking me up and down. "You'll be no more than a whore for them. Just like your mother was."

I didn't miss the look of pure rage on Steven's face as he focused on my father's back. I was equally as angry. So much so that I couldn't even speak.

Why couldn't I stand up to him for once? Why did I always withdraw and cower? I hated that I was too afraid to speak out and I was embarrassed that Steven had been witness to all of it.

"Keep an eye on her for the night," he said to Steven as he headed for the door. "I'll have Marcus contact you once we come up with a plan."

"Yes, sir," Steven replied, staying where he'd been since he entered.

Once my father left, I picked up the stool, tucking it under the counter. I wanted to be alone, to cry and yell by myself. I wished Steven would leave but he didn't move an inch.

He didn't say anything, and neither did I.

Frustrated and sad, I decided to drown my sorrows the only way I could. I went to my refrigerator and pulled out an unopened bottle of wine. I grabbed a pint glass from the cupboard and poured until it was nearly full.

Inhaling a shaky breath, I took a long sip of the bittersweet alcohol. I turned to find Steven still standing there, his hands loose at his sides, eyeing me cautiously.

"You can go," I said, grabbing the bottle and my glass before breezing by him to march down the hall to my bedroom, slamming the door shut.

CHAPTER SEVEN
STEVEN

I ran my hands through my hair, pulling tightly at the ends. Fucking Albert Ricci and his demented parenting. It took everything in me not to knock him out when he threatened Aida and spoke of her mother. Especially when he'd told her the Mafia would use her as a whore. I saw the fear in her eyes, the way she'd gone from angry to deflated in a matter of seconds.

He'd done a good job brainwashing her and making her feel like nothing.

I was hoping to apologize to her and let her know that despite my own reservations about whatever plan they came up with, I'd stop at nothing to ensure her safety.

It wasn't the Mafia that killed Helena Ricci. Gio had confirmed the true identity of Helena's murderer when I spoke with him a few days ago. I believed his evidence because I trusted him and more than that, I trusted my uncle Roman. While I pretended to go along with everything Albert had just said, I had a different plan in mind. One that involved getting Aida away from him and destroying everything he and his ancestors built before.

I'd been sure to keep Gio updated as much as possible, including speaking with him this morning. He currently had a few of our own men staking out local hangouts to see if they could gain more information on where the weapons were. I even spoke with Uncle Roman last night.

He wanted me to continue my task and protect Aida at all costs. I explained her situation and like me, he'd felt bad for her. It wasn't in his nature to demean and ridicule women. He was the one who raised me, who taught me to respect women as much as men. Sometimes more than them.

Of course, Aida didn't know about any of this and instead of hearing me out, or at least giving me a chance, she'd grabbed a bottle of wine and stalked off to her bedroom. Not that I could blame her. Everything her father said had to have hurt her.

I let Patrick know I was good to keep an eye out for her tonight and told him to get some rest. He'd relieve me in the morning.

I entered the kitchen, grabbing a bottle of water from the refrigerator. She'd have to come out eventually to either eat or get more alcohol. I'd wait patiently for that to happen so that I could talk to her.

Sinking down on her plush gray couch, I clicked on the television.

An hour and a half later, Aida came out of her room, walking right past me to the kitchen with an empty bottle of wine. I glanced back at her over my shoulder, stifling a groan.

She was dressed in a pair of shorts that hugged the curve of her ass and rode up her thighs. She was also wearing a tight tank top. Her hair was pulled up high on her head, highlighting her tempting neck.

Jesus, she was going to kill me.

I hadn't been able to stop thinking about her since the other night and even though I knew it was an extremely risky road to go down, I found myself imagining what she'd feel like beneath me. I couldn't get her scent out of my head, or the way the slightest touch of her lips sent a frenzy of emotions through me.

She grabbed another bottle of wine from the refrigerator, pouring some into her glass. How many bottles did she have?

"I thought you'd take the hint and leave," she said quietly, keeping her back to me.

"My orders are to protect you tonight. You're upset and I don't want you to harm yourself."

She scoffed. "It's not like my father gives a shit if I hurt myself. You heard him earlier, he's using me. Once I've served my purpose, he'll put me down like a horse with a broken leg."

She turned around then, her blue eyes glistening in the dim kitchen light. I angled my body to face her fully.

"You know that's bullshit," I said. "Fuck him and what he thinks or wants."

She shook her head. "Yet you're going along with this plan to put me in danger." Her eyes rolled. "You're just as bad as he is."

"Watch it," I growled. "I'm nothing like Albert Ricci."

"Oh yeah?" She set the bottle and glass down, marching toward me. Placing her hands on her hips, she stood over me, her knees brushing my outer left thigh. "Prove it. What makes you better than him?"

"I would never sacrifice you for power," I said, staring into her eyes. "I'd never involve you at all."

Her eyes narrowed. "Why not?"

"Because you don't deserve it," I replied automatically. It was the truth.

Huffing out a breath, she lowered her hands to her sides. "You know, I'm not even allowed to date. I've never had a boyfriend and suddenly I'm supposed to get married?"

Damn. She was totally pure, untouched and enticing as hell. That didn't help the incredibly inappropriate thoughts running through my head. I tried swallowing the lump that formed in my throat.

"He's been keeping me under lock and key my whole miserable life and when I found out that Jonathan was dead, for the smallest moment, I got excited. I felt … hope. But it was fleeting because I knew, deep down, I knew my father would find another way to control me. All to bring to fruition this ridiculous vendetta of his." Tears slipped down her cheeks and I had the urge to pull her onto my lap and hold her.

"Aida …"

Sniffling, she wiped at the tears and went back to the kitchen. "I'm drunk," she said as she sipped more wine. "Stay if you'd like. I'm going to take a shower." She left the bottle on the counter but took the glass with her as she retreated back to her room.

I stared at her now closed bedroom door. She'd never gotten a chance to live at all. Albert had her so dependent on him that she'd missed normal experiences.

Sighing, I pinched the bridge of my nose with my thumb and index finger. Despite all the shit I'd seen and been through, maybe my heart would always be intact. It made me sick to know that Aida was forced to be alone unless it suited Albert. That her own father refused to allow her even something as simple as social interaction with people outside of the business.

My personal burner phone vibrated in my pocket and I pulled it out to see a new text message from Gio.

Gio: We may have a lead on where the weapons are stashed.

Me: Where might that be?

Gio: Looking into it. Will keep you posted.

Well that wasn't at all reassuring.

A sudden crash sounded from down the hall, like something may have fallen in Aida's bedroom. Shooting up, I sprinted to her room, flinging the door open. My heart pounded in my chest as I took in the empty room, lighted by a single lamp on her nightstand. There didn't seem to be anything out of place other than the clothes she'd been wearing before, scattered at the entrance of her closet.

My gaze shifted to the half open bathroom door connected to the room as I heard the water from the shower turn off. Wanting to make sure she was okay; I pushed it open.

"Aida, are you o …" The words died on my tongue as fire licked through my veins.

Aida stood just outside the shower, completely naked and giggling. I couldn't stop my eyes from drifting over her perfect, full chest, down to her flat stomach and voluptuous hips. Her legs were long despite her height.

My cock hardened and I bit down on the inside of my cheek, trying to wake my brain up. I was standing here like a creep and she was none the wiser. Her eyes were closed, her body shaking as she continued laughing. It was then I noticed a mark forming on her temple. I scowled.

"What the fuck happened to you?" I asked in a faint voice, moving closer to her.

Her head snapped up and the laughter died as her eyes widened. She grabbed a towel from the hook near the shower and scrambled to cover her body. I stopped within a foot of her, tucking her soaked hair behind her ear carefully to examine her temple.

"I … fell," she whispered. "I slipped and knocked into the shelf."

She didn't appear to be bleeding, but a faint purplish color was already forming as a bruise. Her eyes flicked up to mine, sparkling in the bright light of the bathroom. Tilting her head to the side, she slowly brought her right hand up, placing it against my cheek.

My body shuddered at the contact of her warm skin. All coherent thought began to wane as my blood heated. I needed to walk away now, get as far away from her as possible.

Why wouldn't my legs move?

"What are you doing?" My voice came out thick. Her fingers slid down my cheek, along my chest, and up my shoulder.

"Nothing," she murmured, her eyes half closed.

Her hand lingered only a moment before gliding back down to my chest and lower to my abdomen. I was beginning to lose my restraint as she splayed her hand over my waist.

I dipped my chin, watching her explore my torso over the cotton of my t-shirt, transfixed with that enticing hand. As it inched closer to the button of my jeans, I grasped her wrist, earning a gasp of surprise from her.

"Careful, babe. You're walking a fine line right now."

She tilted her head back to look in my eyes. I bit back on my molars, staring at that beautiful, full mouth.

"I want to dance," she said, stepping closer to me. Her chest, now covered with the towel, brushed against mine. "Will you dance with me?"

It was then I realized a soft song was playing from a speaker on the vanity. A woman's voice sang about dancing in a daydream and not wanting to wake up.

Lord help me, this woman was going to kill me if her father didn't first. I swallowed roughly, willing my legs to work properly. I still couldn't move.

"Dancing is reserved for lovers, Aida," I began. "We're not lovers. I'm working and you're—"

"I'm what?" She pulled her wrist from my grasp, or maybe I'd let go. Her fingers continued their exploration, descending toward the now prominent bulge in my jeans.

My chest rumbled in a growl. "Fucking dangerous. That's what you are." I grabbed her wrist again, walking her backward until she was against the wall near the shower.

Lowering my lips to her ear, I released a shaky breath and she trembled against me. I was in a whole lot of trouble when she responded to me this way. She had no idea how much I wanted to ease her pain, to make her forget for a while. I wanted to teach her how to kiss, how to fuck. I bet she wouldn't need much training. She was naturally sexy and there was no denying we had a special chemistry.

The only thing stopping me was the fact she was drunk and I'd never taken someone's virginity before. I didn't want to hurt her, didn't want to make her feel pressured.

"What do you really want, Aida?" I curved my free hand over her hip, sinking my fingertips into the soft fabric of the towel, into her skin.

"You," she breathed. The hand I wasn't restraining rose to rest alongside my neck as she lifted her head.

My heart pounded heavily as my mind battled with my body. God, she felt good against me. I hadn't felt a woman's body in so long. Releasing her wrist, I guided her hand back to my abdomen as I met her gaze once again.

"What do you want from me?" I asked. "Show me."

She kept her eyes locked on mine as she walked her fingers down to the button of my jeans again, flattening her palm. My lips parted and my head felt lighter somehow as she moved lower. My eyes closed. For being innocent, she sure seemed to know how to handle me.

I sucked in air through my teeth, feeling the tip of my dick grow wet. If she kept this up, I was going to come in my pants. I needed to stop this, to get the hell away from her. Instead, I opened my eyes as I cupped either side of her face. Angling my mouth over hers, I released a shaky breath. I didn't warn her, didn't give her the chance to reject me.

In an instant, my lips were devouring hers, sucking her bottom lip between my teeth before tugging on it gently. She whimpered, her hand falling away from me as she kissed me back, gliding her tongue against mine, copying my movements.

She tasted like wine and lust and I couldn't get enough.

I grabbed her waist, hoisting her up against the wall. She wrapped her legs around me as I pinned her with my hips, grinding against the soft flesh between her legs. I could feel how wet she was through my jeans, and the way she moaned while clinging to my shoulders nearly undid me at once.

Keeping her steady with my body and the wall, I moved a hand to the button of my jeans, ready to undo them and sink into her. I halted, pulling back from her.

I couldn't take her this way. Hell, I couldn't take her at all. I was responsible for her. It was my job to guard her, to keep her safe, and here I was so wrapped up in the way she looked, the way she felt, that I nearly compromised everything.

Realization flooded through me like a bucket of freezing water. I lowered her to her feet and put a decent amount of space between us. Her breath was ragged as she blinked up at me, her hand resting over her chest.

"Go to bed," I demanded, my voice thick and rough.

I saw the rejection on her face, the look of confusion in those ocean eyes. "W-what?"

Fuck, I didn't want to hurt her, but we couldn't do this. She'd been drinking. A lot. And I wasn't supposed to mix business with pleasure. Getting attached to her would be the stupidest thing I could ever do.

Crossing my arms over my chest, I scowled down at her. This was for the best. She'd regret this in the morning anyway. If she remembered any of it at all.

"Go. To. Bed. *Now*."

Her shoulders squared as anger replaced the uncertainty. "Why?"

I scoffed, shaking my head. "Jesus, you're difficult," I muttered.

Her eyes narrowed. "Tell me why I have to go to bed. Why did you stop?"

My brows rose and I lowered my hands to my sides, clenching them into fists to keep myself from touching her again. My damn body was still ready to go and that made it difficult to think clearly. I decided to be honest, maybe that'd scare her enough to listen.

"Because I want to fuck you. Badly. I want to take your innocence and destroy it until you're left with nothing but what you'll feel when I'm inside you. I want to bite you, mark you so that everyone knows you're mine."

She gasped, her eyes widening slightly. Yeah, that should send her running. I expected her to slap me or storm off, but instead, she shook her head.

"Is that such a terrible thing?"

Holy shit!

Nostrils flaring, I turned for the door. One of us had to be the responsible one here. I shouldn't have allowed this to happen.

"Trust me, you don't want that." I glanced back at her over my shoulder. "I'm trying to be the good guy here. That's not something I'm used to, so please, go to bed. I'm going to spend the rest of the night in the hall. I'll have Patrick check in with you in the morning."

I didn't give her a chance to rebuttal. I walked away from her, back down the hall and out the front door after locking it behind me. I ran a hand through my hair, inhaling a deep breath and letting it out slowly as I leaned against the doorframe.

I fucked up tonight. Big time. I wasn't thinking clearly, I was too enthralled in that beautiful woman with the sad eyes and a desperate need for more.

I slid down until I was sitting on the floor in front of her door. What happened tonight could never happen again. I needed to get this job over with immediately and walk away before I ended up taking it too far again, or worse, breaking Aida Ricci's heart. Because the second she learned who I really was, after everything her father made her believe, she'd regret ever letting me in.

I woke up with a massive headache and the lingering memory of hands on my waist, soft lips, and blazing hazel eyes.

I shouldn't have drank so much last night. I also shouldn't have kissed Steven or touched him the way I had. I couldn't stop thinking about the way he looked at me when he caught me outside the shower. He'd taken in every inch of my naked body with a predatory gaze that left me feeling both desired and terrified.

Even now as I thought about what happened between us, heat flooded between my legs. It was more than just finding him attractive and thinking of how sweet he'd been to me that made me act last night. It was my desperate need to *feel* something. To take something for myself and for once in my miserable life, disobey my father.

The level of control he had over me gnawed at me more every single day. I was tired of not having any freedom and last night, in the privacy of my own home with a man I wanted, I thought I could finally give in.

Just because I was inexperienced, didn't mean I didn't have base wants and desires. I'd watched enough television and read enough romance novels to understand the male and female anatomy and where babies came from. I wasn't a nun just because I was sheltered by my father from the real world.

No, I knew exactly what I was doing last night even if I had imbibed in an entire bottle of wine and another half a glass. I was grateful for the liberation I felt this morning. I only hoped Steven wasn't upset with me.

I wished my head weren't punishing me, too. Last night when I'd slipped, I thought it was funny, but now I was only left with the painful reminder of being a total klutz.

I rolled out of bed, grabbing my robe. I'd gone to bed like Steven wanted but was still reeling from what we'd done. I ended up crawling into my bed to touch myself, to help ease the ache he'd left behind when he walked away from me. I fell asleep naked, wishing he'd come back. Of course, he didn't do that, much to my disappointment.

I made my way to the kitchen, grabbing a couple of pain relievers and a bottled water. I took the pills and guzzled the entire bottle. Within a few minutes, my head already felt better.

I had no idea what would happen when I saw Steven again. Would he make Patrick track me today to avoid me?

He'd said he was trying to be the good guy for once. From what I knew of him; he *was* a good guy. Hopefully, he wouldn't quit because of what happened. Selfishly, I hoped he'd stick around a while. I needed a friend and he was as close to one as I had.

I was pulled from my thoughts by a knock on the door. When I answered it, Steven stood before me with his hands tucked into the pockets of his dark jeans. He regarded me with a look of indifference.

"Hey," I said.

"How you feeling?" he asked.

His eyes drifted to where the robe slightly parted between my breasts and my stomach fluttered. His gaze snapped to mine again.

"I'm okay," I replied, feeling my cheeks heat.

His brow crumpled. "Good."

"Do you want to come in?" I asked, noting the look of unease that settled across his features. Was he nervous to be around me?

He opened his mouth as if to speak, but nothing came out. He scratched at the back of his neck, gazing beyond me into the apartment. "I need you to do something first."

"What is it?" I asked, confused by his behavior. I'd never seen him look so uncomfortable before.

His eyes roamed over my body from head to toe before settling back on mine. When he spoke again, his voice was low, gravelly. "I need you to put some fucking clothes on." His hazel eyes darkened. "Right now."

I couldn't help the grin that spread across my lips. "Am I distracting you?" I asked in an innocent tone. His jaw muscle ticked and I giggled.

Oh, this was hilarious. He didn't trust himself around me, which meant I had a level of control over him. How nice it was for once to have the upper hand. He took a step closer to me, inhaling through his nose.

"I'm serious, Aida."

As entertaining as it was to know I had a certain amount of power over a man, I didn't want to risk him leaving. Releasing a heavy sigh, I rolled my eyes. "Fine." I turned away from him and wandered toward my room to throw on a pair of black leggings and a baggy sweater in hopes that would keep him from thinking impure thoughts. Normally, I was repulsed by the idea of being ogled by a man, but with Steven it was different.

When I went back out to the living room, Steven was standing behind the couch, tracking my every move as I approached.

"Better?" I asked with a raised brow.

He swallowed roughly. "No," he said. "But that's not your fault. I'm sorry." He scrubbed a hand over his face. "This is so fucked up."

Suddenly his reaction to me wasn't so funny anymore. He seemed to really be struggling right now and I felt terrible for teasing him. "Are you all right?"

He huffed out a humorless laugh. "No. I can't stop thinking about you. About the way you touched me and the way your lips felt. You smell like roses." His eyes penetrated mine, making my heart beat faster. "I can't stop it. I'm trying and I can't do it."

I frowned. He looked absolutely anguished and I felt like a terrible person for encouraging what happened between us. For thinking about him, too, and wishing I could kiss him again and touch him.

"I'm sorry," I whispered.

He shook his head. "No, don't apologize. You did nothing wrong, Aida."

I bit down on my bottom lip. That was debatable, but I wasn't going to say that. Instead, I said, "I shouldn't have taken advantage of you last night. I am sorry. I just wanted to … escape for a while, you know? Forget that my life is and has been basically over since the day I was born. You make me feel … free."

Steven closed his eyes for a brief moment. When they opened again, they were darker. "You can't say things like that to me," he growled. "You can't … want me. Not that way, not ever. Do you understand? My job is to protect you and nothing else."

The sting of rejection was like a knife twisting into my chest. I fully comprehended what he was saying. Loud and clear. "I understand."

"Good. Now that that's out of the way, I have some news."

"Oh?"

"Your father was receptive to ideas on how to find out who wants you dead."

My heart sank to my stomach. "What's his plan?"

He licked his lips, dragging his teeth along the bottom one. My stomach tightened. God, why did he have to be so damn attractive without trying? It was totally unfair.

"We're leaving town."

"What?"

"We're going on a road trip up north toward Rochester."

"I don't understand. Why are we traveling hours away?" I asked.

Steven shrugged. "It's the best way to rule out Don Roman."

You'd think being able to get out of the city, out of this apartment, would have me doing cartwheels and cheering. Instead, I felt more like an animal being herded into a reserve to be hunted for sport. This was more than a planned night out on the town or visit to some other group's event. This was putting me out on the road, making me a moving target. What a fun little challenge for my potential murderer.

I loosened a breath, plopping onto the couch. "What's in Rochester?"

Steven moved from the back of the couch to the opposite end, sitting as well. "A safe house of your father's. It's a property he hasn't sold yet. There's also a Mafia outpost linked to the Cuccione family."

My body went rigid. "What?"

He gazed at me for several moments without saying anything. "We'll drive up there on Friday and see what happens over the weekend."

"*We?*"

"Me and you. Albert's staying in town. He has a prior engagement."

Scoffing, I said, "Not surprised. Although, they trust you of all people to take me out of town alone?" I wasn't trying to be rude, but that seemed like an incredibly dangerous idea, even if the thought of spending time out of town with him was appealing.

"I'll be the first to admit, I think the way he handles things are … bizarre. But this is a solid plan. We'll be safe on the road. And Marcus, Demetri, and Patrick will be following us up. They'll be staying in town at a hotel and checking in each day."

"Are you honestly sure it's safe?"

His eyes narrowed at me as if I offended him. I didn't mean it, but this whole thing sounded like a bad idea.

"For starters, I'm trained in self-defense and protective defense," he said. Leaning back, he crossed an ankle over his knee, spreading his arm over the back of the couch. "Plus, I'll be armed and with a car tailing us, we'll have several eyes looking out."

"You have a gun?"

He arched a brow. "Are you seriously asking me that question?"

I rolled my eyes. I knew he was bound to have a gun being in the line of work he was in, I just had yet to see him brandish it. I remembered his initiation interview and the perfect shot he'd taken at the bullseye.

"How often did you use your weapon at your last job?"

"I've killed a few men in my day." He spoke as if it wasn't a big deal and that unsettled me. "Been at the business end of a Glock more times than I can count, too."

My mouth popped open. "Have you been shot?"

His lips tipped up on one side in a half grin, his eyes sparkling. Instead of speaking, he planted both feet on the floor and sat up straighter. I watched as he grabbed the hem of his t-shirt, rolling it up slightly before tugging down his jeans near his right hip.

A small, discolored patch of uneven skin ran about two inches along the muscular V of his hips. I felt my face flame as I leaned forward, inspecting the former wound. I hadn't noticed it before, but then last night I was inebriated and he'd kept his clothes on.

"A bullet grazed me during a shootout a few years ago," he said quietly.

I reached my hand out, gliding my index finger along the scar. His ab muscles twitched and I lifted my gaze to his. "Sorry," I mumbled, sitting back again.

He lowered his shirt. "The point is, I can handle this. I can handle a lot. More than you know or could even imagine. With any luck, we'll figure out who's really out to get you."

I nodded. It'd be nice to figure that out so that my life wasn't in danger any longer. However, I couldn't shake the feeling that I'd never be secure no matter what. As long as I belonged to my father, and he could control me, I'd be a dead woman walking in one form or another.

Whether it was by bullet or forced obedience, I'd surely be dead in the figurative sense soon enough. And if those reasons didn't end me, being alone with Steven in a vehicle on a long road trip surely would.

CHAPTER EIGHT
STEVEN

I had Gio talk to his contact close to Albert and discovered there was a home near Rochester he owned. We happened to have a station of about ten guys in that city which meant if I could convince Aida to leave with me, we'd disappear under the protection of my uncle's men and take out her father.

I still didn't know who the contact was that Gio spoke with and I didn't ask. It was best to treat everyone like an enemy when on the job.

There were more spies than just me working for the Mafia, but we didn't engage with each other. My job was basic intel and getting close with the intention of backing out. There were other men, men like Gio's contact, who made a living by fully embedding themselves in the outfit and dying with their secrets. This particular guy had familial and geographical knowledge but wasn't aware of Albert's newest plans and schemes.

At one time, I thought I might become one of those full time, deep in spies. However, after what happened with Randall Hawks, I decided having the opportunity to walk away was far better. If I didn't have Celeste to look after, maybe I'd think differently. I wanted to be around for her when I could. If I'd taken a vow to go full on member in a rival group, I'd never be able to see her or speak to her ever again.

After leaving Aida's, I called my sister to let her know I wanted to see her. I was leaving town, albeit for only a weekend, but I still wanted to let her know and say goodbye.

We met at my off the job apartment. My place was only about seven blocks from Aida's, so I walked, making sure to keep a look out in case I was being followed.

Celeste brought sandwiches and spent the entire time over lunch telling me about her finals coming up before spring break. I was proud of her for focusing on school and her future.

"We haven't had a vacation together in over five years. I think we should go to Uncle Roman's lake cabin this summer. Aunt Betty wants to do more things like that now that you're back."

"I feel like I've forgotten what it's like to take a vacation," I admitted.

To be honest, the last thing on my mind right now was getting away from it all. I wondered if Aida took vacations or if she'd ever been to a lake cabin. My guess was her father kept her on lockdown even in the summertime.

I needed to stop thinking about her.

Celeste frowned. "Fab, you're home now. I know you have an assignment at the moment, but since you're in town, you should be with family more. It's important and I missed you."

"I know," I said. "I'll do whatever you plan. As long as I'm not needed for work."

She scoffed. "You realize who you are, right? I'm surprised you work so hard when our uncle, the man that raised us, is your boss."

I chuckled. "It's not like underground bosses base their work on federal holidays and follow laws. Uncle Roman can sneak away for a few days if he wants because he has so many men working for him. One of those men being me."

She sighed. "Right."

"I need to figure out a way to get Aida Ricci away from her father and we need to figure out where the weapons are stashed. Once that's solved, hopefully Albert will get what's coming to him."

"Then you'll let Uncle Roman intervene?"

"I have unrefuted evidence of their dealings and intentions, so we could act now if we weren't in the dark on some very dangerous weapons." If Albert and Thompson had hidden them with another group, things could go from bad to worse. I'd feel better once I knew for sure Aida was under Mafia protection. I couldn't leave her with Ricci.

"What is it?" Celeste asked with a mouthful of sandwich. Concern laced her features.

"Nothing," I lied. I wasn't going to talk to her about Aida.

She tilted her head to the side. "Liar." Ripping off a chunk of her bread, she tossed it at me. It missed, landing only halfway across the table. "Does it have to do with the woman?"

My shoulders tightened and I narrowed my eyes at her. "No." She rolled her eyes, picking up on my defensiveness.

Despite our time apart, my sister knew me better than anyone. She had a knack for reading me like a book.

"You like her." She frowned, shaking her head. "Fabiano …"

"I don't like her. She's just a job," I interrupted.

"Oh, you so like her. She's pretty, she's tough, you're smitten. It doesn't surprise me, really. I mean, when's the last time you were even with a girl?"

I groaned. I was not having this conversation with my little sister.

"Would you grow up? I want her to be away from her piece of shit father because I feel sorry for her. That's all," I argued. Who was I kidding? I didn't even believe what I was saying.

I did like Aida. A lot. And seeing her in that fucking robe when she answered the door this morning nearly set me on fire. I wanted to hold her again and kiss her, wanted to make her moan as I sucked on that delicate neck.

I raked a hand through my hair, tugging at the ends. Damn, just thinking about her now had me half hard. I needed to get laid, to get her out of my system.

I was supposed to have the night off tonight since I'd be working all weekend. Maybe I could go out, find a hookup or something.

My sister interrupted my thoughts. "You think she'll leave with you?"

"I hope so. I've already talked to Roman a bit about it. He thinks he can hide her, put her somewhere safe until her father's taken care of and we know she won't be compromised."

"Does she trust you?"

"I don't know." I honestly didn't. "I might have to blow my cover to earn her trust."

Celeste's eyes widened. "You'd risk your cover to get her out?"

I released a sigh, shaking my head. "My vow to the Mafia is sacred and I would die before dishonoring Uncle Roman. But she's … worth it."

She reached out to me, placing her hand on my thigh. When I took the oath to go undercover and do whatever it takes for the greater good of the Mafia, I understood what might happen to me. Even at the age of eighteen, I was prepared to die for the cause.

The more I learned about and spent time with Aida, the more compelled I was to try and save her. Maybe I had feelings for her, maybe it was just in my nature to be protective. I couldn't pinpoint the why's of it all.

It was becoming difficult to be around her with my true identity between us. I wanted her to know who I was and trust that I was on her side. That it didn't matter if we were from enemy families with a sordid past. She was human like me and our names shouldn't matter.

There were times it felt like she trusted me, but knowing how guarded and withdrawn she was, I wasn't so sure. For all I knew, she was simply in need of a friend, someone to talk to and help her not feel so alone. That didn't mean she'd be willing to walk away from her father if the time came. He was all she'd ever known.

I wondered what she'd do if she were finally granted freedom. If she'd get a normal job, marry a nice man and have kids. She deserved whatever dreams she'd been longing for if she were still optimistic enough to have them.

We were a lot alike, me and her. Too much alike in many ways. It's why I felt so deeply about ensuring her safety and giving her those moments of conversation, allowing her to share her feelings. Maybe if I'd had someone like that when I was deep in the job with Randall Hawks I wouldn't have the nightmares. Maybe then, I'd feel worthy of Aida Ricci.

*

Friday morning I was awoken to a phone call from Marcus checking in to make sure I was ready to take Aida up to Rochester. He'd secured an SUV for us to take which was parked in the garage below the building. He and Patrick would be following behind us covertly in another vehicle.

After showering and packing an overnight bag that included two handguns besides the one tucked into the back of my jeans, I headed for Aida's apartment. I told her last night to be ready by ten. The trip would take roughly five hours with traffic and the thought of spending half the day in a vehicle alone with her was already driving me crazy.

I wasn't only worried about the way my body seemed to helplessly react to her, it was what our conversation might consist of that had me nervous. I hated being forced to sound vague in my responses to her, that I had to outright lie about my past. I did receive the scar I showed her from a shootout, but there were other scars, ones that she wouldn't understand unless she knew the truth.

Like the stab wound that healed unevenly on my left thigh that was given to me by Hawks. Then there was the burn scar on my right shoulder from a cigar being put out on me. That was also from Hawks. He'd tortured me a lot because he wanted to remind me that I was nothing without him, that I'd never be.

Normally, I wouldn't take that shit from anyone but being undercover left me vulnerable. If I fought back, he probably would have killed me. If I dipped out and ended the mission, I'd be a disgrace to my family, to the Mafia.

These were things I could never speak to anyone about, and I didn't. But there was something about Aida that lowered my defenses, that brought out parts of me I hadn't seen in

118

years. I was softer with her. I wanted to share every part of my story and find out if it scared her or left her wanting me completely.

The desperation to open up to her grew more and more by the second so I contacted Gio to give him an idea of our itinerary for the day. I'd already provided him with the address of the home we'd be at and while it wasn't intended for our men to watch the place, because Ricci had his own men for that, I felt better in them knowing my whereabouts.

If I could convince Aida to turn on her father and his men, we'd leave for the outpost near Rochester immediately. I was fully prepared to give myself up if it would help in getting her to safety. Although, I hadn't shared that yet with my uncle or his capo. They'd likely be pissed.

With any luck, Roman's FBI officer would know the whereabouts of the weapon stash before the end of the weekend. I'd feel a lot better about moving forward with our plan if that happened. An unknown arsenal of explosives and high-powered weapons could quickly become an annihilation of my family and our people.

I waited for Aida to answer her door and prayed she was dressed in something other than that damn robe. Thankfully, she was wearing a pair of jeans that hugged every curve and a blue sweater that accentuated her eyes. Not much better than the robe but fully dressed was safer.

I wanted to get her out of my system and thought I'd find some company last night, but instead I went back to my apartment, leased by Albert Ricci, and spent the night alone. I jerked off in the shower thinking of Aida, and then again in my bed before falling asleep. I was ashamed of my behavior, but like I said, something about her infected me and I couldn't get enough.

"Morning," I said, slipping by her into the apartment.

I set my duffle bag down by the door. "Hey, when are we leaving?" she asked.

I checked my watch before glancing at her. *Keep your focus on her eyes, nothing else,* I told myself.

"In about ten minutes. Your father has a car in the garage for us." She nodded. "We'll stop when we get about halfway, but other than that, we need to stay on the road and get to the house."

"Got it," she said.

"You ready to go?"

"Yeah." She pointed to a bag sitting on the couch. "We're staying through the weekend?"

"Yeah, two nights." I glanced at the bag again, noting how full it was. "Are you afraid we'll get stranded or something?"

She glared at me. "I like to be prepared. There's nothing wrong with that."

I shrugged, that was true. It shouldn't have surprised me. The last few weeks I'd known her; she'd never worn the same outfit twice. She probably had a wardrobe big enough to wear for an entire year before washing anything.

"Let's go," I said, grabbing my bag and slinging it over my shoulder.

She grabbed hers as well and followed me out into the hall before locking the deadbolt with her key. Our ride in the elevator was silent, as was our walk through the parking garage to the vehicle.

Marcus was waiting next to the SUV with the keys. He nodded in my direction before smiling at Aida. I took the keys from him.

"We'll stay close enough to watch out without being obvious," he said.

I nodded, grabbing Aida's bag from her to put in the back.

"We put out word on purpose, letting everyone know she's headed out of town for the weekend."

"Any new leads on who killed Thompson?" I asked as Aida got into the passenger seat.

Marcus shrugged. "It just doesn't make sense. Someone must know we were working with him and the only ones that did were us."

"What about Gallo?" I asked. It was all bullshit. Grim was the one that made the call claiming he was coming for Aida next. The purpose was to try and take control of the situation which was currently working.

Marcus scowled. "Sebastian's been out of town for a few days now. Unreachable, which is concerning."

I raised a brow. "What?"

The second in command shrugged. "Octavio won't tell us where he is. They may be questioning our agreement since Thompson ended up dead. They're afraid of those Mafia bastards."

Smart men to know when to back off. I nodded, casually. "Here's hoping we sort this shit soon," I said, opening the driver's door.

We said our goodbyes and Marcus told me to text him whenever we decided to stop. He and Patrick would stop with us to keep watch. I didn't like that I was being surveilled by him during the trip, but I had no other choice. I seemed to have his and Albert's trust though, which made offering to stay with Aida at the house easier.

Unless they were on to me and it was a trap. Yeah, that thought occurred to me after suggesting the plan from the beginning, but I was desperate to end this and confident my spy skills were solid.

As I pulled out of the parking garage into traffic, Aida began fumbling with the stereo.

"I hope you don't mind," she said. "I like listening to music."

"Not at all," I said. "I'll let you control the stereo."

She turned to look at me, a small smile playing on her lips. "Really?"

I shrugged. "Yeah. Is that another rule of your father's, to not let you listen to music?"

"Not exactly, it's just that I've never been in a car where I got to control the stereo. I mean, there's always a driver or whatever and typically it's nothing but silence."

I changed lanes, heading for the freeway. "Then let's pretend you're going on vacation. This is a weekend getaway, not a ploy to catch whoever supposedly wants you dead."

She snorted. "Easier said than done."

"I'm serious." I glanced at her briefly. "You can be whoever you want to be this weekend. I've got your back, okay? You're safe with me."

She smiled again, shaking her head. "You're awfully confident in your abilities to protect me."

"That's because I'm always prepared."

"Did you learn that from your bodyguard job in Chicago?" she asked, stopping on a slow rock song.

"It was a lot more involved than I originally anticipated." Not really a lie, but not true, either. I was getting tired of making her think I was something else.

"Is that where you got the scar?"

"Yeah, things were … violent."

Her brow crumpled and she looked at me with remorse. I hoped she wasn't going to question me further. I wasn't sure what I could say when she thought I'd worked for a congressman. Thankfully, she changed the subject.

"You know, my father cut off a guy's finger once. Did it right in front of me to teach me a lesson in stealing."

"What the fuck? How old were you?" I asked, gazing at her again.

She tucked a strand of hair behind her ear. "Thirteen. I got caught in his home office a few weeks before that and then he found out this guy was stealing his street drug product or something."

"I'm sorry," I said and I was, for more than just her crappy upbringing.

"It's okay, I learned my lesson. Besides, like I've said before, I've shot a person. Blood doesn't bother me."

Right, she'd been Daddy's little soldier before he wanted to ship her off like a mail order bride for shady business dealings. It was difficult to imagine Aida having a tremendously violent side. She definitely had a temper and was stubborn from what I'd witnessed, but it didn't set well with me that she'd wield a gun and take bad guys out. Not because she was a woman, but because I was concerned for her safety.

The conversation died off and I drove silently, letting the sounds of Aida's infinite playlist fill up the space between us. She had good taste in music but man was it chaos. One minute, she'd blare a hip hop song, and the next something slow and melodious would play. She'd sing along sometimes and I'd try to listen to what her voice sounded like over the loud music.

After a few hours, I texted Marcus and pulled off the freeway into a town just outside Binghamton. I stopped at a gas station to fuel up, telling Aida to wait in the car. Once that was done, I headed to a small diner that looked fairly empty.

Putting the vehicle in park, I cut the engine. "We'll get out here to eat and use the bathroom. I'm going to get out first and open your door," I explained as I checked the rearview mirror.

Patrick was driving the other vehicle and pulled into the parking lot, taking a spot on the other side. I waited another few minutes, letting him and Marcus go into the diner first, before exiting and coming around to open Aida's door for her then walked slightly behind her, letting her lead the way to the entrance.

We were greeted by a middle-aged woman in a stained white apron and navy blue uniform. I asked for a booth in the corner and she obliged.

"Can I go to the bathroom?" Aida asked quietly after the woman left to get us water.

I scanned the small dining area, scouting where the restrooms were located. "Yeah, you're good."

She nodded as she stood, heading for the women's room door. I stared out the window, once again checking our surroundings. I was nothing if not efficient and cautious. It wasn't my men I was worried about. I was growing paranoid and afraid Albert would roll up or Sebastian Gallo. What if he intended to take Aida while all this shit between Ricci and us was going down?

I ran a hand through my hair, loosening a breath. I needed to quit letting my head run wild with irrational fears. It was just knowing things would be over soon that had me freaking out. Especially since there'd been so much going on at once when it was finally time to end Hawks last year.

I had been constantly worried that he'd discover who I really was or that one of his other men would rat me out when I started training his captive to shoot a gun. I put myself on the line for Claire Evans and what I felt for her didn't come close to what I felt for Aida Ricci. Claire was like a sister to me, Aida was … something else entirely.

After Aida came back to the table, I excused myself to the bathroom as well, slipping my gun from behind me and sliding it into her hand under the table.

"Are you freaking kidding me!?" she whisper shouted.

"Every second you're alone, you're in danger. Keep it under the table," I said before walking away.

She wasn't truly alone since other men were in here to protect her, but I didn't trust them. If anyone, including them, tried to make a move for Aida, she could defend herself. I wasn't going to leave her empty handed.

After I sat back down, I reached my hand out to hers under the table. She passed the gun and I quickly tucked it behind me under my shirt.

"I can't believe you brought a weapon in here," she whispered.

Rolling my eyes, I said, "What are they going to do, shake me down before serving me?"

"It just seems excessive." She turned slightly, gazing in the direction of Marcus and Patrick who were talking. "Are they carrying, too?" She shifted to look at me again.

"I'm sure they are," I said.

She shook her head. "It still feels extreme."

"Not when there's a killer on the loose, gunning for that pretty little face of yours."

Her eyes narrowed and she crossed her arms. Our waitress approached us with the food we'd ordered before I went to the bathroom. Aida'd ordered a double cheeseburger with fries. It was the first time I'd seen her eat something with calories.

Often times, she'd eat a salad or nothing at all. In fact, I didn't think I'd ever seen her eat a real meal since I'd met her.

She took a bite of the cheeseburger, moaning around the food in her mouth. My gaze locked in on her mouth as she chewed. I tightened my hand into a fist under the table. Damn, she even made eating sexy.

"Since we're pretending this is a vacation, I'm eating whatever I want," she said, dipping a fry into a heaping pile of ketchup before popping it into her mouth.

I frowned. "Your father monitors what you eat?"

"Yeah." She took another bite of her burger, chewing slowly.

"That's bullshit," I said.

"I know. He has someone provide groceries for me at my apartment and I don't get a say in what they deliver. At the engagement party, I was under strict orders to not eat or drink too much."

I kept discovering new things about the way she was treated and it pissed me off even more each time. I fucking hated Albert Ricci and every single man that worked for him. How could they allow that kind of behavior?

I took a bite of the sandwich I ordered, keeping my mouth busy instead of saying something I might regret. Like how fucked it was that she couldn't even eat what she wanted. I wanted to tell her that I'd get her out of this, that she'd be safe and away from her father soon. However, I couldn't say any of that right now, so I simply ate.

We both finished the rest of our meal in silence.

I let Aida control the stereo once again and we traveled along the freeway for another two hours before making it to Rochester. The safe house Albert set up was just past the city, up in the hills and secluded. Most of Albert's properties were on the outskirts of different towns within the state.

I'd also learned that he used them as locations for his not so legal business dealings when necessary. Most of what he sold was residential, but some things were commercial as well, which explained the few warehouses where he conducted meetings. I'd made sure to let Gio know about that. For all we knew, the weapons Thompson or whoever purchased were tucked away at one of those places.

I drove up a winding road lined with trees that were just beginning to bloom. The closer we got to the house, the more my anxiety spread. I was used to being in unfamiliar places, but this time, I felt more like a sitting duck than an effective participant. I wanted to be in the line of action, solving a solution to this problem. Guarding Aida was important but so was moving quickly. Being stuck in this house while everyone else did whatever they needed to do seemed ridiculous. It didn't help that when I was idle, my thoughts became more prevalent.

I released a breath as I pulled in the driveway of the rustic looking mansion. The more time I spent with Aida, the further from my original objective I became. And every passing minute had me worried that I'd be made and finally have to pay for my lies and deceit.

I didn't like the idea of being trapped out here in the country for the weekend. I was basically dismissed to find a room while Marcus, Patrick, and Steven talked about the plan and some new development.

It didn't set well with me that my father hadn't come along, that he was remaining in New York City to conduct business. Either he was confident in his men's skills, or there was no hitman after me. I wouldn't be surprised if he were keeping me away for other reasons.

I think Steven was beginning to grow suspicious as well, because he'd been quiet after our late lunch. He'd barely said anything to me and looked tense. I was used to being left in the dark about most things unless it was necessary for me to know, which wasn't often. However, Steven worked for my father and his job was to protect me. Shouldn't he have every bit of information that Marcus and Patrick did?

I chose a bedroom up the long staircase off the foyer toward the end of the hall. Lucky for me, this bedroom had its own bathroom as well. I set my bag down at the end of the queen-sized bed on top of a pink, floral comforter.

Wandering over to the bay window with a bench seat, I sat down and stared out at the expansive lawn. It was more yellow than green because of the early spring weather. It was colder out here than the city.

I glanced down to the right where the driveway was and saw Steven standing out there, arms crossed, as he spoke to Marcus. It was hard to gauge his facial expressions from this distance, though his body gave off a defensive quality that had me wondering if he was angry.

I shook my head, gazing back at the land. It was ridiculous that I could read Steven so well. We hardly knew each other, yet in the last few weeks, we seemed to form a friendship. If you could even really call it that. I mean, we were kind of forced to spend time together with him being my guard and all.

So why did I feel like he understood me more than anyone else? Since the beginning, he'd seemed to have my best interest at heart. There was the time he snuck me an extra glass of wine at the engagement party and the time he took me to the park because I didn't want to be at home.

He was considerate of me at times when he didn't really need to be. Like not agreeing with my father putting me in this situation. It was clear where he stood when it came to my father. He didn't seem to like the man any more than I did. In fact, he'd looked completely repulsed when I'd confessed to not being able to buy my own groceries at lunch earlier.

I wondered why he'd continue to work for a man he didn't like? Why would he keep being my guard if he seemed to disagree with everything the man stood for? Surely, it wasn't because of me? It couldn't be.

Could it?

Just the idea of him sticking around for me made me roll my eyes. There's no way he'd do that. He could so easily find another woman without the family drama I had. He was handsome, with his dark, disheveled hair and hazel eyes that seemed to penetrate straight to your soul when he looked at you. And his body? Even with the scar on his hip, and possibly more I had yet to see, he was the epitome of perfect. At least, I thought so.

My mind flashed to when he'd kissed me a few nights ago. The way he held my face, my hips, as if he were clinging to me to keep him grounded. I still didn't regret what happened. Not when I've been in desperate need to feel a man's touch, to explore something like my sexuality for the last few years since becoming an adult.

I hated that my father wouldn't allow me to at least find myself before marrying me off to Sebastian. I went from childhood, to puberty, to being trained as a soldier because it was "useful," to becoming an object of trade. I was nothing but a mere trophy to some stranger I'd never be able to grow to love. How could I ever love someone who only wanted me because of a business arrangement?

It was awful to say, but I wished Sebastian had been killed instead of Jonathan. It's not like he was a good man and deserved me. He and his father were illegal arms dealers. He was as bad as my father because he'd agreed to take me as a wife without my consent.

Movement in the driveway caught my attention again and I saw an unmarked, black car pull in behind the SUV. The three men turned to see who'd arrived as Demetri stepped out, smiling.

They exchanged a few words and then Marcus followed Demetri back to the car. My brow crumpled as they got in and then backed out and took off down the road. Patrick went to the other vehicle he'd been driving and left as well.

Panic filled me as I feared the worst possible scenario for this weekend. Surely, they wouldn't be stupid enough to leave me alone with only Steven? That was going to make avoiding him more difficult.

Maybe the others were only running into town for something or staking out a different area. They'd likely be back at some point. When Steven said we were staying here, I didn't really think it would be just the two of us.

Releasing a sigh, I stood and unzipped my bag. At least I'd brought a book. I could use that to keep me busy and hopefully avoid Steven for the rest of the night. I'd take his advice and pretend I was on vacation. It was nice to not be under my father's thumb for a while, but the endless possibilities that ran through my mind made me wish for the first time that I wasn't alone.

*

Later that evening, I learned that Patrick, Marcus, and Demetri were in the city of Rochester in hopes of baiting the mystery hitman. Steven let me know that and offered to make me dinner but I declined. My nerves got the best of me with the realization that we were alone, so I thought avoiding him altogether was a better option.

Part of me wondered if the mysterious hitman was even a real threat. It just didn't make sense for someone to kill Thompson out of the blue like that. Unless it was whoever he'd sold the weapons to. I remembered our conversation that night when he mentioned my father knew who it was. Could my father have been the one to call for the hit? But then, why would someone claim they wanted me dead, too? My father sent me to Thompson to check in with him. He wouldn't send me willingly into danger like that.

If it were the Mafia, they would have done more than threatened my death. Very rarely did Don Roman shy away from total annihilation when picking off his enemies. Besides, it would probably be my father he'd kill before me.

I remember hearing a story years ago from my father that the Don had killed my mother out of spite. Our families were old enemies ever since my grandfather, Vincenzo tried to take on the prior Mafia boss. Things had settled for years, but one night while my mother and father were out at a party, hosted by a local politician, Roman saw them and grew jealous.

Supposedly, my mother had left the Don for my father and she'd been caught in the crossfire when Roman tried to get revenge. I believed it to be true, but now I wondered if there was more to the story. As I grew older and realized just how friendly my father was with other women, I began to think his grief was misplaced. He never spoke of her, never offered to take me to where she was buried. I didn't even know what cemetery she was laid to rest at.

I sat up in bed, releasing a heavy sigh. I had way too much on my mind right now. This newfound solitude was drawing out more thoughts than usual. I glanced at the digital clock on my nightstand and saw that it was nearly midnight. I regretted my decision to forgo dinner and was absolutely starving.

I heard the sound of a door closing. A few minutes later, the shower from the shared bathroom down the hall started up. Imagining Steven in the shower did things to my body that made sleep all the more elusive. I needed to get out of this room for a while.

I opened my door, walking quietly past the bathroom, down the stairs to the foyer. The cool hardwood floor helped ease the warmth spreading through me and I inhaled a deep breath before releasing it slowly.

I made my way to the rustic looking kitchen that was located toward the back of the house, past the living room and another small hall that led to an office and half bath.

Everything in the kitchen was made of real wood, including the beams across the cream colored ceiling and the dark, stained cabinets. The floor transitioned to a stone, which was colder than the hardwood. I shivered, wishing I'd put socks on before coming down.

Tucking my hands into the baggy sleeves of my hooded sweatshirt, trying to keep them warm as I rummaged through the cupboards, I was grateful to find food and dishes. Maybe the other men had come back with groceries at some point, or maybe my father sent someone to stock the house before we arrived.

I decided to have a bowl of cereal because it was quick and easy. I wasn't sure if Steven would go to bed after his shower or not, so I didn't want to hang out down here too long. I didn't trust myself being alone with him. Especially when my mind kept conjuring up inappropriate situations between the two of us.

As I spooned a bite of cereal into my mouth, I actually wanted Patrick or Marcus to come back, if only to keep me from the temptation that was my current roommate. I needed to get a grip on my hormones when it came to Steven. I was daydreaming about him when his voice startled me.

"You're up," Steven said, entering the kitchen in a pair of loose hanging gray sweats and nothing else. His dark hair was damp and more disheveled than usual.

I paused my chewing, gaping at him as he headed for the refrigerator. Was he trying to torture me? I needed to say something before he caught me checking him out.

"I'm up," I said, finishing my bite.

He grabbed a bottled water from the refrigerator. His gaze flicked to mine as he closed the door. "Are you feeling okay?"

"Yeah," I said slowly. "Why?"

"You look a little flush. Your cheeks are pinker than normal." Probably because I was staring at his body and remembering the way those hands, now wrapped around that bottle, felt on me.

"I'm fine," I shrugged. "Just have a lot on my mind."

He grabbed an apple from a fruit basket on the counter, then sat across from me at the table, taking a large bite of the fruit.

I watched his mouth move as he chewed, then the way his throat rolled in a swallow. I liked his throat. More than I should. I glanced back down at my now empty bowl.

"We're safe here," he said before taking another bite.

I nodded. "I know." I stabbed the milk with my spoon. "It's just that I don't think anyone is coming here to kill me. This whole plan seems ridiculous."

"I agree, but it's not like we can tell your father, or Marcus for that matter. Once Albert's mind is made up, his word is law."

It was true. That didn't mean he was right though.

"What if it's someone we know?" I risked a glance at him again; grateful he'd set the apple down. "What if it was an inside job?"

Steven's brow lifted. "You think a Gallo or someone on your father's team would kill Thompson and want you dead?"

Shaking my head, I said, "No. I think someone killed him to send a message. Maybe one of my father's men as a distraction or one from the Gallo crew because they found out my father didn't really sell the weapons to an outside buyer. Or maybe it *is* the Cuccione's and they're disrupting from within somehow."

"It's not the Mafia," he said immediately.

My head tilted slightly as I studied his face.

"Why are you so certain of that?" I asked.

How would he know it wasn't them? I thought back to a previous conversation we had when he'd seemed surprised that I even knew the Cuccione name. He had a lot more information on the underground world for someone who supposedly worked for a congressman before this.

Steven cleared his throat. "I just don't think the Mafia would involve themselves in something as trivial as gunning down a nobody like Thompson. He's not as big of a threat to them. Not like your father or the Gallos."

I crossed my arms over my chest, leaning forward to rest my elbows on the table. "How would you know who they'd go after and not go after?"

He stared at me across the table for a few moments in silence. His voice was quieter when he spoke again.

"I used to work for another group."

"Another group? Like part of the Mafia?"

"Sort of," he said. "It was a small outfit, not around anymore. I learned a lot about the history of the Cuccione family and others. That's why I don't think this hitman is theirs. Yes, Thompson was obviously working with your father, but they'd go after the bigger targets first."

I nodded. "Not unimportant children."

His gaze sharpened at me. "You're important. That's not what I meant."

"What did you mean then?"

He ran a hand through his hair, releasing a sigh. "They'd *use* you instead. They'd try to gain information from you first and try to learn all that they could in order to take out your father. The Mafia is organized, precise. Killing people, no matter how vile you may think they are, isn't their mission all the time."

I sat straighter, clasping my hands in front of me on the table. "The Mafia couldn't know about my father and Thompson working together," I said.

"Exactly." He finished off his apple in a few more bites and stood up to discard it. "I'm thinking Sebastian and Octavio

Gallo aren't aware of your father's plans. Which could be why Sebastian skipped town."

I frowned. "What do you mean he skipped town?"

Steven came back to the table and sat down. "Marcus told me this morning that he's gone."

"Do you think he's the one that killed Jonathan Thompson?" I asked. He might want me dead if he found out my father lied to them about the weapon's buyer.

Steven shook his head. "I don't know."

Frustration and fear simmered just under the surface as the weight of everything grew. Nothing made sense and it was driving me crazy. I thought again about what might happen if I tried to turn my father in myself. Perhaps I'd be safer under the protection of Don Roman. But I couldn't just abandon my father and more importantly expect Steven to march me to the Mafia's steps when there may truly be someone out to kill me. What group had he worked for prior? Were they enemies or allies?

I opened my mouth to ask but the words got lodged in my throat. Tears threatened to spill from the corners of my eyes. It was late and I was overwhelmed with exhaustion.

Steven's lips turned down and he rose from his seat, walking around the table toward me. He knelt down beside me, his hands cupping my cheeks while his thumbs swiped away the tears that had managed to escape. "I won't let anyone harm you."

The sincerity in his hazel eyes made my heart stop beating for a second. He continued smoothing my face with the pads of his thumbs and my blood warmed at the touch. Steven cared about me. Maybe not more than one human to another, but he felt something good toward me, and that was enough to break me at the moment.

"I don't want to do this anymore," I cried as more tears flowed. I felt like the dam I'd kept locked tight was finally shattering. I needed release. "I don't want to be in danger. I don't want to marry a man I don't love. I want to be free. I want to run away."

"Shh … it's okay." His hands fell from my face as he pulled me into him, folding me against his chest to hold me.

The action made me sob even harder and I clung to him, digging my nails into the skin of his back, holding on for dear life.

I was angry at my father for ruining my life, frustrated that I had no straightforward way out, terrified at the thought of someone possibly wanting me dead. It was all too much and I couldn't live this way anymore.

I don't know how long we sat there in the kitchen, me wailing against Steven's bare chest that was now covered in tears while he simply held me. I felt awful for my breakdown and it couldn't have been comfortable for him, kneeling on the stone floor.

Eventually, the tears ran dry and I was left feeling completely drained and slightly embarrassed for using him as my personal tear and snot collector. Pulling back from him, I wiped my nose with my sweater sleeve and inhaled a deep breath.

Steven gave me a small smile, smoothing my hair back from my face.

"I'm sorry for crying all over you," I whispered.

"It's okay." He glanced down at his chest and I followed his gaze. It wasn't wet anymore, which I was grateful for.

I noticed that tattoo on his left pec again. I hadn't gotten a good look at it before, but now I can see it clearly. It was some sort of script, but it wasn't in English. It may have been Latin or something else. Italian, maybe?

Even though I had Italian heritage, as did my father, I didn't know much of the native language.

"What does that mean?" I asked.

"*Morte Piuttosto Che Disonore*," he said in a perfect Italian accent, flicking his gaze to mine. "Death rather than dishonor. It's Italian."

"You're Italian?"

"Yeah, um … on my mother's side." He released me, turning away toward the stairs again. "It's late. We should get some sleep."

I nodded. "Okay." I took another cleansing breath before picking up my bowl to take it to the sink.

"Aida?"

I glanced back at him over my shoulder. "Yeah?"

"If you need anything, let me know. I'm here for you, always."

"Thanks."

He offered a tight smile before retreating upstairs.

After rinsing my bowl, I grabbed a bottled water from the refrigerator and headed back up to my room. After my emotional breakdown, sleep was bound to come easier.

I heard Steven's muffled voice through the closed door of his bedroom across from mine. I wasn't sure who he was talking to. Maybe he was checking in with Marcus or my father.

I ran a hand through my hair, sighing heavily as I shut my door. As I slid under the covers, curling onto my side, I closed my eyes, trying to think of something more pleasant than the viciousness of the world I lived in. There was too much violence, too many vendettas, and enemies to keep track of.

Familiar hazel eyes came to mind as I drifted off. I was grateful to have Steven comfort me. Although, there was this nagging feeling in the back of my mind that we might not have much time left together.

CHAPTER NINE
STEVEN

"We got word that Sebastian is back in the city," Gio said. "I think he wants an audience with the Don."

"Why is that?" I asked. If we could form an alliance with Gallo, that would help our cause greatly. After all, they had control of the same cache of weapons. Although, fighting fire with fire wasn't ideal.

He was silent for a few beats. "Ricci is blaming the Mafia for the hit on Thompson and that's causing a lot of paranoia."

"Did you check the locations I gave you? Any sight of the weapons yet?"

"Not yet. Although after doing some digging, James found out the co-owner of The Den is another Ricci client."

I nodded. "So he got the money from a friend to pay his debt and kept the weapons for himself."

"Seems that way. Shady bastard. Once we're sure he won't use his arsenal on us, we can act. Roman doesn't want to risk innocent lives being lost." He was silent a moment. "He thinks it best if you hang tight for now. No sudden moves."

Sighing, I said, "I understand."

"Any progress on turning his daughter?"

I glanced at my closed door, afraid that she might somehow hear me even though her room was further down the hall. "I'm getting closer. I don't think she has anymore intel for me though."

"It wouldn't look good if you left in the midst of this. Stick close to her and see if you can't learn anything new. In the meantime, I'll keep you updated on when you can get out."

I nodded even though he couldn't see me. "Let's hope it's sooner rather than later."

"Do you think you're at risk of being made?" Gio asked, his voice more serious.

"I don't see how I could be. Maybe I'm just paranoid."

"Stay strong, Fab. It'll all be over soon."

"Will do." I ended the call, tossing my phone on the bed.

There was no doubt in my mind that Aida needed to leave. She'd be better off under the protection of the Mafia than with her father. However, now I wasn't allowed to take her and run even if I did have her trust. I was fully aware of what it would imply should we bolt before we were certain where the arsenal was, but that didn't mean I was happy about the decision my uncle made for me.

The sooner we were out of here, the better.

It killed me to see Aida crying in the kitchen earlier, to hear her sobbing in defeat. She deserved so much more than the life she'd been given. It reminded me of my brother's fiancée, Cynthia, and what she'd gone through under Randall Hawks. He'd brainwashed her into thinking she was worth nothing and she believed it.

My brother was dead and couldn't save her, but I did everything I could to make sure she made it back to New York and was safe. Just like I made sure to protect Claire Evans until Mickey Silver came for her.

Aida would be no different. I'd get her out of this hell and place her under my uncle's care. Though the thought of handing her over and walking away made my chest hurt. I'd grown attached to her after the last several weeks.

I wasn't stable when she was near me. Knowing we were alone in this house together kept me up half the night.

At one point, I almost got out of bed and went to her room to check on her. I forced myself to stay put, but if I were any less of a man, I would have caved. I had to fight whatever I was feeling toward her. We couldn't go down that road for a multitude of reasons. The main one being that if we got caught, I'd be a dead man.

It was bad enough I'd kissed her. That moment of weakness itself might cause me a great deal of pain should Albert find out.

I tried to sleep but couldn't fight off the restlessness. Anticipation festered inside me, eager to hear back from Gio on when this would be over. This wasn't a five year stint like last time. In fact, it hadn't been quite a month yet it felt like forever.

Hopefully, I'd get new information tomorrow. If not, I'd keep Aida safe like I was hired to do. I should be able to hold on a little while longer and perform the task without incident. That is as long as Aida didn't cry again or look at me with those sapphire bedroom eyes.

*

As I left my room to head downstairs in the morning, Aida opened her bedroom door across from me.

I froze, taking in her wet hair and the pale pink t-shirt she wore. It fit her body nicely, highlighting the curves of her full chest. She was in a pair of jeans that hugged her hips and thighs before flaring out to her bare feet.

Damn, she was gorgeous.

Her brow lifted at me and I cleared my throat, shifting my gaze down the hall. "Did you sleep okay?"

She nodded, curling her arms around her waist. "Yeah, I was pretty wiped after all that crying." I met her eyes. "Thank you, for being there for me." She smiled and my heart beat faster.

What the hell?

"Don't mention it," I said with a shrug and closed my bedroom door before heading down the hall.

She followed me as I descended the stairs and headed for the kitchen. I ended up making a pot of coffee while she collected eggs from the refrigerator and began scrambling them.

"I'm making breakfast. Do you want some?" she asked over her shoulder as she poured the eggs into a pan on the stovetop.

I couldn't stop staring at her ass in those jeans. God, I was losing my mind. "Sure," I mumbled.

We sat at the table in the kitchen to eat. Aida was a damn good cook. The scrambled eggs were better than any I'd ever had. We didn't speak much over breakfast and it was surprisingly easy just being with her, enjoying a meal.

I finished my plate before she did, sipping my coffee as I stared out the picture window toward the backyard. I had an idea of a way to pass the time, but I wasn't sure if she'd be up for it. I wanted to do what I could to take her mind off our present situation.

I turned to face her, catching her gaze immediately. She'd been watching me.

"I know this isn't really a vacation, and it's difficult to pretend with everything going on," I began. She looked at me curiously. "But I want to make things a little easier for you if I can."

Her lips tilted up in the corners. "You want to cheer me up?"

I smiled back, wishing I could do more for her than what I had in mind.

I stood up, collecting the breakfast dishes and placing them in the sink. "Yeah, grab your jacket and meet me outside," I said, heading for the mudroom just off the back door.

While Aida went to get ready, I set up paper markers on a few of the trees along the edge of the backyard. It was colder than I'd anticipated out here and while I waited for her, I stuffed my hands into the pockets of my jacket, staring up at the sky.

Back in California, when Claire was depressed, I'd distracted her by teaching her to shoot. Not only did she need to learn because of the dangerous situation we were in, but it helped take her mind off things for a while. It gave her a sense of control even though she was being held prisoner.

Aida already knew how to shoot based on what she'd told me, but that didn't mean she didn't need a release. Hitting some targets, perhaps pretending a few were people she loathed, might help her.

I wandered back to the covered patio near the back door when I heard it open. Aida was standing there, staring out at the makeshift targets on the trees.

"What are those for?" she asked as I approached.

I reached for my gun behind my back and presented it to her. She glanced down at it, then flicked her gaze back up to mine.

"Target practice," I said.

Her blue eyes widened. "You're going to let me shoot?"

I extended my hand with the gun in it. "Yeah, go ahead, take it."

Her brow crumpled. "You trust me not to use this on you?"

I narrowed my eyes at her. "Do you want to shoot me?"

She giggled, shaking her head. "No, you're the only person I can think of right now that doesn't deserve a bullet." That was a relief.

"Here." I extended my hand to her again.

She picked up the gun, sliding her fingers along the rectangular barrel. "I haven't held a gun in a long time," she murmured, admiring the weapon as if it were some lost artifact.

The way she stroked the steel barrel and handle had me imagining her touch and my blood warmed. Seeing her holding a weapon was a major turn on. I hadn't expected that.

Clearing my throat, I turned back toward the yard. "Come on," I said.

We walked side by side about thirty feet. We were still a good twenty from the targets. The great thing about this place was the unlimited amount of space outside. I doubted there were any other homes for miles.

Aida stopped beside me, raising the gun and aiming it at one of the trees. I watched as she rested her finger beside the trigger, cupping the base of the handle with her other hand. She closed one eye, focusing her sight.

"You sure you know how to use that thing?" I teased.

She turned her head to look at me. With a small shrug, she said, "You tell me," and then focused back on her target.

She squeezed the trigger and I watched as a small hole formed nearly dead center of the first target. The blast of the gun echoed around us, causing a group of birds to take flight from somewhere beyond the tree line.

"Holy shit …"

She glanced over at me again, lowering the gun and smiling wide. The spark of excitement gleamed in her brilliant blue eyes. I didn't think I'd ever seen her this happy before.

"Impressed?" she asked.

"Yeah." I blew out a breath. "Damn. I didn't think you'd … damn." I shook my head.

She nudged her shoulder against my upper arm. "I told you I could shoot. Can I do it again?"

I chuckled at her eagerness and nodded while stepping back a few paces. "Empty the clip. Show me how it's done."

Aida managed to hit every target the same as before. I was more than impressed at her precision. She did exceptionally well, and while I enjoyed the look of peace on her face as she was in her element, I couldn't help but think of how much more she was capable of. How she could be a major asset to her father's business, to the Mafia even.

I wondered if she'd be interested in working for Uncle Roman once I took her to him. Grim could train her in sniping or she could become a soldier again and use her skills to defend herself and other people with her. Hell, she could handle recon missions if she wanted.

My chest tightened at the thought of her working for us. I didn't want anything to happen to her, so maybe working for the Mafia wasn't the best idea. Although, who was I to tell her what she could and couldn't do? I wouldn't want to treat her like her father and all his cronies had.

Witnessing the joy in her eyes filled me with a different need altogether. One that involved simply making her happy. I wanted to bring her pleasure in a lot of ways, not only when it came to her body. I'd be content seeing her smile every day. That alone made me feel something I'd never felt before. It was a mix of warmth and contentment that didn't exist prior to meeting her.

I handed her the extra clip I had in my pocket and let her continue her target practice until that too was empty. As we walked back toward the house, I couldn't help but notice the color in her cheeks and the brightness of her eyes, so unlike how I'd seen her since we first met.

My mission was to keep her safe, but more importantly, I wanted to keep her smiling. I began to realize that it was more than caring about her, it was the drive to ensure she came before me always. Her happiness meant more to me than anything else and deep down, though I wasn't ready to admit why that was, I knew what I felt for her might break me.

The trouble was, I couldn't stop it. Maybe my heart wasn't nearly as shattered as I thought it was. Not when I was ready to hand it over to this beautiful, broken woman who was the daughter of my enemy.

I hadn't held a gun in what felt like years. It definitely had been a few months. For the first time in a long time, I felt a surge of power and control over my own life. It was liberating to be able to shoot again, to breathe in the crisp spring air and just let go for a while.

I'd been desperately trying to feel something and as I shrugged out of my jacket and kicked off my shoes in the mudroom, my body hummed with adrenaline. I wanted to chase this feeling and never let it go.

I couldn't help the smile that was permanently etched on my face now. I was happier than I'd been in a long time and it was all thanks to Steven. He gave me something more important than words could ever express, and I wasn't entirely sure if he realized just how much that meant to me.

I was struggling more and more to hold back with him. We didn't know each other well and yet in the last month, he'd been kinder to me than those closest to me. He was protective but didn't treat me like a helpless woman. He treated me like an equal.

It didn't hurt that he was incredibly attractive and thinking about the way he'd kissed me still sent fire coursing through my veins. Now more than ever, I wished things were different. That he was just a normal guy and I was a normal woman. If this were a weekend getaway and we were two regular people, perhaps I'd kiss him again. Maybe it would lead to more.

It was difficult to deny the chemistry that sizzled between us. Especially right now as I curled up at one end of the couch in the living room while he sat at the other. He'd gone upstairs to call Marcus to check in after we'd come back inside. I was surprised that he'd come back down to hang out with me, although I didn't mind his company.

We were hovering on this line between a make believe domestic situation and the reality of whatever darkness loomed outside. I wanted to get lost in the fantasy of what could be if I didn't have a father like Albert Ricci and was a regular twenty-two year old woman.

Because the house was a property on the market, there wasn't much in the way of furniture or décor. I knew my father occasionally used these places as safehouses, which meant they didn't spend much quality time here. It's not like there were puzzles or board games to play or movies to watch. In the living room, there was only one couch, a small coffee table, and a television mounted above the natural stone fireplace. This house had a very cabin-like feel to it, which I kind of loved.

Maybe one day, if it were possible, I could have a house in the woods where I'd be able to curl up and read or bake cookies. Although, having been secluded for as long as I had, I sought the bustle of a city, too. I craved adventure and travel.

"In another life I'd want this," I said.

Steven, who'd been channel surfing basic stations because there was no cable hooked up, turned to look at me. I tucked my hair behind my ear.

"A house at a similar location," I clarified. "If I could find a way to get away from it all, I'd like to live outside the city."

He nodded. "It's peaceful,"

"What about you? Did you live in the city before working for my father?"

"Yeah, I have an apartment near the park. It's not really big, but it works for me. I don't need much and I stay pretty busy."

I remembered he'd mentioned working for another group in New York. I wanted to find out more about that. I wanted to know everything about him.

"I imagine you're not home often. How long did you work for the group in New York?"

"I was young when I started in the underground business. At twenty I went to … Chicago and that's where I worked the last five years."

I frowned. During his initiation he mentioned being military trained. The timeline didn't add up. "So you haven't been back that long."

"I got back about three weeks before I started working for you."

I was taken aback by the fact he'd said me, not my father. Did he truly feel his loyalty was more to me than Albert Ricci? My chest tightened at the sentiment.

"What did your parents think about you working underground at a young age?" I asked.

"They died when I was little. I was raised by my uncle."

There was only a slight twinge of sadness in his tone. I didn't know if he'd trained himself to not show emotion, or if he'd moved past the great loss.

"I'm sorry," I said. "Does your uncle mind what you do for work?"

Steven shrugged. "He's cool with it. My sister hates it though. She worries about me." I forgot he'd mentioned having a sister before.

"What's her name?"

He set the remote control on the arm of the couch, leaving the station on some old sitcom.

"Celeste. She's in her last year of fashion school. I want to help her as much as possible, which is why I'm in the line of work I'm in. I paid for her education."

I gaped at him. Paying for college wasn't cheap. Whatever he did in Chicago must have been incredibly lucrative. It was admirable to do something like that for his sister. Maybe he really was a naturally caring guy, albeit mixed up with the wrong crowd. He had a big heart to do something so important for Celeste.

"That's incredible. Is it just the two of you? Do you have any other siblings?"

His gaze shifted to the wall behind me and his lips thinned. "No, it's just us," he said quietly.

We were silent for a while after that. Him lost in his thoughts and me wishing I didn't ask so many questions all the time. I'd struck a nerve somehow and wondered if he did have other siblings that weren't around anymore.

I settled into the couch and Steven turned his attention back to the television. We ended up watching two and a half episodes of the show he'd left it on before he spoke again.

"I had an older brother, but he was murdered. That's why I left the city five years ago," he said in a low voice.

I turned my head slowly to look at him. He was staring at the coffee table, his hands resting atop his thighs.

"That's terrible. I'm so sorry," I said.

He nodded and licked his lips. "I watched him die. The man who murdered him also kidnapped his fiancée. I had to track her down and eventually he paid for his sins."

"Is she safe now?" I asked. My heart dropped to my stomach.

He glanced up at me. "Yeah, she's safe. Still pretty fucked up from the whole ordeal, but that's expected."

His story was familiar. I'd heard it before. "Thank you for telling me."

"I had to go through hell, had to engage in a lot of terrible behavior in order to get her back. I killed a lot of people." He blew out a breath, running a hand through his hair.

I frowned at him. What was he trying to say?

"Is that the real reason you went to Chicago?" I asked. He bit down on his bottom lip, gazing down at the couch cushion between us. "You weren't really working for a congressman, were you?" He'd lied to my father, to me.

If he was out seeking revenge for his brother's life, for his would be sister-in-law's, then I understood why. I knew how the business ran, how snitches were hung out to dry and traitors were put to death. As a soldier, I'd track down people of the same class and act accordingly. It's why I shot that man years ago at just seventeen. He'd betrayed my father and he had to pay.

"I wasn't working for a congressman. I'd infiltrated the man's group, befriended him, became his right hand." He shook his head, flicking his gaze back to mine. "I did what I had to do."

It was no wonder he knew as much as he did about the Mafia then. If he'd worked for a group in New York and went to Chicago to avenge his brother, he was more aware than I originally thought. He'd gone deep into enemy territory for vengeance. Not a lot of people did that and came back out alive.

Realization struck me then and ice flooded my veins. I remembered why his story sounded familiar. He wasn't in Chicago and he didn't work for some *random* group.

My throat went dry and I swallowed. "You were … a spy?"

His eyes locked with mine, piercing straight through me. My heart hammered in my chest. Steven remained silent, though his head bobbed in a quick nod.

"Oh my god," I breathed. "Were you really undercover for five years?"

He muttered a "Yes," and my jaw dropped as I stared at him, suddenly seeing him differently, yet still the same. I was confused, angry, and terrified. Most of all, I was hurt.

Everything slowly began to make sense. The fact that he worked for my father, a man he didn't seem fond of. He'd asked before if I'd go up against him if I could. At the time, I thought it more of a generic question, but then he'd been surprised that I knew as much as I did about the Cuccione family. He encouraged me to go to Don Roman and tell him about my father, to turn on him.

My stomach rolled as a wave of nausea ran through me. All of the pieces fit together in the miserable puzzle of my life.

That night in the car after meeting with Jonathan, Steven had been upset with me. He'd said if I died, he'd lose everything. At the time, in my naivety, I thought maybe that meant he cared about me. But then he'd also stressed that he *had* to work for my father. Then there was the phone call he made as we were leaving.

"Straight shot. The Den. Immediately."

Minutes later, Jonathan Thompson was dead.

My eyes lowered to his chest, to the white fabric of his t-shirt over his left pec. I could make out the faint markings of the script on his skin. It felt like I couldn't get enough air to my lungs as I met his wary gaze again.

"Steven Cline isn't your real name," I said.

His shoulders tightened and his eyes narrowed slightly. "No, it isn't."

I swallowed the lump in my throat. "Am I in danger?" I whispered as tears clouded my vision.

He frowned. "No. Not from me."

I wanted to believe him, but it was difficult to do that when he'd been lying to me this entire time. More than that, the pain of his betrayal broke my heart. I thought he was different, that he was better than everyone else I'd met and I was wrong.

"Who do you work for?" I shouldn't be asking anymore questions. I should be bolting up to my room and locking the door. Instead, I was frozen in shock and disbelief.

I wanted him to confess to the truth. I needed him to tell me in his own words. He would have killed me already if that's what he'd wanted. Wouldn't he? If he was who I thought, then I wouldn't still be here. At least not according to what my father had told me.

"I can't tell you that right now." He scooted closer, leaning toward me and I sat back, my legs which were curled beneath me straightened, and my feet touched the floor. "Aida, you're safe with me. I promise."

"You lied to me," I argued, shaking my head. "All this time you've been a spy. I don't trust you, I can't." I shot up off the couch and ran up the stairs.

I had to get away from him, away from here. I needed to tell Marcus or my father, but I didn't have a phone with me. Damn them for trusting this stranger with my life! He'd fooled everyone, including me.

As I reached for the door handle of my room, Steven grabbed my wrist, spinning me around. He walked me backward to the wall of the hallway, his body pressed against mine, keeping me from fleeing. I hated that I enjoyed his touch, that my body responded in traitorous ways to him when he was an enemy.

I squeezed my eyes shut, tilting my head back to rest against the wall. I tried to regulate my breathing, tried to calm down and think of a rational way to get out of here. God, I was such an idiot.

Anger took hold as I realized he'd only gotten close to me in order to gain information. That's what spies did. He'd been pretending. Every word he said was a lie in order to gain my trust. He'd used me and I let him. I opened up to him more than I ever had to anyone.

I was absolutely mortified at my actions. The only thing he ever said that wasn't a lie was that I was stronger than anyone gave me credit for. I could be stronger than *him*.

Opening my eyes, I lifted my free hand quickly, smacking him across his jaw. He barely flinched and I whimpered as he took hold of that wrist, too. Raising my arms, he pinned them above my head, tilting his head down until his lips were hovering over mine.

"You can't hurt me, Aida. You have no idea the pain I've been dealt, the torture I've been through."

Squaring my shoulders, I met his gaze. "Let. Me. Go."

"Everything I told you, apart from my résumé, has been the truth. I … like you. I want to keep you safe."

"You're an enemy!" I spat, disgusted with myself and with him for continuing to try and use me. "You're only here because your job is to take down my father."

He leaned back slightly, his jaw tensing. "The Gallos, too. Those weapons of theirs need to be destroyed. They may be willing to give them up, but your father won't let go of his personal vendetta. That's my job." He exhaled roughly, his breath warming my lips. "But I'm not your enemy."

I glowered up at him. "I don't believe you."

His jaw muscle ticked. "Then don't. But if you tell your father or anyone who I am, you'll ruin everything."

"I don't care!" I shouted, using my body to try and push him away from me. He didn't budge and I growled in frustration.

"You'll care when I'm forced to kidnap you and take you back to New York. You'll care when you're placed in the custody of Roman Cuccione without ever knowing what will become of your father."

"You're going to kill him, aren't you?" Tears stung my eyes. I didn't know why the thought of my father being killed bothered me. He deserved it for what he'd done in life. Just yesterday, I'd contemplated turning on him.

Everything was different now though. Steven was the one who lied to me and it was impossible to believe he'd keep me safe. I had no one.

"I thought about letting him live, until I learned how he's treated you, how he's controlled you. Now, I'll take him out myself." There was a certainty in his voice that terrified me.

I hated Albert Ricci, probably more than anyone else because of what he'd made me do, what he'd done to me. But the thought of him being gone forever sent a strange pang of sorrow through my heart. He was my father and he gave me life. I didn't know a world without him. Even if that world was completely wrong.

Some of my anger dissipated as I realized what he just confessed to me. Did he even realize what he'd done? He'd just blown his cover. In a matter of minutes, he'd slipped up in great detail. He told me *everything*.

He said I'd be turned over to Roman Cuccione. The only way he had the authority to do that was if he was exactly who I suspected. I wanted him to say it. I needed to know if he was being honest about not lying to me. "Do you work for the Mafia?"

His nostrils flared and he closed his eyes, inhaling a deep breath through his nose. When he opened them again, they were softer than before, earnest. "I fucked up." He released me then, shrugging away from me and running both hands through his hair, tugging at the ends. "Damn it, I fucked up," he mumbled as he paced the hall.

I remained where I was, watching him, wondering what he'd say next. I knew enough about the way this world worked to understand how a spy is trained and dedicated to their mission at all costs. They will die before dishonoring their group. If he was a spy for Don Roman, he'd just sealed his fate and given himself a death sentence.

Morte Piuttosto Che Disonore.

His tattoo, death rather than dishonor, was a dead giveaway. He'd shown it to me last night. Why hadn't I picked up on it then? I really was blind when it came to him.

Steven had taken the vow and yet he'd been so careless in giving me details. Maybe he meant what he said earlier. If that were the case, then he wasn't my enemy at all. He genuinely wanted to keep me safe because he really did care about me and more than that, he trusted me.

Peeling away from the wall, I risked a step toward him. He stopped moving and hung his head, clenching his fists as his sides.

"Why?" Why did he tell me? Why was he working for the Mafia? Why hadn't he just kidnapped me and used me as leverage from the beginning? Why did he kiss me? There were a lot of responses he could have given.

When he finally responded, my heart nearly lept out of my chest.

"I trust you." He lifted his head to peer into my eyes. "Maybe it's partly because I'm eager to get this over with. Or maybe it's due to the fact that I've developed feelings for you." He blew out a breath, shaking his head.

I swallowed the lump that formed in my throat. *Feelings?*

"I ordered the hit on Thompson," he said, frowning and staring down at the floor again.

It felt like my knees were going to buckle. I knew it, deep down, I already knew the truth, but having the words spoken out loud made it all the more real.

He shook his head. "We can't act until we find those damn weapons that your father pretended to sell. It's safer to maintain my cover until we know where they are."

"*We* as in … the Mafia?"

His head lifted, eyes meeting mine. "Yes. My uncle is Roman Cuccione."

I had to grip the doorframe behind me for support. He *was* Roman's nephew! He was … I gasped. "You're … you were on the West Coast. You took out two groups over there. You killed Randall Hawks."

He raised a brow. "How do you know about that?"

"I may be stuck in hiding all the time, but I'm not deaf. They talked of you, everyone in the underground did. Randall Hawks murdered your brother, Dante, and you killed him for it."

His lips twitched slightly. "Technically, someone else pulled the trigger, but I helped set up the shot." He gave me a quick bow. "Fabiano Cuccione, at your service."

My stomach fluttered at the sound of his name. It was surreal to be standing in front of a Mafia legend. I almost felt star struck and that only amplified the mix of emotions running through me. I had some serious issues.

"You really worked for that guy for five years without being caught?" I asked incredulously. "I thought those were just rumors."

"It wasn't easy," he admitted. "He was abusive and power hungry. I took the brunt of that in order to protect others."

"I can't believe this," I said, shaking my head. "I told you to get out while you could and all this time you've been *the* Fabiano Cuccione? I … can't believe I made out with you." I was in a daze of information overload.

"Kissing you wasn't part of my plan."

I huffed out a laugh, despite the heaviness of this unexpected conversation. "I groped you; I threw myself at you. Why did you let me do that?" I felt incredibly embarrassed and so stupid for wanting him. Even if he was being honest, I had no idea who he really was.

His brow crumpled as he stalked toward me, sliding his hand over my cheek. My breath caught in my throat.

"I let you do that because I wanted it, too." His chest rumbled against mine, sending a flood of warmth between my legs. "I don't want you to think I'd ever use you like that, Aida. Of all the things I've confessed, that's the most honest." He lowered his head until his lips brushed over mine.

My heart beat unsteadily. I couldn't keep myself from reacting to him, even after everything he'd told me. Knowing he wanted my father dead and still planned on taking him down, I couldn't stop the way I felt when he was near me.

I lifted onto my toes to meet him, feeling the softness of his mouth, the sweep of his tongue against mine. Everything would change now that I'd been told the truth. It was difficult to imagine what might happen from here, but I wasn't going to let that stop me from whatever we had right now. Because in this moment, regardless of his name, I still wanted the freedom that only he could give.

CHAPTER TEN
FABIANO

Telling Aida the truth went against everything I was trained for. Opening up to her wasn't something I planned on doing exactly at that moment, but she kept asking me questions, and I couldn't bear the thought of lying to her anymore.

Each day that passed, I was growing closer to her and that terrified me, but I trusted her. On my life, I knew she'd have my back. I don't know if it was intuition or kismet. Maybe it was the fact that I'd discovered just how deep my feelings ran for her. Either way, I had to blow my cover for her.

I wasn't sure if that was a good thing or a bad thing yet. It didn't matter right now anyway. I had more pressing matters to attend to.

Aida moaned against my mouth as I kissed her deep and slow, unable to control my dire need to be as close to her as possible. The fact that she still wanted me after everything I'd told her made my feelings that much stronger. I was shocked, but I wasn't complaining. Being with her just felt right.

When I tried to break the kiss, she wound her arms around my neck, lifting up onto her toes to keep me in place. My hands slid over her hips, to the curve of her lower back. I gripped her and lifted until she wound her legs around me.

Pressing her into the wall, I rolled my hips and she whimpered against my mouth. God, she was perfect. I was hard as hell and knew I should stop before things went too far, but not yet. I needed a few more moments with this beautiful creature to calm my nerves and clear my head. She was a sedative, a painkiller, my addiction.

My lips traveled down her chin to her throat and I slid my tongue along the soft skin before biting down gently. I wanted to taste every last inch of her.

"Fabiano," she murmured between gasps and my heart nearly burst in my chest. I liked the way my name sounded when she said it. No, scratch that, I fucking *loved* it.

She tightened her legs around me, creating an earth shattering friction against my cock and I trembled. God, she was going to undo me right here. She had no idea how much power she held over me. I needed to control myself because she was new to this and still very much an innocent. I couldn't take that from her.

Still holding tight to her, I kicked open her bedroom door and walked over to the bed, lowering her down atop the crumpled comforter to inhale the scent of her skin. Roses. Even the sheets smelled like her.

I kissed her again as she slid further back to allow me to kneel between her legs. Her hands flew to the hem of my shirt and within seconds, it was tossed to the floor. Placing my hand against her neck, I bent to kiss her once more as she explored the dips and planes of my upper body.

Damn, I loved when she touched me.

I wanted to touch her, too. Everywhere. I wanted to feel the fullness of each breast beneath my palms and slide my index finger along her wet center. I wanted to know what flavor she was, even though I could already guarantee it'd be my favorite.

My cock strained against my jeans as she trailed a finger down the center of my stomach. I sat up, grabbing her wrists and pinning them beside her head.

"We … have to … stop," I panted.

It felt like my heart was going to leap out of my chest. She drove me crazy.

She frowned up at me, her chest rising and falling as fast as mine. Her blue eyes were full of fire and want. Jesus, this was a bad idea. I shouldn't have kissed her.

I began to rise from the bed and she sat up, gripping my bicep. "Wait. Please?" Her voice was raspy, sexy.

I groaned, dropping my head. "You're fucking killing me. Do you understand that?"

She sighed. "Please, I need this. I want you to … be my first."

I snapped my head up, growling. Yep, she'd be the cause of my death. "No. You don't."

She shifted to kneel on the bed, squaring her shoulders as she straightened. "Yes. I do," she said in the same tone.

My brows shot up. "Don't get all tough on me right now," I warned.

"Why?" She placed her hands on her hips. "Does it scare you?"

I scoffed, "Nah, babe, it doesn't scare me." I leaned closer to her, staring at her swollen lips. "It turns me on."

Her mouth parted in a gasp and I kissed her once again.

I was officially a dead man, but Aida Ricci was worth whatever price I had to pay.

I was prepared to beg if I needed to. I wanted to escape for a while, to forget about the business, the truth of who he really was, everything. If only for a little while, I wanted to experience something new and exciting, normal, and the only time I ever experienced anything close to that was with Fabiano Cuccione. In this moment, with the uncertainty of both our futures, I wanted to give myself a memory to cherish.

Feeling confident, I kissed him back when he leaned into me again. I'd only ever known him as Steven, but his real name was like a second language to me.

I don't think he understood how often I'd heard of him. How much I'd secretly admired his ability to do what he'd done. Of course, that wasn't something I could ever broadcast openly. He was the enemy, after all, even if he wasn't mine.

I pushed him down on his back and climbed on top of him, straddling his hips. I could feel him straining against his jeans between my legs. A jolt of electricity traveled along my spine, creating a flood of warmth as I rocked into him.

He groaned, closing his eyes and grabbing my hips, sliding me over his hard length. A moan crawled its way from my throat as I let him guide me at a steady pace, my head clouding with desperate need.

His eyes opened, burning up at me with such a fierce intensity that my lungs tightened. "Damn, Aida," he murmured, sitting up.

His forehead rested against mine and he tangled one hand in the back of my hair while steadying my waist with the other. He kissed me again, his tongue sweeping over mine before gently biting down on my lower lip. I whimpered against him, trying to move my hips again, seeking that incredible feeling.

He chuckled as he lifted his head, meeting my eyes. "I want you," he whispered. "Trust me, I don't want to stop this. But you've never had sex before and your first time—"

"Should be what I want," I interrupted in a shaky voice. He frowned. "I want this, right now. I don't care that we don't know each other well. I don't care who you are or who I am or what happens an hour from now."

His eyes searched mine as he opened his mouth to speak but nothing came out.

"If you want me and I want you, then just let this happen," I said. "Let's forget who we are and the mess we're in right now. Escape with me." I kissed him once, twice, and then pulled back to look at him again.

He was silent for a few minutes before releasing a heavy sigh. "Are you sure this is what you want? That *I'm* the one you want?"

"Yes," I said and I meant it with my whole heart.

It's not like I was in love with him or anything, but I liked him a lot. And who better to lose my virginity to than someone I trusted? Someone that seemed to know me better than anyone else even in the short amount of time we'd spent together?

He dragged a hand through his hair, releasing yet another heavy breath. I thought he was going to deny me, but then he said, "Let's go to my room."

I didn't want to move away from him, but did, standing beside the bed on unsteady legs. He stood as well, grabbing my hand before leading me down the hall to his bedroom. Once we entered his room, he closed the door and locked it.

I wasn't sure why he felt the need to do that if we were alone, but now wasn't the time to question it. Besides, he brought me in here with him so I didn't really care. This was actually happening. My body trembled in anticipation and nervousness.

He went to his duffle bag at the end of the bed and dug for something in an inside pocket before placing the bag on the floor.

Turning to me, he presented a small, square foil packet and said, "Do you know what this is?"

I snorted, rolling my eyes. I may have been a virgin, but I wasn't uneducated or a prude. "It's a condom, Captain Obvious."

He narrowed his eyes playfully. "Just checking."

"You do understand that just because my father never allowed me to kiss boys or get close enough to have sex, doesn't mean I'm oblivious to the science behind a man and woman getting together?"

"I wasn't sure how much you knew. He may have kept you completely in the dark."

I nodded. "He did. But he didn't ban the internet which is an amazing tool to learn from. I've had orgasms before."

His hazel eyes burned into mine. "You have?"

"I've touched myself. I … touched myself that night after you left. While thinking of you."

Suddenly he was standing in front of me. "Don't tell me things like that, Aida," he murmured before kissing me.

He peeled my shirt off slowly, his hand moving over my right breast to palm it before moving on to the other one. Even through the fabric of my bra, I could feel every nerve ending as he explored me, igniting a need within me so great I thought I would combust right then.

Kneeling in front of me, he placed a kiss against my stomach, undoing the button of my jeans. He slid the zipper down slowly, his mouth traveling to each new piece of me he unveiled.

"I want to go slow, make it count," he murmured as he tugged my jeans down my thighs.

I stepped out of them and lifted each foot so that he could take off my socks. Only left standing in my bra and panties, I suddenly felt self-conscious. It's not like he hadn't seen me naked before, thanks to that night I slipped in the shower. But this moment was entirely different. Now, he was taking his time, perusing my body as if he were memorizing every curve, every spec of skin that he could see.

He rose, standing in front of me. "You're so beautiful, Aida." He stroked a finger down my cheek and I shivered. "Lay down."

I crawled onto the bed and laid on my back. His eyes roamed from my head to my toes and back up as he stalked toward me, staying beside the bed.

"I want you to touch yourself. Show me what you did when you thought of me." My mouth popped open in a gasp and a wicked grin tilted his lips. "Don't be shy." He winked.

With trembling hands, I kept my gaze locked on his, sliding my right hand down to my panties, between my legs. I used my left hand to cup my breast over my bra, squeezing lightly.

My eyes closed on their own accord as I swirled my finger over the tight nub, drawing out more wetness. My breath grew heavier as I worked myself and it sounded like Fabiano made some sort of strangled noise. I opened my eyes to find him now at the end of the bed, staring at my hand between my legs. His jaw was tight, his chest rising and falling rapidly.

"Do you want me to do that to you?" he asked in a breathless voice. His eyes flicked up to mine.

"Yes." I nodded.

He knelt on the bed, running his hand over mine before moving it to my side. His fingers brushed over the fabric of my panties and my body jerked when he used his thumb to continue what I started. I was so close to tipping over the edge.

Suddenly he stopped, placing his hands on either side of my hips.

"I want to take these off. Can I see you, taste you?" he asked.

"Taste me?"

He bit down on his bottom lip. "Yes."

I nodded slowly and let him undress me, my body heated as he studied me with hungry, hazel eyes that sparkled in the sunlight of the bedroom window.

He kissed my left thigh, then my right, making his way between my legs. He released a breath and any nerves I had about him being so close dissipated as fire erupted within me. He started by kissing me right where I ached for him. I writhed beneath him, crying out as he ran his tongue along me, sucking and soothing every so often.

Before long, my eyes were screwed shut and my fingers tangled in his hair as the orgasm rocked through me. I felt like I was floating. My heart hammered in my chest erratically. When I came down, I opened my eyes to find him watching me.

I sat up, reaching for the button of his jeans, undoing them quickly and pulling down the zipper. He fisted my hair, bending to kiss me with such intensity that I felt it within my entire body. I ran my hand over the length of him and he sucked in air through his teeth, releasing me. He stood again, tugging his jeans down along with his underwear and my eyes zeroed in on his cock.

I reached behind me, removing my bra as I met his eyes. God, he was perfect. Seeing how ready he was for me brought on an even deeper desire for him. I wanted to please him. I always wanted him.

"I'll go slow," he said, sounding nervous. "You have to tell me if I hurt you, if it's too much."

"Okay."

He knelt between my legs again, opening up the foil packet and placing the condom on. He fisted his cock as he moved over me, settling between my legs. We both moaned at the same time when he slid himself over my opening.

"Jesus, you feel good," he breathed against my temple, bracing himself with his free hand beside my shoulder. He pushed into me slightly and I gripped his bicep. "You're sure you want this, Aida?"

"Yes," I said, my body trembling as he sunk in further.

Our gazes stayed fixed on each other and I bit down on my bottom lip as he pulled out and slid back in again, a little further each time.

"Fuck," he groaned as he moved in and out slowly.

There was a slight pinch within as he filled me completely and then stopped moving as he lowered his mouth to mine. He kissed me, distracting me from the painful ache before sliding in and out again. He continued kissing me, relaxing me as my hips lifted to meet his.

I wrapped my legs around his thighs when he increased the momentum. "Does it hurt?" he asked in a breathy voice, his lips at my ear now.

"No, it feels … good." I moaned, sliding my hands to his back, holding him to me.

He panted in my ear, his breathy moans igniting me further as we continued moving together. It didn't take long before I was close to tipping again. My pulse beat in my ears and I closed my eyes, crying out.

Fabiano muttered a curse, increasing the pace. His body shook with a violent force and his lips crashed into mine. His movements slowed to a stop seconds later and he broke the kiss, straightening his arm to look down at me.

His brow crumpled as he studied my face. "Are you okay?"

I swallowed the lump that formed in my throat. The heaviness of what just happened sank into my chest like lead. I nodded.

I felt amazing, better than I could have ever imagined. But I couldn't quite form the right words to tell him that. I was speechless, on the verge of laughing or crying. What we'd just done was intense and the fact that I felt closer to him than ever frightened me.

It was as if I was breathing for the first time or seeing brilliant colors that I didn't know existed until now. Fabiano Cuccione quite literally rocked my entire world.

He brushed his lips against mine. "Stay here," he mumbled as he pulled out of me, rising up from the bed and unlocking his door. He retreated to the hallway bathroom.

I continued laying there, trying to catch my breath. I was a little sore now that it was over, but it wasn't too painful.

Exhaling a shaky breath, I began to stand. Everything suddenly felt overwhelming.

"This should help," he said as he came back in the room with a damp washcloth, handing it to me.

"Thanks," I said. I needed to get out of here and wrap my head around what just happened.

Without another word, I headed straight for my room, closing the door behind me and leaning against it.

I was officially a woman now and while I didn't regret what we'd just done, I couldn't help but feel a sense of panic inside. Reality came crashing down with a vengeance.

Steven was Fabiano Cuccione, a spy for the Mafia. I'd done more than sleep with the enemy, I'd given him a part of me, one that I could never get back. I hadn't expected what we did to affect me so strongly, yet I found myself already craving more of him. Wanting him to kiss me again, to hold me.

I wanted more from him than what we'd just done and that epiphany was like a dagger straight to my heart. Because we'd never have more than what we just shared. We couldn't.

He needed to finish his mission and I'd either be dead right alongside my father or stuck in hiding under the thumb of Roman Cuccione. Surely, he wouldn't offer me a job or allow me to come and go as I pleased?

Even if he did, I knew deep down that I could never have more with him. He was dedicated to his work, to the Mafia. He didn't have room for me.

I closed my eyes, inhaling a deep breath. Maybe I'd made a mistake. I wasn't even sure if I could face him right now. I walked to the garden tub, turning the faucet on. As steaming, hot water filled the tub, I braced my hands on the marble countertop and stared at myself in the mirror.

I didn't look any different on the outside, though my lips were swollen and brighter in color. My eyes sparkled under the soft, fluorescent lights. I was the same woman. But I was missing something now, and I worried everyone would know the extent of my betrayal.

If my father ever found out, I'd be punished to the full extent for my moment of freedom. I'd be labeled a traitor, a harlot, the same as my mother was. That's what my father always said that she'd let Roman use her and that caused the Don to kill her once he got what he wanted. What if history repeated itself?

Once the tub was full, I shut off the water and sank into it, submerging my entire body. Maybe I'd just stay here forever.

*

After spending longer than necessary in the tub, I decided to shower. The water turned cold halfway through, but I didn't care. My goal was to scrub the scent of Fabiano from my body. To hopefully cleanse my mind along with it and forget about what we'd done.

That was the only way I was going to be able to look him in the eyes again. The alternative would leave me shattered, because I knew we'd eventually part ways and based on what he'd told me, it would be soon.

I couldn't stand the thought of losing him. I know it seemed dramatic and farfetched, but it was the truth. In a short time, I'd grown to like him, and after sleeping together that feeling only amplified. I've heard people say that sleeping with someone changes things, and I thought I'd hardened my heart enough to defeat that. I was wrong.

Thankfully, Fabiano wasn't in his room when I went back to retrieve the clothes I'd been wearing. Once I was dressed again, I decided to muster up the courage to confront him. He probably thought I was weird for leaving him after what we did.

How was I supposed to know the proper etiquette of afternoon sex? It was my first time. Hopefully, he'd go easy on me.

As I descended the stairs, I heard his voice, which I followed to find him sitting at the dining table wearing only his

165

jeans. He rested his forehead against the palm of his left hand, holding his phone with the right.

"You can't turn him out on the street again," he growled. He paused, listening to whoever it was he was talking to. "We'll head back to the city tonight."

I froze. He must have sensed my presence because he lowered his hand and peered up at me. "I'll take her with me to Roman."

We were leaving tonight? It seemed far too dangerous to just up and go. Especially knowing my father's men weren't far from the house. If they realized we left and suspected that their hired guard kidnapped me, we'd be in danger. I couldn't allow that.

Fab ended the call, placing his phone on the table.

"We could be caught," I said.

"We won't be." When he stood to move toward me, I backed away. He stopped, running a hand through his hair. "What's wrong?"

I crossed my arms over my chest, shaking my head. "Nothing. It's just … I don't think we should leave tonight. Marcus is with Patrick and Demetri in Rochester. They're close. If they catch us …"

"If they catch us, we fight back and run." He shrugged as if the thought of that didn't bother him. It sure as hell bothered me.

"So that's your plan?" I asked, growing irritated. "Just run? Shoot them if we have to, *kill* them? Then turn me into the Mafia boss and walk away?"

He gaped at me, raising a brow. "Walk away?"

"Yeah, isn't that your plan? You said earlier that I would be protected under Roman. You're a spy, *Fabiano*. You have to end this."

"And you think I'll just dump you at my uncle's compound and take off, right? That I wouldn't want you next to me?"

That's exactly what I thought.

"Listen," I began, "what we did, what happened between us, was because I wanted it. It was more freedom than I've ever felt before. A way to get back at my father even. You don't have to worry about protecting me or coming back."

He placed his hands on his hips, narrowing his eyes. "Why are you pushing me away?"

I blinked at him. What was he even saying right now? Did he think that I'd cuddle up with him on the couch and declare my undying love for him just because we had sex?

I trusted him, I'd admitted that to him and myself already, but that didn't mean anything. We went as far as we could ever go with each other. He wasn't making this any easier on me by pretending that wasn't our reality.

"I'm. Your. Enemy's. Daughter," I said slowly, and that earned a glare. So what if I was explaining it to him like he was a child. I wanted to make sure he got it. "Do you understand? Just because I let you fuck me doesn't mean that I want to be with you. That I even want to do it again!"

A low growl rumbled from his chest as he advanced on me, causing me to back into the counter at the island. "I didn't *fuck* you," he bit out. "Believe me, you'd know the difference."

My mouth popped open as I stared into his burning hazel eyes.

"I'm still bound to keep you safe outside the realm of work I was doing for Albert Ricci. It's my duty. You're innocent and I won't have you staying behind without me to be killed alongside your father and his men. I won't allow you to do that."

"*Allow* me?" I snapped. Raising my arms, I pushed him to stumble back slightly. "Allow me? As if you or anyone else can tell me what to do! Do you think because I like you, because we were intimate, that I'll just cave to your whims and allow *you* to treat me like a helpless woman? You're just like the rest of them."

His face fell as I managed to brush him aside.

"We stay here together until tomorrow morning. Pretend that we don't know anything and that nothing

happened. When we head back for the city tomorrow, you'll
drop me at my apartment and go to your uncle. Tell him
whatever, devise a new fucking plan for all I care."

"Aida …"

"No!" I shouted and he recoiled as if he'd been struck.
"I won't be controlled anymore. Not by you, or by my father,
or Roman Cuccione. I don't want to belong to the Mafia like
you do. I want out, completely."

He crossed his arms. "How do you intend to do that?"

"I'll leave. By myself. Albert will be so busy dealing
with you that he won't even know I'm gone until it's too late."

I didn't say anything else as I turned toward the stairs. I
didn't care if I hurt him, or if he thought I'd react differently.
No one told me what to do anymore and maybe being with him
helped that. I wasn't going to let him tell me how to handle
this. I wasn't going to be trapped again.

He didn't want me left behind because he was afraid I'd
be killed alongside my father? Well, what about him? I didn't
want him to die trying to protect me.

CHAPTER ELEVEN
FABIANO

There was no way in hell I'd be letting Aida out of my sight. Not when things were about to get even more dangerous. I'd been on the phone with Gio when she'd come in, finally done with what I assumed was her bath or shower.

I couldn't understand why she'd retreated into her bedroom after what we did. It was as if she were avoiding me now that she'd gotten what she wanted. In a pathetic turn of events, I felt like I'd been used.

I was angry at her and myself for letting the situation get out of hand in the first place, frustrated that I let my guard down as well as the walls I'd built up so steadily over the years. I lost myself in her entirely and I thought she'd done the same.

However, now that the moment had passed, she seemed colder than ever. It was almost as if she finally discovered the key to her freedom and was taking it without regard of how it might feel to others. Especially me, who was trying incredibly hard to drive the point home that I gave a shit about her.

She deserved a life apart from her father and he'd be dead soon enough anyway if I had my way. But she walked away from *me*. She told me she didn't need me, or anyone, to help her.

I hadn't intended to come off as controlling when I'd said I wouldn't allow her to stay behind. I simply wanted her to understand that I had a plan and needed to ensure her safety. She needed to know what was going on before doing something stupid. It was difficult not to get caught up in the moment of arguing with her though. That woman riled me up constantly and I couldn't help but push back.

There was something about her that I couldn't shake. A void that she seemed to fill in me, so long lost after the time I'd spent with Randall Hawks. Even fighting with her brought joy to my miserable existence.

I made my way upstairs and went to her bedroom door, which was closed. Knocking on it, I waited for her to answer. I could hear her shuffling around in there, clearly ignoring me.

"Aida," I called through the door. "Will you please open the door?"

"Go away!" she hollered. I scowled.

Why was she choosing this very moment to act like a damn child?

"I'm not going anywhere until you open the door. Please?"

"I don't care what you do. I've made up my mind and I'm not leaving with you."

"You have to go with me or you'll be in more trouble than you are now. Do you realize you're an accessory now? I'm compromised here," I growled.

I heard her stomp toward the door and it swung open in a flash.

"I don't care. *You* made that decision, not me." She moved to slam the door on me and I caught it with my knee.

"Stop acting like this," I said. "I'm your friend. I'm trying to help you."

She shook her head. "You're not my friend. You're my bodyguard and a spy!"

I scoffed. "That didn't seem to bother you earlier when you were in my bed."

Her blue eyes narrowed. "I regret it," she said, but I knew she was lying.

"You made a decision for yourself, seized a moment of freedom. You don't regret that."

She let out a frustrated groan, stamping her foot. "Don't tell me what I feel or what I'm thinking."

I could see tears forming in her eyes and all frustration eased as concern took over. Before I could stop myself, I reached for her, pulling her into my chest. I dipped my chin, resting my cheek atop her still damp hair.

"Fab ..."

"No," I whispered. "What's wrong? Why won't you leave with me?"

Her breath hitched and she relaxed into my body. I normally wasn't the type of person to give hugs, let alone touch many people in general, especially after what I'd been through, but it felt right in the moment. I held her tighter.

"I'm scared," she said in a low voice. "I'm afraid of what I felt with you and what I feel now. If I go with you, I know what that means for my father. I hate him, but knowing he'll die breaks my heart."

"You can't stay with him," I said. "Aida, you're in danger with him now that you know who I am. You'll be safer with me."

She pulled back and I let her go. Swiping her eyes, she sniffled and looked up at me.

"With the Mafia, not you. You're taking me to another person who will find a use for me, who will control me. That's not freedom."

Suddenly her outburst made sense. She thought if I took her to Uncle Roman, she'd be forced into a life she didn't choose. While there were certain rules to follow, namely staying hidden for a while just until shit blew over, she could still live a somewhat normal life. Better than what she'd experienced. Celeste was protected and couldn't share what she knew of the family business, but that didn't mean she couldn't have a normal career and go to school like she was doing.

"He won't control you like Albert does," I said. "Aida, I want to keep you safe. Regardless of whatever job I have, I care about you. I've told you that."

"Why? How am I any different than your brother's fiancée?"

I released a sigh, running a hand through my hair. I couldn't pinpoint exactly why I had such an affinity for her. It was a number of things that were difficult to explain right now.

"You're different than anyone I've ever met," I said. "You're not helpless, you're strong and capable. You understand the business and you were a soldier, but you're soft, too, feminine. I'm attracted to you, obviously, but it's more than that. When I was with Randall Hawks, I was never alone. I was always surrounded by him or his men. I was always … on. It's exhausting trying to pretend to be a completely different person. To act as if you agree with someone you want to kill in order to learn what you can."

"You never grew attached to anyone during that time?" she asked.

I shook my head. "No, I couldn't. It was mostly men and the women that were around were either his helpless victims or prostitutes." She gasped at that.

It was the truth. I'd fallen into temptation a handful of times out of boredom and a way to relieve stress, but none of those women wanted me for anything.

"With you, I don't have to be something I'm not. Even when I first met you, it was as if you could see right through me. I know you're not weak and you're fully able to do whatever you want to do. I also know what it's like to feel captive, to push others away because you're afraid of being vulnerable. You're afraid of actually needing someone."

She nodded slowly, seeming to process what I was saying. "I've never met someone who listens to me like you do. Who has offered to help me."

"I'm not going to my uncle right away. I'm staying with you and continuing to work for your father."

"What?"

Shrugging, I said, "I trust you. Our capo thinks I'm crazy, but I have to make sure you're safe. I have a plan."

"But on the phone—"

"You walked into the tail end of a conversation with my uncle's capo. They want to release Sebastian Gallo."

She gasped. "They have him?"

I nodded. "Yeah, he's been incredibly cooperative."

"What happens now?"

"I think Albert will do whatever it takes to get his way. The co-owner of The Den gave us a lot of information, as well. He talked at length about your father's plans to take out the

Gallo gang once he got their weapons. You never heard anything about that?"

She shook her head, wandering over to her bed to sit down. "No, I had no idea. Why did he want to marry me off to Sebastian then?"

"To gain their trust, to prove he was willing to work with them completely. He used you as collateral." I didn't mask the venom in my voice. I fucking hated her father and she deserved the truth.

"What are you going to do?" she asked, gazing up at me with tear-laced eyes.

I crossed my arms. "I'm going to tear apart your father's group from the inside. Marcus trusts me enough and Patrick is oblivious."

"How?"

As much as I wanted to be honest from here on out, there were certain things I wouldn't admit. Like how I planned to set up her father's men to be picked off one by one until Albert was paranoid. Some of them I could kill on my own, others would be taken out by Grim. We'd scare Ricci into thinking Gallo knew the truth and was retaliating.

I wasn't totally against my uncle's plans to wait, but I wanted things to hopefully play out quicker. I had to try because as of right now, Thompson's business partner wasn't sharing where those weapons were. He could very well be tortured to death before surrendering information. Without those weapons, Roman feared Albert would be able to attack at the press of a button.

"I want to kill the men who came with us to Rochester."

Her eyes widened. "You're not serious?"

"I am," I said. "I was going to call Marcus and say there were Mafia men on the property. Then when he and the other two arrived, I was planning to shoot them."

Aida sat in stunned silence and I released a sigh. This was why I didn't want to tell her my plan. She was probably realizing just how dangerous I was. Hell, she was probably regretting everything right now.

When she finally spoke, her voice was soft as if she was talking to herself. "That's why you said we'd head back tonight when you were on the phone."

"Yeah, then I'd lie to your father about an imaginary ambush and hopefully scare him."

She ran a hand through her wavy hair and let out a heavy sigh. "This is dangerous."

I uncrossed my arms and approached her slowly. "I know it is. That's why I want you with me, because if you don't stick close, and your father finds out who I am or what we've done, he could hurt you. I don't want that, Aida." I shook my head. "I can't bear the thought of him hurting you, not because of me, not for any reason."

Whether I wanted to admit it or not, I was falling for her. The way I felt about her, right or wrong, was uncontrollable. I'd die before dishonoring her. If that meant taking my own life or being labeled a traitor by Roman, so be it.

I risked a step closer to her, then another. She watched me as I approached, not retreating this time. I lifted my hand, tucking a stray strand of hair behind her ear.

"We're in this," I spoke quietly. "Whether we want to be or not, it's the truth. The question is, are we in this together?" I searched her misty blue eyes, waiting for a response.

Her breath hitched and a single tear rolled down her cheek. "Together," she replied.

I bent down to kiss her, using one hand to hold her face while the other curled around her waist. She wrapped her arms around my neck, kissing me back. Before long, I was hovering over her and pinning her to the mattress with my hips while I tasted the sweet skin of her throat, reveling in the way she encouraged me with soft moans.

Aida ran her fingers through my hair before grabbing my face and drawing my lips back to hers. "I don't want to leave yet," she admitted in a breathy moan as I pressed against her.

"I know, babe." I sucked in a breath when she fisted my cock. I hadn't realized she'd unbuttoned my jeans.

"Can we stay a while longer?" she asked sweetly, flicking her tongue against my ear lobe.

My body shuddered. "You'll be the death of me," I growled, claiming her lips.

I was giving in because I didn't want to leave yet, either. I wanted more moments like this with her, and for all we knew, we wouldn't have much more if any. Taking a vow to end your life at a moment's notice changes your perspective on timing. It makes you say and do things you might otherwise hold back on because you never know when your next breath will be your last.

I carried Aida into my room and grabbed another condom. I was grateful I had them on me. I hadn't planned on needing them, but they'd been tucked in the inside pocket of my duffel bag since I'd gotten back from Seattle.

I settled over her in my bed, sinking into her body slowly. I still had to be careful with her and didn't want to cause her pain. I gripped the sheets beside her head, trying like hell to control myself. She felt so warm, so tight. It was difficult to hold back, especially when she made those noises in the back of her throat, urging me to keep going.

I kissed her lips, her forehead, her neck, all the while claiming her body until she wrapped those smooth thighs around my waist, forcing me deeper.

"Holy shit," I breathed. "Fuck, babe, you're going to make me come." I panted, curling my fingers in her hair and tugging gently.

She cried out, bucking her hips up to meet mine. I felt her muscles clench around my cock and that familiar tingle shot down my spine, forcing me off the edge. I grunted out in pleasure, letting her milk every last drop from me.

I lowered my head to the crook of her neck, nuzzling against her warm, sweet skin. She wound her arms around my shoulders, trailing her fingers up and down my back. It was difficult to move, but I reluctantly rose from the bed and went to the bathroom to discard the condom.

When I came back, Aida was still lying there waiting for me. I crawled back in the bed, settling into her warmth and shifting slightly so that I didn't crush her beneath me. I wrapped my arms around her waist, pulling her close.

We lay there silently, catching our breaths, and I felt my eyelids grow heavy with each passing second. For the first time in years, I wasn't haunted by the past that gave me nightmares.

Fabiano fell asleep beside me, his arms circled around my body, holding me tightly to him. I studied his peaceful face, taking in every freckle and scar I hadn't noticed before. He had the gunshot wound on his hip and a jagged line across his upper thigh that I'd seen when he took his clothes off earlier but hadn't yet asked about. I also found a round scar near his right shoulder that looked like he'd been burned by something.

He had a freckle on his cheekbone under his left eye and his long lashes were almost black, fanning out in a way that made me envious. I wondered how many fights he'd been in because he had several tiny, pale scars near his right brow, as if he'd been punched and the skin split. Even with all his markings, he was handsome.

His lips were clear of any scars, the top one slightly thinner than the bottom, yet both quite full. I had the sudden urge to kiss those lips but refrained. I didn't want to wake him, yet. Instead, I ran my finger over the tattoo above his heart, following along with the Italian script.

Death rather than dishonor.

I still couldn't believe he was Don Roman's nephew, a man who was known for maintaining order in the chaotic underground of New York since before we were born. What's more, Fabiano Cuccione was a legend in his own right. The East Coast Mafia was now in charge of several areas on the West Coast, and it was all because of the man sleeping next to me.

Having that same man hold me right now felt incredibly bizarre, yet also right.

Fabiano's lips parted in a small gasp and he mumbled something unintelligible. I watched his eyelids flutter and his breathing grew quicker. Was he having a nightmare? He groaned as if he was in pain. The arm he had draped over me spasmed and his hand clenched into a fist against my lower back.

"Please," he whispered. "No, don't …" He whimpered, sucking in a sharp breath.

I lifted my hand from his chest, slowly running it down his arm until my fingers tangled with his behind my back. He released a sigh, nuzzling into me further and pulling me close to his body.

"Aida …" he murmured huskily, his lips finding my jaw. He slowly made his way toward my mouth. "Aida …"

I turned into him, letting him kiss me. He slid his hand from mine, cupping my chin as he continued kissing me in a way that made my heart flutter. He pulled back and his hazel eyes sparkled as he drank me in. He trailed a finger along my jaw, down my neck, and over my shoulder.

"I fell asleep on you. I'm sorry." His voice was thick.

"It's okay," I said. "Do you have nightmares often?"

He swallowed, nodding slowly. "I don't sleep a lot at night. I have pills to help, but I can't escape my past."

I frowned, my gaze shifting to the scar on his shoulder. "What happened there?" I asked.

He leaned back to inspect the pinkish circle. "Hawks burned me with a cigar." He shifted, sitting up and raising his left arm. "Stabbed me with a letter opener here." He pointed to a small scar near his ribs.

"Why did he hurt you if you were his second in command?" It didn't make sense to me. I knew my father was a cruel man, but he'd never hurt Marcus or any of his other employees that way unless they crossed him with betrayal.

"He had a temper and I was usually in his path when he'd get angry. Sometimes I fought back and he welcomed it. Other times, he used me as his personal punching bag." He shrugged. "It was me or them, and the choice was a no brainer."

"Them?"

"The women who worked for him and his victims like Cynthia and Claire."

"You protected them." It wasn't a question, but a statement of amazement. Fabiano was inherently good despite the family he belonged to.

His lips tilted up on one side. "I tried to. Cynthia had been beaten a lot before I got there, but he never touched her after I arrived. I found ways to distract him, kissed his ass a lot and acted like I wanted to grow up to be just like him." His eyes narrowed and he gazed down at his thigh, running his index finger along the jagged scar.

"He stabbed me here when he found me talking to her one day. He thought I was trying to have sex with her because I'd been in her room. I think he was jealous."

"That was your brother's fiancée, right?"

He nodded, dragging a hand through his hair. "It was the one year anniversary of Dante's death. She was hurting and I didn't want her to be alone. We talked about memories of him."

"You don't belong in the darkness of the underworld," I said, placing my hand over his. "You're so good."

His eyes met mine. "I'm not all good, Aida. I've done a lot of bad things to protect the people I care about. I've even done bad things just because I wanted to. My first kill was an innocent man."

My spine stiffened and I gaped at him.

"I'd like to say I had a motive, but I didn't have all the facts. I thought he was involved in my parents' death and I shot him. It turned out the person responsible for their accident was the guy's twin brother and was already dead."

"That's awful."

"I paid for his funeral though. It was the least I could do for his family. I carry that burden with me."

He'd made it right despite the fact he'd ended a life. Well, as right as he could. I shook my head. "You have a good soul though. You've never killed anyone else who didn't deserve it, have you?"

He lifted his hand, tucking a strand of hair behind my ear. "No, but I'm walking a very thin line between good and evil lately when it comes to you." I shivered as he leaned closer to me, placing his lips at my ear. "I'll ruin you if you let me in." He pulled back, rising from the bed.

I stared at him as he pulled on his jeans, then a t-shirt. "I need you to get dressed and pack up your stuff." He grabbed a cell phone from his front pocket, appearing to text someone.

I got up and began collecting my clothes to get dressed. Steven's phone rang as he held it in his hand. He scowled, answering it immediately.

"Marcus," he said, his gaze drifting to mine. I managed to get my underwear and jeans on but hadn't put my bra or t-shirt on yet.

Steven listened to whatever Marcus was saying and lifted his index finger, curling it inward at me. I stepped close to him and he tilted his head down, kissing my cheek. He placed his free hand on my hip, drawing me into him. His lips traveled to mine, hovering there for a few beats.

"We can head back tonight." He spoke in a low voice and I shivered as his thumb traced a circle along my hip. "Yeah, that sounds good. I'll make sure she gets home safe."

He flicked my upper lip with his tongue and I released a shaky breath. Pulling back, he smirked at me. "Sure thing, later." He disconnected the call and tossed his phone on the bed.

I wanted to ask him what was going on but didn't get the chance. Suddenly, he hauled me against him and claimed my mouth, kissing me until I was breathless and dizzy. His hands slid over my backside, forcing my hips into his and I moaned against his mouth.

I ran my fingers through his hair, over his shoulders, and down his chest. He growled low, taking a step back from me, tucking his hands behind his back, his chest rising and falling rapidly. I stood there, attempting to catch my breath.

"We've got to roll out, babe. Your father just found out that Sebastian Gallo is with the Mafia. Marcus wants me to get you home."

"What about your plan?" I asked, still standing there topless. My body felt like a livewire after that smoldering kiss.

"Dead in the water. On a good note though, our capo found the arsenal your father stashed. I had a missed text from him."

I finished dressing and nodded. "What are we going to do?" I asked.

His face fell, his jaw flexing. I frowned at the sudden shift in his mood.

Shaking his head, he stared at the floor. "I'm not sure yet," he said quietly. "Go get ready."

I left his room, feeling the sting of our horrible reality with every step. We were going back to New York, back to the prying eyes of my father and his men. The chances of anything ever happening again were incredibly low. Was that the reason for the sudden shift in his mood?

As I packed my bag, a sense of disappointment clouded my earlier optimism. Fabiano would go back to pretending to be Steven, my guard. I would be left in the dark, waiting for everything to blow up around us. My father would end up losing his life along with countless others. I really wished we could just run now, but my father was not stable with Gallo weapons in his possession. For all we knew, he might already be ready to attack now that the Mafia had Sebastian.

I headed downstairs once I was done packing and found Fabiano sitting at the bottom of the stairs. He gazed up at me, giving me a short smile. I set my bag down on the floor and sat next to him.

"Thank you for … getting lost with me for a while." He slid his hand around mine, squeezing gently. "You don't know how much—" He cut himself off, shaking his head. "We should get going." He stood then and I followed.

A wave of both relief and anxiety flowed through me. "What happens now?" I asked again.

He ran a hand through his hair, his lips turning down. "Once we get back to New York, I'll figure that out." He headed for the door, opening it.

"Do you regret it?" I blurted, tears springing to life.

I understood the disappointment of having to go back, but his mood had already changed toward me and we hadn't even left yet. How could he close himself off to me so quickly after he'd been upset that I'd done the same to him?

He turned around to face me, his eyes searching my face. "What?"

"Me and you. Do you regret it?"

I don't know why I suddenly felt like crying. I couldn't shake this sense of fear building in the pit of my stomach, like something bad was going to happen.

"Aida, we have to be extremely careful. You know my identity now."

I nodded. "I know that. I understand what's at stake here and that what we did can never happen again. I just want to know if you regret it. Because even when I said that I did, I didn't mean it. Not at all. I need to know that we're on the same page before we walk out of here."

He dropped his bag and strode over to me, curving his palm against my cheek. "I'll *never* regret anything when it comes to you." His other hand lifted mine and he pressed it against his chest. "Do you feel that?"

I nodded, feeling the steady beat of his heart beneath my palm. Our gazes locked and the intensity in his hazel eyes gave me butterflies.

"That's for you, Aida."

I wasn't sure what I was expecting him to say. He opened something up within me and I knew from that moment on I'd never be the same. I recognized that despite how he may act from here on out, his truth toward me would never waiver.

His heart belonged to me.

CHAPTER TWELVE
FABIANO

Nothing was going according to plan. Yes, we had eyes on the weapons stash and could stop Albert Ricci from obtaining them, but he was on to us now and knew that Sebastian Gallo ratted him out. I needed to contact my guys and figure out what the next plan of action was while also trying to placate an extremely angry Albert.

Marcus was his usual unpleasant self when meeting Aida and me at her apartment shortly after we'd arrived back in the city. The drive had been quiet and pensive most of the time. It felt like the further away from that random house on the outskirts of Rochester we got, the further from safety we were. It also felt more and more like what we'd done was a dream instead of reality.

Aida spent most of the drive staring out the passenger side window, sighing every now and then as if lost in thought. I wished I could say something to make her feel better or to bring that smile I'd witnessed earlier in the day back.

When she asked me if I regretted our time together it killed me. There was a fear of rejection in her curious gaze and all I could do was say exactly what came to me in the moment, which was the truth. My heart did belong to her. She gave me a reason to live, to stay alive and see this through until I knew beyond a shadow of doubt that she would be free from the burdens her father put on her. I wouldn't rest until she was finally able to live her life on her own terms.

It was more than just doing my job. There was a connection we shared before we ever touched. Something about Aida Ricci spoke to me on a spiritual level. It was like we understood each other without even trying.

Now that we were back in the city of New York, I had to focus on the task at hand which also included not letting on just how close Aida and I had become.

I was currently sitting on the couch in her living room, glancing at her every once in a while as she sat in her chair by the window, picking at her nail polish. She was angry and rightly so. Marcus had just told us Albert's new plan which involved Aida doing something that made me want to track him down and punch him in the balls.

"I understand your aversion to leaving the country; however Albert feels it best to ensure your safety."

"I won't leave!" she screamed, standing from her chair. "Call him up. Tell him to come here and say that to my face."

Marcus rolled his eyes, taking a sip of wine that he'd helped himself to in her kitchen when he arrived twenty minutes ago. "He's busy. We know you're safe here for the time being, but it may not last."

"Will you at least tell me why my father wants to ship me off to Sweden?"

"I told you; it's for your safety. His plans are being put into action sooner than expected."

"This is bullshit!" She stomped down the hallway to her bedroom, slamming the door loudly.

It took everything in me not to chase after her and tackle her onto her bed. God, she was sexy when she was all worked up like that. Marcus turned his attention to me, raising a brow.

"I'm sorry I left you alone with her for twenty-four hours." He finished off his wine.

I shrugged. "She doesn't scare me. I have a sister."

Marcus chuckled. "Ah, so you're used to a hormonal woman. Thanks for keeping an eye on her. I've let Patrick know that he'll be guarding her tomorrow. You can take the day off."

I nodded, standing from the couch. "Does Albert need any help?" I asked casually.

Marcus shook his head. "No, he was prepared for this unfortunate event."

Raising my brows, I asked, "What do you mean?"

He winked at me. "The weapons were a diversion tactic."

I tried to reign in the shock coursing through me. "What does he intend to do?"

He waved his hand dismissively. "It's not your concern. Have a good night and report Monday morning at the warehouse for a meeting."

I nodded. "Got it," I murmured, making my way to the door.

"Hey, Cline!" he hollered as I reached for the handle. I glanced at him over my shoulder. "Thanks for taking such good care of our girl." He angled his head toward Aida's room.

My jaw clenched. "No problem," I said, getting the fuck out of there and immediately regretting it. I wanted to get away from Marcus Pelossi, but I'd left him alone with Aida. If he so much as breathed on her, I'd blow his dick off with my 9mm.

I'd check on her later. For now, I had my own business to take care of. I went back to my apartment down the hall and called Gio right away. Luckily, he answered even though it was late into the evening.

"You back in town?" he asked by way of greeting.

"Yeah." I ran a hand through my hair, sitting at the edge of my coffee table. "We've got a problem. They want to ship Aida off to Sweden before the week is out."

"What the fuck?"

"That's what I was thinking."

"What is Ricci planning?"

"I don't know."

A low growl rumbled from the other end of the line. The capo was pissed and that wasn't good. I'd seen the vicious side of Giovanni Daleo and it wasn't pretty. He didn't earn his job sponsoring Girl Scouts.

"Do you have any idea when they'll act?" he asked.

"I have no clue. The second in command wouldn't give me any information when I asked. He seemed different than normal, more arrogant, like he knows something. He was running his mouth a lot but said nothing significant."

"Do you think you're made?"

I considered that, but it wouldn't make sense. They never would have hired me if I was that easy to peg. "I think he's just a dick."

Gio grunted in agreement. "Without knowing their timeline, we need to be prepared for anything. Where's the girl right now?"

"She's in her apartment. She's safe. I'm going by to check on her later."

"Fab …"

"Don't," I bit out.

"Fab, listen to me. Did you fuck up?"

I didn't respond right away and that told him everything he needed to know.

"Jesus, Fab. What in the hell were you thinking? You realize you can't have her, right? That's not something possible when she's the enemy's daughter and you're, well, *you*."

"I'm well aware of the consequences, Gio," I snapped. "It's different. She's different. She trusts me completely."

"Fuck. Does Roman know?"

"No."

I couldn't tell my uncle what I'd done. He didn't care if I took the girl to save her, but getting close to her, blowing my cover for her, that would earn me a demotion. I was his star employee, the apple of his eye. He'd find out soon enough, but we didn't need the drama at the moment.

"I won't say anything, but you know he'll figure it out. What do you expect to do with her when this is over?"

"Nothing. There's nothing I can do. She wants freedom and I have my vow."

"You're a good kid, Fab. Don't think with your dick anymore, yeah?"

"Yeah."

"I'll call Roman, give him a heads up on Ricci. Keep your head down, stay out of trouble until you hear back from me."

"Will do."

I ended the call and inhaled a deep breath before releasing it slowly. Running a hand through my hair, I stared at the door of my apartment.

Gio was right. I needed to maintain a level head from here on out. My plan to take out the group by picking off their members blew up in my face before I even got to test it. I needed to figure out how they were planning on taking out the Mafia and what method of destruction they'd choose.

Knowing I wasn't working tomorrow made every passing minute away from Aida agony. I shouldn't be thinking of her and I needed to steer clear of her, but it was difficult after spending so much time with her today.

I unpacked my bag and started doing laundry in the stackable washer and dryer in my hall closet. I was trying to find all kinds of ways to keep myself from marching down that hall to her room. Once the few items of clothing I had were clean, I took a shower.

I was absently channel surfing on the television when something Marcus said earlier came back to me. Albert was prepared for his weapons to be confiscated by the Mafia.

"The weapons were a diversion tactic."

Shit. I jumped up from the couch and sprinted to my room to grab my boots, tugging them on as I made my way to the door. I needed to talk to Aida. Now.

I hated Marcus for ruining my already shitty mood with his ridiculous news about me being shipped off to Sweden. He left an hour ago, telling me that he'd see me at some point tomorrow. I flipped him off behind his back. I would have stayed in my room, if not for my desperation for some water.

Since he'd gone, I'd been lying in bed, trying to fall asleep. I didn't even get to say goodnight to Fab and while it was a foolish reason to be upset, I wished I'd been able to at least see him leave. It might sound cheesy, but in a way, I sort of missed him.

I heard a soft knock on my front door and cautiously got up to check it out, flicking a gaze at the digital clock on my stove. It was after midnight. Glancing through the peephole, I saw a familiar mess of dark, disheveled hair and hazel eyes. My stomach erupted in butterflies.

I opened the door quickly and stepped back to allow him to enter. He closed the door behind him; his gaze trained on me. He gave me a slow perusal, biting down on his lower lip.

"Is that what you usually sleep in?" he asked in a whisper.

I glanced down at my pale blue silk tank top and shorts that matched. "Sometimes …" I was immediately interrupted when his lips crashed down on mine.

He shoved me into the door, pressing into me. I tangled my hands in his hair, whimpering when he swept his tongue across mine. He was such a good kisser and I was a complete and total mess in his hands.

I slid one of my hands from his hair over his chest and lower until I felt his abs. He caught my hand, pulling back from me.

"We need to talk," he panted, tugging me with him to the couch.

He sat me down and took the spot next to me, keeping his hand wrapped around mine. His thumb made idle circles against my skin as he studied my face.

"Did Marcus say anything to you after I left?" he asked.

Confusion filled me. He came over in the middle of the night to talk about Marcus? "Not really, why?"

"Did your father ever explain to you why he wanted those weapons from Gallo?"

"No. He only said he thought they could work together since he knew Thompson had a buyer and he wanted to pay his debt. You know this."

"That's all?"

I slipped my hand away from his. "What is this about?" I asked, feeling like I was part of an interrogation and not an innocent conversation.

"Marcus basically said that your father expected the Mafia to find the weapons," he replied and my stomach turned. "He said it was a diversion tactic."

"What was he creating a diversion for?"

His eyes narrowed, his jaw ticking in thought. "You selected me at the initiation. Who chose the candidates?"

Ice filled my veins. "Marcus …"

A darkness fell over Fabiano's face and he muttered a curse. Shooting up, he began pacing in front of the couch. "They know who I am. They have to," he said, glancing at me again.

"Why would my father bring you in intentionally?" I asked. It didn't make sense.

"Leverage," he said, halting his pacing. He ran a hand through his hair. "It makes sense."

"Maybe Marcus lied to you. What kind of benefit is it to have you know their business?"

"He wants to take my uncle out, Aida. Who do you think he'd like to use as a threat to get Don Roman to cave?"

I shook my head. "Maybe Marcus just wanted to scare you. We did spend a full night together alone. Maybe he thought you'd crack."

He resumed his pacing. "Maybe."

I watched him continue his thinking for several minutes, feeling cagey myself. Fab could just be paranoid now that he'd told me the truth. Marcus was always messing with the guys and making comments. He was probably trying to get this exact rise out of him since things were heading toward war. He couldn't know Fabiano Cuccione was working for my father. If he did, he certainly wouldn't be in my apartment right now.

I stood abruptly and stepped in front of him, keeping him from moving any further. He frowned. "You're driving me insane," I said.

His lips tilted up on one side. "Likewise, babe. Those pajamas leave little to the imagination and I'm trying to behave myself."

Rolling my eyes, I said, "That's not what I meant." I'd have to remember he liked these on me. "You can't let something like what Marcus said eat at you. I'm sure he was just messing with you and you're over here freaking out about it for no reason."

He raised a brow. "Freaking out?"

"Yeah, you're going to wear down a hole in my floor."

He released a sigh. "Sorry, I shouldn't have come here. I just want this over with." He lifted his hand, cupping my cheek. "I want you safe."

I nodded, wrapping my hand around his wrist. "I know, I want that, too. But if you don't maintain a level head, you're going to blow your cover. Maybe you should go to your uncle now. Get out while you can before they capture you."

He frowned. "No. I'm not leaving without you."

I didn't want to believe that Marcus and my father truly knew who they hired, but the thought of them using Fabiano to get to Don Roman scared me. They could torture him for information or outright kill him to prove a point. It didn't matter what happened between the Don and my mother in the past, I refused to let history repeat itself.

"Why did Don Roman kill my mother?" It didn't matter, not really, but I was curious. Perhaps if I knew what really happened, not just my father's side, I could fix this somehow before anyone else had to die.

Fabiano released a breath, dropping his hand from my face. "He didn't."

I blinked up at him in confusion. "Then who did?"

He glanced down at the floor, rubbing his fingers over his left brow. "Aida, I don't know if I can tell you the truth." His gaze flicked back to mine as he dropped his hand.

I squinted at him. "Why?"

"Do you know why she died?" he asked. "Did your father tell you how it happened?"

Crossing my arms over my chest, I nodded. "He said that they were at a party and Roman showed up and saw them together and shot her. He was mad because she chose my father over him."

He scrubbed a hand over his face, shaking his head. "Jesus Christ," he muttered. "No, no, Aida, that's not how it happened." Anger flooded his features when he looked at me again. "I promise you that your father is as good as dead. And I'm sorry if that hurts you, but what I'm about to tell will probably change your mind, although it will likely hurt you more."

"What are you saying?" I demanded, growing frustrated. Why couldn't he just tell me?

He bit down on his lip, thinking of how to say whatever it was. "Helena was murdered for choosing the wrong man. The man she chose wasn't your father. The man she chose didn't kill her. Why do you think Albert hates Roman?"

My mouth popped open as tears formed. No! No, that couldn't be true. But then, the only thing I knew for certain about my father was that he always lied to me. Always. More often than not. Oh god, how could I have ever felt any sort of loyalty to him? He'd lied to me my entire life.

"He murdered her for choosing Roman."

Fabiano gently wrapped his hands around my waist. "Roman met Helena shortly after you were born before he started dating my aunt. I don't know all the details, but I was told your mother was miserable with Albert. Her and Roman grew close and she was going to leave your father, but when Albert found out, he killed her. I'm sorry, Aida. I didn't want to be the one to tell you. I only found out a few days ago, but it's true. I swear, I wouldn't lie to you about this."

I swiped away the tears that spilled out. I'd always had a gut feeling that my father may have been behind my mother's death. It was strange to imagine what my life might have been like if my mother and I had gotten away.

"Thank you for telling me. I think …" I choked on a sob and shook my head. "We have to go."

He nodded. "We will, but not tonight. I need to talk to Gio again and figure out how we do this. If I'm made, I don't have much time and you might not, either. Leaving now is a risk I'm not sure we can take. For all we know, the doorman will stop us."

I hadn't even thought about that. It was going to be difficult to pretend like I didn't want to kill my father myself at this point, but patience was important. Fabiano was right. I trusted him completely.

"I can talk to my father tomorrow. See if I can't figure out his true plans," I said.

"I'll come by tomorrow night if I can't sooner. I'm going to come up with a plan to get us out of here. Patrick will be working the day shift."

Disappointment flooded me, but I had to get over that. He couldn't be with me all the time and honestly, I'd rather not have him near my father until we figured out exactly what was going on.

"Okay, just be careful."

He tilted his head to the side, smirking playfully. "Are you worried about me?"

I bit down on my bottom lip, nodding sheepishly. "I kind of like you."

He chuckled, lowering his lips to mine in a simmering kiss. When he pulled back, I was breathless. "When you say things like that, it makes me want to keep you."

My stomach dipped. Keep me? Like forever?

Before I had the chance to process what his words meant, he kissed me again and said goodbye. I locked my door after he left, leaning my forehead against the wood. Despite the happiness Fabiano brought when he was near, I knew deep down we were walking an extremely dangerous line right now.

Nothing good could come of this.

I called my father first thing in the morning to set up a time to meet with him. Questioning his business practices was a good way to end up on his bad side, but I had to know what was actually going on. If he knew that Steven was actually Fabiano Cuccione, things could go downhill quickly.

Lucky for me, he agreed to let me come to his office in Manhattan. Patrick escorted me and made small talk on the drive over. Once we arrived at the building, he stayed in the lobby as I made my way up to the floor of my father's office. He was sitting behind his desk, speaking on the phone to someone. I took a seat in one of the chairs across from him, clasping my hands in my lap.

"The transaction will take place on Tuesday then," he said to whomever he was speaking with. "Yes, that will work for me. Let's plan on eight-thirty." He hung up the phone and gave me a quick once over.

"Who was that?" I asked indifferently.

"Marcus."

"Oh, our beloved second in command?" I rolled my eyes.

My father chuckled. "He said you weren't happy about the news. I thought you'd enjoy a vacation."

"By myself while you do whatever it is you do?" I shot back, glaring at him. "You're shipping me off. Again!"

He waved his hand, his mouth thinning. "I have little time for your attitude, Aida. What do you want?"

"What's happening on Tuesday?" I asked.

"Cuccione didn't get all my weapons. I have a handful in hiding."

I inspected my nails, pretending to be uninterested. "So you're finally putting your number one plan into action?"

"I'm working toward it, yes."

"I don't get to stick around to see how it plays out?"

He narrowed his eyes at me. "You want to help take down the Mafia?"

I rolled my eyes. "I'm worried about my safety. What if something happens to you and I'm out of the country?"

"You'll be fine. Besides, Don Roman will be the one with a bullet in his skull."

"How are you so sure?" I asked, leaning forward. He scowled at me.

"You're full of a lot of questions. What's the meaning of this?"

"Even if you have a handful of automatic rifles or machine guns or explosives, how are you so sure you can draw out Roman Cuccione?"

Resting his elbows on the top of his desk, my father matched my posture and leaned forward as well. "That's none of your business."

"Am *I* in danger?" I asked, biting back on my molars. "Sebastian Gallo talked to the Mafia and I was engaged to him. Am I still? Will they be gunning for me, too?"

"Your ticket is for this upcoming Friday. You'll be out of the country before we act and you'll be safe. Don't worry about Gallo. He's as good as dead, too."

"Why did Marcus say that the weapons were a diversion?"

My father looked genuinely surprised and I instantly regretted my question. Damn my curiosity. It would surely get me killed one of these days.

He cleared his throat. "I don't know why he said that."

"Maybe I misheard him," I said quickly.

"Are you done with your questioning?" he snapped. "I have work to do."

I sat back, loosening a breath. "Yes, I suppose I am. Any jobs for me since it's my last week here for a while?" I stood from the chair, heading for the door.

"No. You're clear for the week."

I nodded and hung a left toward the elevators.

"Aida!" my father called out and I stuck my head back in his office. He crossed his arms, leaning back in his chair. With an evil smirk he said, "Watch your back, daughter. Be careful who you speak with from now on."

A deep fear washed over me and I blinked at him. Was that a threat?

"Go home. Make sure that guard of yours does his job properly."

I walked numbly to the elevators, then through the lobby and out the doors. Patrick followed behind me as we headed for the car waiting at the end of the block. I got in the back mechanically, my mind racing as we navigated through heavy traffic back to my apartment.

Once I was safely tucked inside, I locked the door and sunk down to the marble floor. My chest felt heavy and a wave of nausea rolled through me as I replayed what my father said to me.

That was most definitely a threat. He was warning me and that could only mean one thing. Albert Ricci knew the truth about Fabiano Cuccione.

*

I spent the rest of the day counting down the hours until Fabiano would show up. He'd said last night that he'd check in and as the clock approached midnight, I began to grow worried. Just as I was considering going to his apartment, there was a knock on my door. I opened it quickly and he slipped in like the night before.

Locking the door, I whirled around on him. "He knows. He knows everything," I said in a rush as tears stung my eyes.

His jaw hardened. "Are you certain he's not just baiting you?"

Shaking my head, I wrung my hands together. "He threatened me. Told me to be careful who I spoke to and to watch my back."

A low growl rumbled from his chest. "I'm going to kill him."

"He's going to kill *you*," I sobbed, throwing my arms around his neck. He wrapped his arms around my waist, pulling me into his body.

"Hey, it's okay," he murmured against my hair.

"It's not okay," I said against his shirt. "He said to make sure that guard of mine does his job." I pulled back, meeting his worried gaze. "That was after I asked him about what Marcus said. You know, about the weapons being a diversion."

"Oh, Aida." Steven ran a hand through his hair, releasing a shaky breath. "Fuck." He closed his eyes. When they opened again, there was a fear in them that only made me cry more. "You told him what Marcus said to me?"

I nodded. "Yeah, I had to know if it was true. I didn't think—"

"If that was a test to figure out if I was more than a guard, then we failed miserably. You weren't supposed to tell him anything you wouldn't already know."

Oh God. What had I done? "I didn't know," I cried. "How was I supposed to know that?" My lungs constricted as I tried to control my breathing.

Steven gripped my upper arms. "You wouldn't have known. I should have told you that, I'm sorry." That didn't make me feel any better. He was still on my father's radar.

My stomach turned and I felt dizzy. "What do we do now? You have to go before they question you." If my father was coming for Fabiano, I already knew what the outcome would be. He had to get out before it was too late and there was nothing left for me here anyway. I wasn't any safer under his protection than I would be with Don Roman.

"We go together or not at all," Steven said in a clipped voice. He raised his hands to cup either side of my face. "Aida, I'm not letting you stay behind. It's too dangerous."

"If I go with you, my father will burn the Mafia to the ground."

His eyes sparkled as he peered down at me with a wicked grin. "The Cuccione's don't let anyone get close enough for that to happen."

I had spoken with Gio at length earlier in the day Sunday, to formulate an escape plan for me and Aida.

Without knowing when Ricci planned to attack and not being certain if I was truly made or not, we decided a quiet exit would be best. The doormen changed shifts every three hours, so we could get out of the building easy enough.

I had to be prepared for anything and that included fixing my own mistakes. I shouldn't have told Aida who I was, should have held out a little longer. It wasn't that I regretted telling her. My only issue was that this brought her closer to danger than it should have. She knew too much now and that made her a liability. Not to me or the Mafia, but to her father.

He might decide to question her now that she'd confessed to something she shouldn't have known. I refused to imagine how he planned on gaining intel from her. He might go as far as torturing her or threatening her life. He basically already had.

I rested my forehead against hers, inhaling the scent of roses. "We'll leave early in the morning, during the shift change at the front desk," I said. "I'll have a car waiting for us."

"This is really happening?" Aida asked, sniffling as more tears fell from her brilliant, ocean eyes.

"It has to. We've got to get you out of here." I gently tilted her head back until she met my eyes. "Do you trust me?" She nodded. "With your life? Aida, do you trust me to take care of you and keep you safe no matter what the cost?"

She searched my serious gaze, her brow creasing in the center. "What cost?"

I removed my right hand from her cheek, pointing to the tattoo on my chest. I took a vow and I'd never break it. She had to understand the importance of what I'd done when I blew my cover to her. If she didn't, she was about to. "Death rather than dishonor."

"You?" She shook her head. "You can't risk your life for mine."

"It's my duty, Aida. Do you understand? I will die before I let anything happen to you. I made that decision the moment I laid eyes on you."

She didn't speak right away and I was worried that she'd refuse me. I needed her to accept whatever might happen and trust that I'd get her out of this for good. Instead of saying anything, she lifted her hand to mine still against her cheek.

She raised up on her toes and kissed me. I kissed her back, my heart pounding around in my chest like a drum. I placed my hands on her hips, pulling her against me. I wanted her as close as possible; I needed to prove to her that she belonged to me.

Aida put her hands on my shoulders and I hoisted her up, holding her tight as I made my way down the hall to her bedroom. I set her down on the bed, immediately crawling on top of her and settling between her legs. I stroked her hair, her skin, the silk of her tank top. When my thumb slid along her hard nipple, she moaned into my mouth.

I loved how she responded to me, how she allowed me to touch her wherever I wanted. I wanted to worship her body before claiming it fully.

My lips descended to her neck and beyond as I slid down the bed, licking and sucking her skin over the silky fabric of her pajama bottoms. She fisted my hair, crying out while I worked her with my tongue, tipping her over the edge.

Fuck, she was stunning. The way she unraveled because of me made my chest squeeze tight. I'd never had a connection with someone this way, never been their first. It was intoxicating.

Sliding her shorts down her legs, I stood and removed my shirt, then my jeans until I was left in only my boxer briefs. Aida's eyes opened slowly, her gaze lingering on my rock hard cock. I gripped it lightly, groaning at the sensation of touching myself.

"You want this?" I asked with a wicked grin.

Her lips parted in a gasp and she nodded, tugging off her tank top so that she was completely naked. She sat up, kneeling on the bed and crawled over to me. Her sapphire eyes sparkled in the dim light coming from the small lamp on her nightstand, making her look like some sort of ethereal princess.

I was either incredibly lucky or completely stupid, but I didn't care at the moment. Not when she placed her lips against my chest, over my tattoo. She kissed down to the waistband of my underwear and I shifted my hand to my side, staring down at her in anticipation.

My breath came out ragged as she flicked her gaze up at me while removing my last article of clothing. Without warning, she held my cock and slid her tongue over the tip.

"Oh, fuck." I moaned, clenching my hands into fists. "That feels … incredible."

She continued her exploration and I let her learn on her own, sucking, licking, even lightly nibbling on me. Every once in a while she'd let out a small moan as if the act of giving me head was turning her on and that made it difficult to restrain myself. When she suddenly stopped, I whimpered and she glanced up at me again, her brow creased.

"Fabiano?" The way she said my name in that husky voice completely undid me. I felt it in my soul.

"Yeah, babe?" I murmured, tangling my fingers in her hair and guiding her up so that I could kiss her mouth again.

She pulled away after a few moments, her cheeks coloring to a faint pink. "Will you show me your favorite position?"

My gaze pierced hers and I clasped her jaw. What was she doing to me? Why did I suddenly feel like I couldn't breathe? I kissed her deep and slow, tugging her bottom lip between my teeth as I lowered my hands to her hips, clutching the soft skin there.

"Turn around," I demanded in a rough voice.

Staying on the bed, she turned until her back was to my front. I slid my right hand up the front of her body, over her delicate neck. With my left, I guided her back by the waist until her ass pressed against my cock. She moaned, tilting her head back against my shoulder.

I placed my lips to her ear. "Do you trust me?" I breathed, releasing her hip and grabbing my cock to position it at her entrance from behind.

"Yes," she moaned, squirming against me.

I slowly eased into her and then out, teasing her. She was still so very wet for me and I loved that. My sexy queen.

"Lie down, on your stomach," I growled in her ear.

I eased her forward until she was flat, her hands already clutching the sheets on either side of her. I grabbed a condom from my jeans pocket and placed it on quickly before kneeling between her legs. My hand slid over the curve of her ass to her hip and I positioned her so that she was slightly on her knees, lining up with me.

I bent to kiss between her shoulder blades as I entered her from behind, my body trembling. I heard her gasp and I froze.

"You okay, love?"

She glanced back at me over her shoulder with a smile that made my heart race. "Yes. I like this," she said.

I began moving again, building a slow, steady rhythm until she was panting and begging me not to stop. I picked up the pace, clutching her hip with one hand and gripping her forearm with the other, holding it against her side as I plunged deeper and harder into her sweet body.

I felt her muscles tighten around me and I clenched my teeth, trying like hell not to come. I wanted to stay like this forever; it felt like the purest form of heaven.

She lifted onto her knees, her hands planted firmly on the mattress and I tangled my fingers in the hair at the back of her head, pulling lightly so that I could kiss her. The moment my lips touched hers, she lost all control, sinking back into me until she was practically sitting on my lap. I held her steady, keeping her close as I felt my own climax build and break.

I continued kissing her, not wanting to let her go as I slowly came back to earth. Aida melted into me, lifting a hand to place it behind my head. A flood of warmth spread through me at the contact and I held her tighter.

"Stay with me." The words were out before I could stop them. At first, I wasn't sure if I'd actually spoken them out loud, but then Aida pulled away from me, turning to face me fully.

Her eyes were lined with tears as she searched my face.

I traced her bottom lip with the pad of my thumb. "Stay with me," I said again. I wasn't sure if I was asking for the night or forever, but I needed to know she wouldn't leave. I needed confirmation that she wouldn't disappear like most of the people in my life had.

She nodded slowly and wrapped her arms around my shoulders. I wasn't sure how long we stayed there, skin to skin, simply holding each other. I didn't care. It was just me and her right now and for the first time in so many years, I finally felt at peace. My mind was at ease, my body relaxed.

I was only certain of one thing. I wanted more of her, more of this. I had to find a way to make that happen, after I killed her father.

CHAPTER FOURTEEN
FABIANO

Aida and I ended up falling asleep in her bed with my arms curled around her and her head on my chest. As much peace as she brought me, I was still startled awake by a nightmare. I rubbed my eyes and glanced at the clock on her nightstand. It was after five in the morning. We were off to a late start.

Aida stirred when I sat up, her blue eyes slowly focusing on me. Her lips tipped up in a smile and I couldn't help but lean forward to kiss her.

"What time is it?" she asked in a sleepy voice when I pulled back and rose from the bed.

"After five," I said. I began getting dressed. "We need to get out of here. I'll text Gio."

She immediately sprung up from the bed and started getting ready, packing a bag with random clothes. "When will they know we left?" she asked as she zipped up the bag.

"I don't know." I ran a hand through my hair. "Stay in here, I'll be right back," I said, making my way down the hall.

"Where are you going?"

"I have to grab my stuff from the apartment."

I was able to change my shirt, brush my teeth, and grab what little belongings I'd initially brought without incident. When I got back to Aida's apartment, she was fully dressed and waiting for me where I left her.

I shot a text to Gio, telling him it was time and that we'd meet him near the park which wasn't too far of a walk from here.

Aida inhaled a deep breath, wringing her hands together as she stood near the edge of her bed. I hated that we had to leave like this without much preparation, but we had no choice. Her father was likely planning my demise at this very moment and if we didn't disappear quickly enough, who knew what he'd do?

If it were just me, I wouldn't care so much. I've gotten out of some near death situations plenty of times, but I wasn't certain how Albert Ricci would treat his daughter now that he realized we'd been talking on a personal level. I didn't trust him at all.

I set my bag down and stepped toward Aida, palming her cheek. "We'll be okay. I'll get us out of here to safety. I just need you to be ready for anything, okay?"

She nodded. "Okay."

"We'll get through this soon, I promise." I pressed my lips against hers. "Are you ready to go?"

She exhaled soundly. "Yes. Let's do this."

I shot her a wink. "You're such a brave woman, you know that?" She smiled and I kissed her again, nice and slow. I couldn't get enough of her, but now wasn't the time. We had to move.

A sudden, loud bang sounded from the front door and we both froze.

"What was that?" she asked.

I released her, moving toward the bedroom door. I motioned for her to stay quiet and stepped partly into the hall, listening for anything else.

Heavy footsteps sounded on the marble floor in the living room and my heart plummeted to my stomach. At the mouth of the hallway, I saw an armed Marcus with Patrick following close behind.

Marcus rushed me, grabbing ahold of my arm and spinning me until my back hit the wall. His forearm came up to my throat to apply pressure to my windpipe. Aida screamed as Patrick lunged for her, grasping her wrist and holding her still.

"Who are you?!" Marcus snarled, pressing his arm into me further.

I clenched my teeth, angling my body away from the wall to try and push him off. So he didn't know who I was, only that I was Mafia. That was something.

"What's going on?" Aida demanded, struggling to break from Patrick's hold.

"Don't play dumb with me," Marcus said, still looking at me. "We already know you're Mafia scum."

"What are you talking about?" she cried. "He didn't do anything!"

"Go find his phone," Marcus told Patrick. "Tie the girl up first. The last thing we need is her running."

"Don't touch her," I growled.

Marcus raised a brow. "She does not belong to you!" he spat.

Patrick dragged Aida out of the room and she screamed again. I moved to punch Marcus in the ribs but he stepped back, aiming his gun at my face. Frozen, I stared at him.

"The Mafia found our weapons. We've been trailed everywhere we go since Thompson was offed."

"He worked for Albert Ricci. Why wouldn't they end him?" I bit out.

"We haven't stepped on their precious toes."

"You sure about that?" I asked, my fingers twitching. I wish I had my damn gun on me; I'd lay him out right now.

Marcus narrowed his eyes. "Who are you?"

I didn't answer him and that pissed him off further. I was fucked either way at this point so it didn't matter. I wasn't going to blow my cover yet. "You're going to have to kill me."

He eyed me up and down with a sneer on his face. Lowering the gun, he pressed his forearm into my windpipe again and leaned forward until his face was a mere inch from mine.

"There is nothing I would love more than to blow your brains out, *Cline*. Unfortunately, the boss wants you alive for now. You're coming with us."

"Like … Hell …" I choked out. Stars danced in my vision as he continued applying pressure to my trachea.

He said something else, but it sounded muffled and far away. *Shit.* I was blacking out and while I tried like hell to hold on; to push forward and remove his arm from me, it was no use. The last thing I heard before darkness took over was the sound of Aida's screams.

*

I came to with a tingling sensation that began in my fingers and slowly crawled its way up my wrists, forearms, and shoulders. I attempted to shake the feeling away and realized I had my hands behind my back. I kept my eyes closed; my chin tucked to my chest as I listened for any sounds of movement. I heard what sounded like a chair scrape across a floor but that was it.

As my eyes blinked open, I saw a dirty concrete floor beneath me. I was in a wood chair with a high back and my chest was held tightly to it with a thick nylon rope. My hands were cuffed, resting between the leather of my belt and the wooden rungs of the chair back. My legs were bound together and tied to the front two legs of the chair as well. They had me nice and secure then. I wasn't getting out of here anytime soon.

When I lifted my head, the room tilted and I screwed my eyes shut again. I had no idea how long I'd been here, but it must have been awhile because I had to piss and my entire body felt stiff. I lifted my head, slower this time, and examined the small room.

There was one window to the left of me but it was covered on the opposite side by a thick piece of cloth, almost like canvas. I couldn't tell if it led outside or into another room. The single metal door to the right was painted black with flecks of it missing in places, revealing a grayish color.

What the hell was this place?

As my body became more alert, I shivered and it was then I noticed I was missing my shirt. They must have checked me for weapons. I shifted my shoulders, trying and failing to loosen the nylon rope around my chest. Next, I attempted to stretch my legs but they didn't budge. I was completely trapped and panic began to surface as I recalled the last thing I remembered.

Aida was screaming. I didn't know if she'd been hurt or was simply worried for me. What had Patrick and Marcus done with her after I was knocked out? Was she with Albert?

I felt dizzy, almost as if I were hungover or drugged with something to keep me down for a while. It was difficult to keep my eyes open.

A sharp, buzzing noise sounded from the other side of the door and I heard a heavy lock turn before it swung open. Albert walked in with Marcus trailing behind him. The latter had a short, black instrument in his hand that looked a hell of a lot like a Taser.

I narrowed my eyes at him and he smirked, crossing his arms.

"Seems your plan didn't work out too well, spy," Albert said, standing directly in front of me. "Cuccione may have Gallo, but I don't need him, nor do I care if they kill him."

"They'll come for you next," I said. "You'll all be picked off one by one until there's nothing left. *Traitor.*"

He chuckled. "Just because I'm not siding with the almighty Don Roman doesn't make me a traitor."

"Maybe not in your delusional world." I growled. "Let me dumb it down for you. Treason is the crime of betraying one's country, especially by attempting to kill the sovereign or overthrow the government. *We* are the country, the government, and every other ruling in New York City." I memorized the definition of the word during my training. It was ingrained in my brain like a phone number or home address.

"You're quite arrogant for a boy strapped to a chair in my possession," Albert snarled. "What is your name?"

A slow smile spread across my lips. "You know my name."

"Steven Cline is an alias. We ran an extensive background check on you last night and found nothing," Marcus said.

I glanced at him, shaking my head. "You didn't do your job properly if you just found that out. Way to fuck up, second in command."

I deserved the wrath of his fist against my jaw, but I hadn't expected it to hurt as badly as it did. He'd lunged for me, grabbing my throat and laying a solid uppercut to the right side of my face. Blood pooled in my mouth from the impact of biting my tongue. I spit it out at Albert's feet, glowering up at the two men.

"You think beating me will change my mind? Do your worst!" I shouted. "Unlike you, I'm not a rat."

Albert stared me down for several minutes, not saying a word. He reached into the pocket of his slacks, producing a utility knife. I clenched my aching jaw as he stepped closer to me, bending until we were eye to eye.

"I may have underestimated you in the beginning," he spoke in a low, menacing voice, "but you honestly didn't think I'd allow you so close to my flock without a few safety measures in place. Did you?"

My shoulders tensed. He slid the blade up from its casing, resting it against my jugular vein. I held my breath, afraid that if I even swallowed, the knife would pierce my skin.

"Thanks to my inquisitive daughter, we discovered you've been talking to her by planting little seeds to catch you in the act." I only glared at him, refusing to speak. "But you couldn't just spy, could you? No, you had to try and turn her. You've been entertaining her with ideas of running, haven't you?"

My hands clenched into tight fists behind me, the movement straining the sore muscles in my arms from lack of use. Rage filled my stomach and chest, creating a dangerous urge to headbutt this motherfucker and drop him.

The only thing keeping me in check was understanding it wouldn't end well for me or her if I reacted. It's not like I could get out of this damn chair quickly enough before Marcus tased me or put a bullet between my eyes.

Albert straightened, holding the knife to the rope at my chest. "She does not belong to you and she never will." He slashed the rope and it fell to the floor. Pointing the tip of the blade against my vow tattoo on my chest, he said, "Death rather than dishonor. What a crock of shit."

The pain of the blade scraping across my skin ripped a vicious scream from my throat. I grunted and jerked as he continued slicing the skin on my chest, warping the tattoo. My head felt hazy by the time he was done, falling to the side as I groaned in agony.

Hearing Fabiano's screams sent a wave of horror through me and I bolted from the chair I'd been sitting in, rushing to the closed door. I began beating on it, screaming at my father to stop whatever he was doing. He couldn't kill him.

"Leave him alone!" I shouted. "Please, please, stop hurting him!"

The door swung open and I nearly fell forward. Marcus gripped my arm to steady me, squeezing harder than necessary.

"Shut your mouth!" he demanded.

My gaze slid behind him and bile rose in my throat. His head was tilted to the side, his eyes closed and lips parted. His shoulders were rising and falling rapidly as if he were breathing heavy and it was then that I saw why he'd been screaming.

Fabiano's left pec was marred, blood trickling down his abdomen from what my father had done. He'd cut a large X over the top of his tattoo. It wasn't deep enough to do any damage internally, but it would become an angry scar if he lived long enough for it to heal.

Tears fell from my eyes and I choked on a sob as I pushed Marcus, trying to get by him. He held me tighter. My father wiped the utility knife clean with his necktie before closing it up and placing it in his pocket. He turned to look at me, a wicked gleam in his eyes.

"Who is he?" he asked me. It was probably the hundredth time since yesterday morning when we'd been caught.

"I don't know," I lied. I refused to tell my father the truth. I refused to do anything that might give him more leverage against Fabiano and his uncle.

His jaw twitched as he glared at me. "You fell in love with him, didn't you?" he sneered. "Ungrateful whore!" His gaze shifted to Marcus. "Get her out of here. She's of no use to me right now."

"You have to let him go!" I shouted as Marcus dragged me away from the room through the larger one in an abandoned warehouse outside city limits.

We were near the docks, at the line of Gallo territory and I wasn't sure if my father planned that or not. The Gallo patriarch fled town hours ago, taking half his crew with him. Any working relationship between him and my father was severed the moment Giovanni Daleo sent a special package containing the severed head of Sebastian Gallo.

I was tossed into the back seat of an awaiting car by Marcus. Demetri was in the driver's seat and started the engine.

"Take her to the Brooklyn office," Marcus said before slamming the door in my face.

Demetri immediately pulled away, heading out of the large, near empty parking lot.

"Where are you taking me?" I asked as I sat up, frantically gazing out the window. I wasn't aware of an office in Brooklyn. For all I knew it was code for something.

Often times, my father would call a location "the office" even if that's not at all what it was. Like when I had to take a drug dealer who'd kept his cut to an apartment in Queens so Marcus could teach the guy a lesson.

"You're lucky you aren't being treated in the same manner as that spy," Demetri said. "Your father doesn't trust you, but he won't off you."

"I'd rather die than work for him anymore."

"Where would you go? Do you think Don Roman would take you as a soldier? You're a helpless woman. Worthless." He took a sharp left, heading back toward the city.

"The Mafia is going to come for him, you know?" I said.

"We're counting on that. That's why we have men stationed around that building and hiding out in the shadows. If a single enemy steps foot near there, they'll be shot on sight."

There had to be a way to get Fabiano out of there and save him. If I had to do it myself, I would. I leaned against the seat, closing my eyes. I hadn't slept since the night we'd spent together and I was exhausted.

After Marcus had successfully detained Fabiano, I'd been forced by Patrick to stay on my couch. They injected him with some sort of tranquilizer and tied him up while ransacking my apartment for any information on him.

They found a burner phone he had in his pocket but there were no contacts, only one phone number and it didn't trace anywhere worthwhile. When Marcus tried calling the number several times, no one picked up. Of course, the person wasn't going to answer. Mafia men were smart, careful.

Sebastian Gallo called my father early yesterday morning. He claimed the Mafia was going to execute him in twenty-four hours if he didn't give them the location of their spy. My father refused to offer any information and that proved his loyalty only rested within himself. Not that anyone should be shocked by that development anymore. When push came to shove, it was only ever about Albert Ricci.

I could give up the information if I'd only get a damn moment alone. Either Marcus, Patrick, or Demetri were hovering me at all times. Not only that, but I also had no idea where to go to give Don Roman insight on what I knew. There was an office in Manhattan, but I wasn't sure which one. There were hundreds of potential locations in that area alone.

I must have dozed off, because I was jolted awake by flying forward into the back of the passenger seat. The car's tires screeched to an abrupt halt and I heard Demetri curse loudly. I gazed out through the windshield and saw a man exiting a large SUV, his face was covered with a ski mask.

"Who the hell is that?" I gasped.

"Who knows?" he muttered. "Stay down, don't do anything brave or I'll shoot you. Unlike your father, I don't care if you live or die."

I stared out the windshield, watching as the stranger lifted a gun in his gloved hand, aiming it at Demetri. Only in New York could a man slam on his breaks and exit a vehicle without incident. Passersby blared on their horns, driving around the scene without so much as a second glance. Granted we were on a side street and there wasn't much in the way of traffic in the middle of the day here, but still.

I gathered it was a man by his tall build and broad shoulders. He was dressed in head to toe black. He approached the driver's side door, still aiming the gun, and motioned for Demetri to roll down his window. I was surprised when Demetri actually complied.

"Who the fuck do you think you are?" Demetri demanded.

The man cocked the gun, keeping it trained at my father's henchman. He had pale green eyes that shifted to mine briefly before narrowing back at his target. "The Grim Reaper."

I didn't have time to brace for the blast that made my ears ring in the car cab. One minute, Demetri was sitting there and the next, he was slumped over the center console as blood splattered the interior. I was fairly sure I was wearing some of it, too.

The man opened the driver's door, clicked the unlock button and then opened the back door. He tucked his gun into the waistband of his dark jeans and held a gloved hand out to me.

"Come with me if you want to live." I gaped at him in horror and confusion. Did he just quote *Terminator 2*? His lips twitched through the hole of the ski mask. "I've always wanted to say that." He chuckled, but then quickly scowled at me. "For real though, let's go." He angled his head toward the SUV.

"Who are you?" I asked, staying put. I wasn't getting in another car with a stranger.

"A friendly. You know Fab, right?" Was this guy with the Mafia? I gave a quick nod, wondering if I should trust him or not. He crouched down, shifting his hand as if wanting to shake mine. "The name's Grim. I'm here to rescue you."

I could certainly see why his name would be Grim based on what he'd just done to Demetri. I squeezed my eyes shut to keep from looking toward the front seat again. I couldn't believe he'd gone down so easily. You'd think I'd start freaking out after witnessing that, but I was only numb. Maybe I was still in shock.

Not wanting to be alone, and certainly not about to stay in a car with a dead body, I reached out and let Grim take my hand. He helped me out and led me to the passenger side of the SUV. I climbed in and he closed the door before settling in the driver's seat.

He easily merged back onto the road, turning onto a busier street alongside traffic like nothing ever happened. I was still reeling from it all and this guy acted like he didn't just murder someone at point blank range. He glanced at me for a moment and then started speaking.

"I'm taking you to the capo. He wants to talk to you, see if you can help in getting Fab out before Albert kills him."

"He cut him pretty bad thirty minutes ago," I said, shaking my head against the memory of his bloodied chest. "He crossed out his tattoo."

"Damn," Grim murmured. "Where's he at?"

"A warehouse near the docks. Just outside the city limits." I wasn't completely sure if I could trust this man but if he was mentioning Steven's real name, I figured he was telling the truth.

He nodded. "Gio will want the address if you have it. You can draw a map if you need to." Gio was a name I recognized. Fabiano had mentioned him before. He might have mentioned this guy, too, but I couldn't remember.

"They're heavily armed. No one's getting in there without risking several men," I said.

"Snipers?" He merged into the far left lane, running a yellow light toward downtown.

I shrugged. "That and traps probably."

He nodded, hanging a right and heading for the freeway. "We can formulate a plan of attack at the capo's place. Octavio Gallo?"

"He ran," I said.

Grim's hand tightened on the top of the steering wheel. "Smart man."

The rest of the drive was silent as Grim navigated through traffic, taking me to Don Roman's capo. I was officially in custody of the Mafia, something I'd never expected to happen. Demetri was dead and I couldn't help but wonder who was next. Would it be Marcus and my father? Would Fabiano be killed before we could act?

"You're stronger than anyone gives you credit for." His words filled my mind.

I *was* strong and capable. He believed in me and more than that, I believed in myself. The only thing that mattered right now was getting him out and ensuring he lived. Even if what we shared over the last few days was simply a way to escape, it meant more to me than anything. If I was being honest, he meant more to me than anything.

Fabiano had a sister to look out for, she needed him. The Mafia needed him. The world needed him. Despite his affiliation, he was a good person. I knew that deep down in my soul. He was nothing like Albert Ricci and I knew that if it came down to a choice between the two of them, my father would have to die.

CHAPTER FIFTEEN
AIDA

Grim took us to Little Italy, turning off Mulberry, which was the main street, into a paid parking lot near a pizzeria. There were many people wandering around here. It was strange, knowing they were none the wiser of the dark dealings happening around the city. This was the most I'd been free since birth and while I was nervous to meet Don Roman's capo, I was also trembling with anticipation.

We pulled into a reserved space directly behind the building. Grim cut the engine and looked at me.

"I need to know you're not going to run if I let you walk in there of your own free will." He pointed to the building in front of us.

My brows raised. "You don't trust me?"

He didn't hesitate in his reply. "Not at all."

Rolling my eyes, I sighed. "That's fair, I guess. I won't run. I don't want to. Helping Fabiano get out alive is more important than fleeing away from my father right now."

He cocked his head to the side, eyeing me carefully. "Capo mentioned Fab had a soft spot for you. I'm guessing the feelings mutual?"

Had he told them about me? What we'd done? I licked my lips, dragging my teeth along the bottom one. "Listen, I'm not sure what he said regarding me or our ... friendship, but it doesn't matter. Even if we hadn't grown close, I'd still want to help him. I hate my father." Those were the truest words I'd ever spoken.

Grim nodded, opening his door. "Let's go."

I climbed out of the SUV and walked beside him to the metal door in the back of the black painted, brick building. He was still wearing his ski mask and I wondered if I'd ever see his face. After giving two solid knocks on the door, it swung open and a young guy, maybe in his early twenties or late teens stood there.

"That was quicker than I expected," the guy said, waving us in.

Grim placed his gloved hand on my upper back, nudging me into the building. "They were easier to spot than I thought."

I gazed around at the black walls with gold accents everywhere. Beyond the area we were standing in was a small sitting area with black booths and gold tables. The walls in there were adorned with golden skulls and matching framed paintings in a Renaissance style. I think we were in some kind of nightclub.

Grim lifted his hand to the bottom of his ski mask and pulled it off. His green eyes were a stark contrast against his golden brown skin and short, black hair. His full lips tilted up on one side, revealing a charming dimple.

He appeared to be around Fabiano's age, maybe twenty-six or twenty-seven at most. He was cute, and definitely not what I expected for a man who just gunned down one of my father's men without batting an eye.

He plucked off his gloves next, revealing a tattoo of a rose on the back of his left hand. "You're probably wondering why I waited until I was inside before losing the mask," he said and I slowly nodded at him. "I'm one of the top three hitmen for Don Roman. I've killed more men than the years I've been alive, including that Thompson guy. No one knows my true identity and I want to keep it that way." He winked. "Like Batman."

I scowled at him and he chuckled. "You're so … young," I said.

He shrugged. "Grew up in the business. My father was one of the top sharpshooters for Don Roman up until he got capped a few years ago."

I frowned. "I'm so sorry."

He shrugged it off. "Shit happens. Come on." He began walking through the room with the booths and I followed.

The guy who'd opened the door for us disappeared down a hall, leaving us alone. Grim led me up a flight of stairs to a closed office door. It was the kind with the frosted glass window that you couldn't see through. He didn't knock before entering, just grabbed the handle and pushed the door open.

"She says he's injured but still alive," Grim said by way of greeting.

I glanced up at the man he was speaking to, a man who was taller than both Fabiano and Grim. He had to be several inches over six feet. He wasn't overly built, though the pin striped suit he was wearing fit him perfectly, displaying strong thighs on long legs.

He swirled a crystal glass of amber liquid in his large hand. There was an initial on his index finger that looked like the letter M. My gaze slowly lifted from that hand, over the black tie, and up to the stark white collar of his shirt beneath his suit. He had dark stubble on his tanned, square jaw, his lips outlined with it. When I finally reached his rich, brown eyes, I startled.

Giovanni Daleo was intimidating as hell and the long scar starting from the top of his dark brow, down to his cheekbone, didn't help matters. He stared at me, studying my face for a long time before slowly perusing my long sleeve shirt and faded jeans. I swallowed the lump that formed in my throat.

"Aida Ricci, daughter of Albert the asshole," Giovanni said before tipping back his drink. He set the glass on the top of his desk. "Why should I believe anything you say?"

I squared my shoulders, inhaling a deep breath. He was testing me and I understood why. My father used the same tactics with newbies. I'd done it myself before.

"Because your spy is bleeding out all over a concrete floor in a warehouse near the docks. The likelihood of the utility knife he was cut with being sterile is small. If my father doesn't kill him, an infection will."

He raised his brows, crossing his arms. He smirked at me and it threw me off. The look didn't match with his harsh features. "Fair enough," he murmured. "Where is this warehouse?"

"The border of Gallo territory, by the harbor."

"How many men are on site?"

I shook my head. "I don't know. I was only inside, near the room Fabiano was in. The man he killed," I angled my head toward Grim, "mentioned there were men everywhere to keep you guys from getting in."

"We need firearms and at least twenty men then," Giovanni said.

It was a suicide mission. If my father had access to any of the weapons Gallo and him were selling, things could blow up, literally. Grim and the capo began discussing a plan of attack and resources, but I ignored them.

There was only one way we were going to get Fabiano out and that was walking in there and taking him. My mind was made up hours ago. I couldn't sit back and let someone else rescue him, not when I knew my father better than anyone. He wouldn't realize I was turning before it was too late. While he trusted me, he refused to believe I was intelligent enough to handle things. His underestimation of me would be his biggest downfall.

"We can take out the guards and breach the door."

"That'll cause a shootout and risk your man's life further," I said and both men looked at me as if I'd spoken another language. I glanced between the two of them. "I can get him out."

Giovanni narrowed his eyes at me. "You?"

"Yeah, me," I bit out. "I know my father better than you. He trusts me. I can walk right in, drop him, his right hand, and whoever else is in there. Then I free Fabiano Cuccione and we exit out the back where you'll be waiting with a car and medical supplies."

Giovanni scoffed, standing to his full height. "A car and medical supplies? Who the fuck do you think you are, little girl? You don't tell me how to save my man."

"You don't tell me how to save *mine*," I snarled, marching up to him. I could do this. I knew I could. There was no way in hell I was letting this guy treat me like nothing because of my gender. I didn't care if he was Don Roman's capo.

Grim chuckled. "Damn, man. She's fierce as fuck."

"What about the men outside the building?" he growled, peering down at me. I had to tilt my head back to look at him.

"Take care of them. Although, they may have set traps." I shook my head. "I'm not certain if they're using Gallo weapons or not. My father mentioned still having a few things even after you found his cache."

"That could be a problem. Those weapons are highly illegal and can obliterate everything within a few block radius."

I nodded. "We need to find a way to get those weapons out if they're inside."

"Are there other warehouses in the area? Perhaps a building close enough where we can place men to snipe from."

"I think so. I can map the location, do a perimeter check and report back."

Giovanni blinked down at me. "Where the fuck did you learn all that?"

I smiled sweetly. "Albert, the asshole, Ricci," I said. "Clearly you don't know everything."

He clenched his fists at his side as if he were restraining from striking me. I wasn't fazed. I didn't care if he was irritated with me, I was their only way in that wouldn't end in unnecessary bloodshed.

"How long before your father kills him?" the capo asked.

"I don't know. One of his men was killed by your hitman, so he's likely to retaliate as soon as he finds out. However, he's arrogant and would prefer to end the Mafia entirely, especially Roman. He doesn't know that Steven Cline is actually the Don's nephew. He might like to use him as a bargaining tool instead. That could buy us some time."

"He won't blow his cover," Grim said and I looked at him. "That guy takes his vow seriously. He spent five years enduring a ton of shit to maintain his secret identity."

Fabiano didn't speak a lot about his past, but the scars on his body and what I did hear about his former boss, Randall Hawks, made me glad the guy was dead now. My heart squeezed. He didn't deserve that, not when he was trying to save his brother's fiancée and others. He was a good man with a big heart. In the last month, he'd shared himself with me in the most intimate ways and opened me up to a world of endless possibilities. I got the feeling that I could ask him for anything and he'd find a way to give it to me.

The desperate need to save him strengthened me and a surge of confidence sprang to life within. He said he'd die for me and if that didn't prove just how much he felt for me, nothing did. The only way to repay him would be to do the same and in that moment, I understood his vow more than ever and realized I couldn't live with myself unless he was alive.

Even if it meant the end of me, I'd save him. I would risk my life to save his.

I couldn't feel anything apart from the burning sensation on my chest where I'd been carved like a damn pumpkin on Halloween. There was a single light bulb hanging from the ceiling, allowing a soft yellow glow in my peripheral vision.

I was in the same room and it was quiet, the door surprisingly open. I could make out faint voices coming from another area, though I didn't hear exactly what they were saying. I'd been awake about fifteen minutes, after passing out from the pain. I'd been counting in my head, trying to gain a sense of time although I had no idea how long I'd been out this time. I'd faded in and out so many times that even my tally of alert minutes was difficult to count.

I attempted to shift my legs and realized I was no longer tied to the chair. My wrists were still cuffed which made things difficult, but not impossible to get the fuck out of here. I shivered against the cool breeze flowing in from the open door and it was then I realized I'd pissed myself. *Nice.* The rage roiling within me helped warm my blood. I sucked in a sharp breath as I stood from the chair.

I needed to hear what those bastards were saying, wanted to figure out where Aida was and whether or not she was safe. I hobbled toward the door slowly, my head pounding like crazy. I'd kill for some water right now and a giant bottle of hydrogen peroxide to pour on the wound Albert gave me. I'd kill that bastard for crossing out my tattoo.

"They found his body in the front seat of the car. He was shot in the head," someone said.

"Where is she?" That was Albert. I recognized his slight accent and gravelly tone. Was he talking about Aida?

"We haven't found her yet. There was blood in the backseat as well, she may be injured."

My stomach dropped and I attempted to swallow as my throat clogged up. No. She couldn't be hurt. She had to be okay. I needed to find her.

"If she were bleeding, she'd be easier to track," Albert growled. "What if they took her? Have you heard anything new from the Mafia?"

"They've gone silent, boss." I realized it was Patrick that was speaking.

"If they have Aida, they'll likely try to bargain with her." That was Marcus' voice.

It sounded like someone punched something wooden. A fist hitting a desktop, maybe?

"I need her found. *Now!*"

"I'll go canvas the city again," Patrick said. I heard his footsteps retreating to somewhere off in the distance.

"What should we do with the spy?" Marcus asked after a few minutes. I leaned closer to the open doorway. "I can kill him now."

The fuck he could. I wasn't going down easily.

"Not yet," Albert snapped. "We need to find out how important he is first. Maybe we can use him as leverage. A trade if they have Aida."

"What if they turn her and she doesn't want to come back?"

"I don't care what she wants. I never have. I'll beat her into submission if I have to. I've done it before, Marcus. All I have to do is threaten and she'll cower to me."

My nostrils flared and I clenched my teeth. Before I could stop myself, I sauntered out, quite languidly, into the larger room. It appeared to be daylight through the square windows lining the top of the walls. I saw seagulls flying in the sky. We were near water. The docks, maybe?

"You touch her and you'll be sorry," I seethed, trying to stay upright. God, I was fucking dizzy and probably not at all intimidating right now. I didn't care though. I wasn't going to let him hurt Aida.

Both Albert and Marcus turned in my direction from a small, round table near the center of the room. Marcus gave me a once over, smirking at my soiled jeans.

"You look like shit."

I shrugged. "At least I have an excuse." I eyed him up and down. "You're just fucking ugly."

He stood abruptly, marching toward me with his fist cocked back.

"Marcus …" Albert warned. "Ignore the kid." His gaze shifted to mine. "You ready to tell us your name?"

"That depends," I said. "Do you have a fresh pair of jeans for me?"

"Tell me who you are and I'll see what I can do."

There was a sudden burst of cold air as someone barreled through a side door from outside. My gaze flew to Aida who looked like an avenging angel, dressed in black from head to toe. She was wearing a long sleeved shirt, cargo pants, and combat boots. Her hair was pulled back from her face and her brilliant blue eyes were trained on her father.

"Hello, Father." She smiled sweetly at him, barely glancing at me.

"Where the hell have you been?" Marcus demanded, moving to approach her.

She lifted her hand, signaling him to stop. "Demetri was killed in front of me. I've been running for my damn life the last several hours, worried I was next," she said.

"Who shot him?" Albert asked.

Aida didn't respond. Instead, she pulled a cell phone from her back pocket and handed it to him. "You'll be receiving a call in ten minutes from Giovanni Daleo. He's willing to trade for their spy." She looked at me, her face a controlled mask.

I couldn't read anything from her gaze and I wondered if she was playing them or me. What happened to her? I wanted to ask her, but she couldn't tell me the truth in front of her father and his right hand. Or maybe she wouldn't tell me the truth anyway.

"Did he give you this phone?" Albert asked her, stealing her attention again.

"It was in my apartment. I think they were there. He left this note." She pulled a piece of paper from her front pocket and handed it to Albert. "I was covered in Demetri's blood and needed to change. I risked going back and found that sitting on my kitchen counter."

He read the note silently before passing it to Marcus. "They're threatening to use the weapons they stole," Albert murmured.

"They're trying to keep you in your place," Marcus sneered. "We need to take them down once and for all."

"That's going to be difficult considering you have no backup," I said.

That earned a glare from both men. "Why did you untie him?" Aida asked, looking at me again. Her eyes traveled over me slowly, her brow crumpling. "He's filthy."

"This isn't a day spa," Albert said, standing from his chair. "Tie him back to the chair." He waved his hand dismissively in my direction and Marcus reached for my arm.

I kept my eyes trained on Aida as he dragged me back to the room, not breaking contact until I was pulled out of view. Before I lost sight of her, she shot me a coy wink.

A surge of energy sprang to life along with hope. This woman was going to save the day. I just needed to try and hold on a little longer.

Fabiano looked terrible. The left side of his chest was an angry red and purple where his tattoo had been scratched out. His stomach was caked with dry blood, and his jeans hung low on his hips, looking darker in the front. I doubted they let him go to the bathroom, let alone disinfected his wound.

Despite his appearance, there was still that familiar sparkle in his eye when he looked at me, and while his voice sounded hoarse, I didn't miss his confidence in the Mafia getting him out and ending my father for good.

Hopefully, he could hold on just a little while longer while we put our plan into action. The first goal was to figure out where my father had men staked out and report back to Giovanni and Grim. I was able to spot a few of the obvious locations as I drove into the lot, but there were likely more than the handful I saw. I ended up taking a walk around the perimeter, feigning boredom.

Lucky for me, I was known for my curiosity, so the few soldiers lingering about answered all my questions. One guy even offered to take me up on the roof and see their rifles. I declined, of course and once I left them, I texted Gio to tell him where all the soldiers were posted. Grim was working on setting up a takedown area with a few men and also setting up a vantage point that offered what he called "clean kills." I didn't ask what that meant and didn't want to know.

Before walking in to confront my father, I'd received word from Grim that one of their soldiers located the weapons cache. My father had nothing but whatever was left on his person.

The final task was to create a diversion while the Mafia closed in. I needed to keep my father busy so he wouldn't catch on.

I sat down at the table with him. He stretched out his hand, resting it atop mine. "I'm glad you're okay," he said quietly.

I offered him a small smile. "I'm resourceful. You know that."

"Did you get a look at the person who shot Demetri?"

"No. They were wearing a ski mask and gloves. I have no idea who they were and I didn't stick around to find out," I lied. "I took off running through traffic the moment the gun went off."

He opened his mouth to speak, but the phone I'd given him began to ring. The shrill sound made me jump. My father picked it up, hitting the answer button and then the speakerphone. He rested the phone back atop the table.

"It's a rarity to receive a phone call from you, Mr. Daleo," my father said in way of greeting.

"Seems your daughter did the right thing," Giovanni said from the other end. His voice was just as ominous as his looks. "She obviously didn't learn that from you."

His comment was ignored. "She managed to get away from your man and report back to me with this phone. Her loyalty will be rewarded."

Giovanni chuckled. "What exactly do you have to offer her or any of your men for that matter? We have the weapons you tried stealing from Octavio Gallo, and your location."

My father's jaw muscle twitched as he glowered down at the phone. "You'll be dead before you ever set foot near us."

"Come on, Albert. You know that's just not true. Roman is sick of you living in the past and trying to stir up shit. You lost the battle and the war."

"You know nothing!" My father's face turned red in anger.

Marcus came out from the room he'd taken Fabiano to, wiping his hands on a handkerchief. My shoulders tightened and a lump formed in my throat. What had he done to him now?

"According to a special contact, your plan was to use the weapons against us and Gallo if he stood in the way."

"I have little time for your ranting, Daleo," My father growled. "What do you want?"

228

"I want our spy back."

My father scoffed. "You're lucky I haven't offed him yet."

"You do that, and you'll end up gutted like a pig before being fed to one," Giovanni snarled. "He's more than a spy, and you'd be better off returning our property to us unless you want Don Roman to obliterate everything you've created, including your daughter."

"I am tired of Don Roman ruling New York City. *My* city. It belongs to me!" my father roared and I flinched. "It was my grandfather who built that empire!"

"It was Vincenzo Ricci who grew power hungry and cared more about his bottom line than the people he affected," Giovanni argued. "Seems that's a hereditary trait."

My brow crumpled as I stared in confusion at my father. I remembered hearing about my great-grandfather and the Don's father being friends at one point. I had no idea they'd worked together. The fallout was greed, which in the present situation didn't surprise me. Clearly, my father was no different than his ancestors.

Marcus approached my father, bending to whisper something in his ear. I watched as my father's eyes grew wide, his hand clenching into a fist next to the cellphone.

"I've been biding my time, but it ends now," my father said. "Don Roman will surrender control of the city to me or I'll kill his nephew, Fabiano Cuccione."

I froze, my head whipping to the direction of the room Fabiano was in. Why did he blow his cover?

Marcus grinned as he straightened. "It's incredible how quickly someone will cave when pain overwhelms the senses."

I shot up from my chair, nostrils flaring as I glared at my father's second in command. "What did you do?" I demanded.

A low rumble sounded from the phone. Giovanni spoke and even though I was on his side, his voice sent a shiver of fear straight through me. "You're a dead man," he said before disconnecting the call.

"What did you do?!" I shrieked again at Marcus.

He chuckled, placing his hands on his hips. "See for yourself."

I immediately bolted for the room and saw Fabiano kneeling on the concrete floor, uncuffed and holding his left forearm. I gasped as I moved closer, seeing his hand hanging limply with what looked like a small bone poking out from his wrist.

I fell to my knees in front of him. "He broke your wrist."

Fabiano's shoulders trembled and when I glanced up at his face, I saw tears falling from his hazel eyes.

"Why are you here?" he asked in a broken whisper.

"To get you out," I replied quietly.

I removed my long sleeve shirt; grateful I'd worn a tank top beneath it. I pulled a knife from the cargo pocket of my pants and cut the fabric. Putting the knife back, I glanced up at him again, reaching for his broken wrist.

He pulled it away from me. "You have to get out of here, Aida." He whimpered when I gently grasped his forearm, laying it in my lap.

I began wrapping the material of my shirt around his wrist, setting the bone back in place as best I could. "I don't know if any tendons are damaged, but this should help a little."

"Aida …"

I made sure to keep the make-shift tourniquet tight and tied it off. "There, that should work."

"Aida …"

I glanced up at his face, shaking my head. "I'll see if I can get you something for the pain."

"Aida, listen to me," he said slowly, his voice hoarse. I met his eyes. "I'm not getting out of here."

"Yes, you are," I argued, glancing at the doorway to make sure Marcus wasn't listening. "I have a plan," I added in a low voice.

He shook his head. "They know who I am now. I gave up my cover in exchange for something more important."

"What are you talking about?"

He swallowed, his eyes searching my face. "You."

"Me? What do you mean?"

He opened his mouth to speak and was cut off by Marcus who marched into the room and grabbed me by the arm, forcing me to stand. I shook off his grip. "What are you saying?" I asked Fabiano.

He lifted his head, glaring at Marcus. "You promised not to touch her," he growled.

Marcus lifted his hands in front of him. "I was simply helping her stand." He smiled tightly. "She's safe."

"What in the hell are you talking about?" I demanded, growing more frustrated by the minute.

My father came into the room, a gun in hand. "He's exchanged your life for his own."

My lungs restricted and my heart pounded heavily in my chest. They were going to kill me?

My father grinned, winking at me. "You think I'm stupid enough to believe you hadn't been sent here by Giovanni Daleo? You think I'd trust *you*?" he spat, aiming the gun toward me.

No!

I underestimated him, took him for a careless fool and I was wrong. Dead wrong.

Panic sprang to life and the realization that if I didn't act now, neither one of us would make it out alive, spiked my adrenaline. Screw the plan, hopefully Grim was already working on the men outside.

"Look at you," he eyed me up and down, "acting weak for a man who already got what he wanted from you."

Glaring at my father, I marched toward him until we were toe to toe. "He has more of a heart than you ever did and what he got from me was *mine*."

His face fell slightly, a simmering anger shown in his eyes. "I expected you to be better than this," he said with disgust. "Falling for an enemy, a traitorous man who isn't even who you think he is. Do you understand what he's done? Who he's harmed for that tyrant uncle of his?"

"What about you?" I questioned. "You've killed men for looking at you the wrong way. Your ego is far bigger than your empire and it always has been. You'll never take over the city. You killed my mother and for that, you *will* pay." As good as it felt to finally say the words I'd been thinking for years, I knew I was walking an extremely dangerous line.

Standing up to my father was something I should have done a long time ago, back before the consequences were this severe. I had no doubt he'd kill me without a second thought. He had nothing left to lose and my intentions were clear.

Inhaling a deep breath, I closed my eyes and counted to ten. This wasn't the plan, but I had no other choice. Before I could second-guess my actions, I knelt down and pulled the gun I had concealed from the holster at my ankle. I squeezed the trigger without hesitation, imbedding a bullet directly in the middle of my father's chest.

I whirled around and shot Marcus in the shoulder and he stumbled backward into the main room. I heard the sound of another gunshot ring out and turned to see my father aiming toward Fabiano who was now standing. I choked out a sob in relief. His aim was off.

Fabiano stepped over to him, now lying on the ground and breathing heavily as the blood poured from his chest, staining the white button down shirt he was wearing. He kicked my father's hand, forcing him to release the gun and bent to pick it up.

My hands shook as I lowered my gun, staring into my father's eyes. He tried sitting up and began coughing, blood trickling out of his mouth.

"You left me no choice," I murmured. "I'm sorry."

"Let's go," Fabiano said in a clipped voice as he brushed by me through the doorway.

"I'm sorry," I said again, gazing down at my father for a final moment before turning to follow Fabiano.

He scanned the room, frantically searching for Marcus. I wasn't sure how many rooms were in this warehouse. For all we knew, he was hiding in a dark corner somewhere. I glanced up at the few windows and saw that the sky was growing darker by the minute.

"How many men are outside?" Fabiano asked, turning toward me.

"I don't know," I replied in a shaky voice. "It depends on whether or not Grim started. Four on the roof for sure. Maybe more surrounding the building on the ground." I saw the phone Giovanni had provided me to give to my father. I picked it up, dialing his number.

"Ten minutes out," he said when he answered.

"Fab's wrist is broken. Albert's lying on the floor, dying. Not sure where his right hand man went. Got him in the shoulder and he took off." Fabiano lifted a brow, staring at me. "Tell Grim to start now. Things took a turn."

"What the fuck happened?" Giovanni asked.

"They threatened to kill me if he didn't blow his cover." I narrowed my eyes at Fabiano.

He held his hand out for the phone. "Let me talk to Gio."

"He wants to speak with you. But get here quick, I've only got a few more bullets and I'm quite sure we won't find more ammo lying around." I handed the phone over and kept my back to the wall, raising my gun.

We weren't safe in here if Marcus managed to get outside. He could be readying the men for an ambush. I prayed all the weapons that the Mafia needed to confiscate were in their hands after I'd walked in here.

I watched Fabiano as he began talking to the capo. The hand connected to the broken wrist looked purple and he placed the gun he'd stolen from my father on the table so he could hold the phone.

I'd almost lost him for good. He gave up his identity for me and while I was angry with him for breaking his vow, I was also in awe of the lengths he would go to protect me. He sacrificed his life for mine.

Everything he'd said before about keeping me safe was genuine. It was an indescribable feeling to know that he'd given me his heart and cared for me so deeply. Almost losing him helped me recognize that I'd never be able to walk away from him. It didn't matter who he was or what he did.

I was in love with Fabiano Cuccione.

Aida Ricci was badass. I couldn't believe I'd just witnessed her not only stand up to Albert but take his life with zero hesitation. I only wished she would have killed Marcus, as well. He would die eventually. Everyone who backed Albert Ricci would.

Of course, there wasn't a hell of a lot I could do with a limp hand. I'd broken some bones in my life but had never felt the kind of pain Marcus dispensed. It still made me queasy to think of the way he bent my wrist, ensuring a bone snapped completely.

I inhaled a deep breath through my nose. "I can't protect her with a bum hand," I growled into the phone.

"It seems she's able to handle herself," Gio retorted. "I'm getting there as quick as possible. She's got a tracker on her, so we know exactly where you are. Grim's positioned on a nearby building as we speak to take out the snipers."

"We need the whole fucking cavalry," I said. "I overheard Albert speaking earlier. They have a small army and the weapons—"

"The weapons aren't an issue. Aida got that handled. They were tucked in a chest outside the building. We've got this, Fab. *She's* got this. We'll be there soon."

I was surprised at how much trust he was putting in Aida right now. Not that I didn't believe she was capable, but that Gio himself had reservations about even taking her in mere days ago. I wondered what happened to her after she'd been taken away the last time I'd seen her. Someone in the Mafia had to be behind the killing of Demetri and I knew Grim never missed a golden opportunity to show off.

"Okay," I replied.

"We'll get you two out. Hold tight if you can and if you have to, shoot to kill."

I disconnected the call and handed the phone back to Aida who slid it into her back pocket. Even though I was sure I looked like shit, and probably smelled like it, too, I had the sudden urge to just hold her for a minute. It felt like a lifetime since we'd last touched each other.

Cautiously, I stepped toward her, sliding my good hand over her shoulder and up her neck to cup her cheek. She gazed up at me with those ocean eyes that captivated me.

"Thank you, for saving me," I said softly.

Her lips tilted up in the corners, but it wasn't a full smile. "Don't thank me yet. Wait until we're out of here."

I nodded. "I owe you and I intend to make good on that the second this is over." Tilting my head down, I placed my lips against her cheek, inhaling her sweet scent. I felt her shiver against me and her breath quickened as I kissed a path to her ear. "My heart belongs to you, too."

If we were in a different situation, I'd kiss her lips and hold her. I'd explore her body and confess the one thing I'd been holding back from her. Now wasn't the time. Pulling back, I grabbed the gun again and glanced around the room.

"How is there no one else in here?" I asked, spotting another exit door across the wide room.

"My guess is Marcus wants to be the one to kill us. He's selfish like that," Aida said with a shrug. "We can each cover a door, but the odds of survival aren't good."

"What happened with Demetri?" I stayed close to her side as we both backed toward the wall.

"Grim shot him and took me to Little Italy to meet up with Gio and come up with a plan. I like him," she said with a small smile.

I raised a brow at her. "Gio?"

She laughed. "No, Grim. He's nice and surprisingly level headed for someone that kills people without remorse. You know, he quoted Terminator?"

Yeah, I could never quite understand his method of thinking. I'd killed enough people myself in the heat of a fight, but I didn't enjoy it. In fact, there were times I felt guilty. Grim didn't seem fazed ever. It was like he was missing his conscience or something.

"Giovanni is a bit … harsh." Her voice was low, her eyes flitting around the room, looking for signs of danger.

I nodded. "He's had a violent life. He's more loyal than anyone I've ever met though."

The sound of several gunshots rang out from outside and I instinctually stepped in front of Aida, pressing her into the wall as I lifted my gun toward the main door. The phone rang and she answered it.

"Hey." She slid out from behind me. "Okay, how many?" I heard another round of shots being fired and a few people shouting. "Grim took out the guys on the roof. No sign of Marcus," Aida said to me and then spoke into the phone again. "Go toward the back like we talked about." She hung up and I frowned at her.

"You're way too good at this," I said.

She shrugged. "I told you I had skills. We're going out that door. Soldiers have moved in to take out my father's men." She pointed to the one furthest away on the other side of the large space.

I followed her as she slowly made her way toward the back, keeping close to the wall. We had the growing darkness on our side to stay out of sight, but so did our enemies.

Aida was all business right now, taking charge and sticking to the plan. It was incredibly hot to see her like this.

"It's a good look for you," I said and she glanced back at me over her shoulder.

"What is?"

"Taking the reins on this escape, rescuing me. I don't think you realize how incredibly sexy it is to see you like this."

She rolled her eyes playfully and shook her head. "You have an open wound in your chest and a broken wrist. Are you seriously thinking about how I look right now?"

"I could have a bullet go straight through my heart and I'd still be thinking about you." She stopped abruptly, causing me to bump into her back.

Her head lowered and she let out a heavy sigh. She spun around and caught me by surprise when she clasped my cheeks with her hands and lifted up to kiss my lips. I used my good hand, with the gun still in it, to press into her back, bringing her closer to me.

Maybe it was the adrenaline of what was happening, or the desperate need I had for her in general. I kissed her fiercely, giving as much as I was getting. When she leaned back, her breath was erratic and tears laced her eyes.

"I need you to do something for me," she said quietly.

"Anything," I replied, releasing her.

She swallowed roughly. "When we get out there," she hitched her thumb behind her toward the door, "I need you to head directly for the vehicle. Don't stop until you've reached it. There's medical supplies and Gio is in there. He'll take care of you."

My shoulders stiffened. "What?"

"I need you safe. I need you alive. They'll get you somewhere away from here and clean you up."

My eyes narrowed at her and anger licked up like vicious flames in my stomach. "You're not serious?" I snarled.

"This is how it has to be."

"No! What the fuck, Aida?! You think I'm going to let you stay here and shoot it out with your father's men without me?"

Her jaw hardened and I could tell she was growing as angry as I was. Honestly, what did she think I would say? There was no way in hell I'd leave her behind. Not in a million years.

"You're more important right now. Do you understand?" She growled and I blinked at her in surprise. "You're Don Roman's nephew. You have a legacy, a job. My purpose right now is to get you safe and out of here. That's my job. I've got backup, I'll be fine." I didn't miss the slight waiver in her voice.

"I'm not leaving you."

"You have to," she argued. "It's part of the plan."

"A plan I had no say in!" I shouted, stepping closer to her again. "A ridiculous plan that I did not agree upon."

"Don't you dare try to pull rank on me," she warned in a low voice. "*I'm* the one who implemented this plan and I am seeing it through. You will go to that waiting vehicle, get your ass in it, and let them take you to get fixed up."

I gaped at her. Holy shit, she was standing up to me and it was turning me on. She was also scaring me a little bit and I wasn't sure what to say. I was dumbfounded by her tenacity.

"I'm not backing down on this," she said when I opened my mouth to speak. "I've got several of your men to help me out here, plus Grim."

Shaking my head, I said, "You expect me to walk away from you just like that? You think after everything we've shared, the way I feel about you …" I released a frustrated groan as Aida nodded.

"I didn't say it'd be easy. But you're no good to me if you're dead. I can't bear the thought of losing you. Not yet." Her eyes pierced mine. "I think you know why that is, even if it's not right. Even if it doesn't make sense." Her breath hitched and a tear slid down her cheek.

I exhaled a breath, swiping the tear away. "Aida …"

"Just do what I say, please. We can argue about it later, after I take care of Marcus."

My lips twitched despite the heaviness of our situation. "I'll do what you say. But you have to promise me one thing."

She frowned. "What is it?"

"Come back to me." I bent to kiss her again, conveying everything I could without words.

She clung to me, savoring the kiss as much as I was and I felt more tears fall from her, soaking my chest. When we finally separated, we were both breathless.

"Cover me," I said, "and don't let them take you down. You've got this, do you hear me? Shoot to kill, *murder* that son of a bitch."

She nodded and her lips tilted up in a smile that stopped my heart. God, she was beautiful even in the midst of a violent showdown. I kissed her once more before we made our way to the back door. Aida turned the handle and pushed it open with one hand while aiming her gun outside with the other.

Night had officially fallen and darkness surrounded us. I heard shouting from the front side of the warehouse and a series of shots. An SUV was parked several yards away and I could make out at least six men surrounding it, holding their weapons out toward us. Fear took root as Aida stepped forward in their direction. I was about to stop her when I noticed one of the men wasn't in tactical gear, but a suit.

"Go to them," Aida urged. I gazed down at her, my chest tightening. Fuck, I didn't want to leave her. "I'll be okay, Fab," she said with a smile that made my heart beat faster.

Nodding, I turned back toward where Giovanni and the men were waiting. "Remember your promise," I said.

She nodded. "I'll see you soon."

As I walked away from her, I muttered a prayer that she'd be safe, that I would see her again. It killed me to leave her, but I was no use to her in my current state. I'd only hold her back and I didn't want that. Not when she was fully qualified to take out Marcus and many other men on her own.

Gio took my gun from me once I reached him and I climbed in the back of the SUV. He followed me in and the driver immediately took off, heading away from the warehouse. I glanced out the back window, trying to see Aida, but it was too dark and we were moving quickly.

All I could do was remind myself that she would be okay. She promised she'd come back to me and once that happened, I didn't think I'd ever be able to let her go again.

I kept myself in the shadows, pressed against the brick exterior of the warehouse. I got Fab to safety. Another step complete. I didn't stick around to watch the vehicle pull away. I didn't have the time. Marcus had to be lurking around here somewhere unless he'd managed to find a ride out of here, or Grim or one of the other guys managed to take him out already. That would disappoint me. I wanted to be the one to finish him.

I made it to the corner of the building and peered around toward the front. I saw several men lying face down with blood pouring from random wounds. Movement to the right caught my attention and I saw two men with what looked like automatic rifles stalking someone. I followed their line of site and saw a man, his back to them, heading for the main door.

I took aim and fired off a clean shot to one man and then the other before he could even turn and run the other way. They both fell to the ground and their target whipped his head in my direction.

"Thanks!" he hollered. I stepped out of the shadows, all the while gazing around as I approached him.

"No problem." I recognized him as one of the soldiers for the Mafia.

Most of the men were dressed in all black like me. My father's men were clad in their camouflage gear, which I never really understood seeing as how we were in the damn city and not the wilderness.

"How many are left?" I asked.

The man shook his head. "Hard telling, but we've dropped at least twenty so far."

My brows rose. "Damn, that was quick."

He chuckled. "Your father had a good plan, but ours was better."

"Isn't it always?" I asked with a teasing smile.

He lifted his hands in front of him. "I wasn't going to say that."

I laughed. "What about Marcus Pelossi. Any eyes on him?"

He shook his head. "He may have gone back inside. Three guards just entered, that's where I was heading."

"That should be all of them," I heard Grim call from behind us. I turned in his direction. "There's two left alive being carted off to Don Roman."

"Nice job," I said.

He grinned at me. "Likewise, killer." He pulled a 9mm from his back and handed it to me.

I tucked the gun I'd brought with me back in my ankle holster and readied the new one. "We should get inside and drop the rest of these guys."

"Fab is safe then?" Grim asked.

"Yeah, he was in no shape to hang around. It took a minute to convince him to leave though."

"Let's go." He angled his head toward the door and we made our way over, ensuring our movements were careful.

I didn't know the other guy's name, but it didn't matter right now. He stood in front of me, gripping the handle, ready to pull it open. Grim was beside me, preparing a wicked looking automatic rifle. I noticed a tear in the long sleeve shirt he was wearing, near his stomach.

"Were you shot?" I whispered.

He shrugged. "Probably. That's what the vest is for." He patted his front and I realized he was wearing a bulletproof vest.

I blinked at him. He wasn't even affected by getting shot at. What an odd guy. Ignoring the multitude of questions that came to mind because now wasn't the time, I focused back on the door in front of us.

"I'll swing it open wide. Grim take the right, Aida the left. I'll stay in the center. Be ready."

I grunted out an okay, raising my gun in front of me. I didn't have a bulletproof vest and suddenly felt like maybe I should have gone with Fab and Giovanni. Inhaling a deep breath through my nose, I released it slowly from my mouth and steadied my trembling hands. I'd made it this far. We were almost done. I could do this.

The Mafia soldier counted down from three, not hesitating to open the door when he was finished. I slipped by him, veering to the left and tucking into the corner while Grim fanned to the right and the soldier took center.

It was nearly pitch black inside but I heard rustling coming from the far corner, toward the back door.

"Stay back and stay low," the soldier said as he bent his knees, taking slow, measured steps further into the warehouse.

I hung back, scanning the darkness for any sign of movement. We continued moving forward when suddenly Grim stopped and began firing off several rounds to the right. I heard a grunt before the body hit the floor.

"How many are there?" he asked.

"Two more not including Albert's second in command," the soldier said.

We made our way toward the middle of the room and the sound of a chair scraping across the floor in front of me had me aiming and shooting.

"Nice hit," Grim muttered as the guy dropped to the floor.

A loud buzzing noise filled the air as the lights came on, temporarily blinding me. Once my eyes focused to the brightness, I saw Marcus standing against the wall across from us. His shoulder was wrapped with some sort of bandage. How nice for him to have medical on hand.

Movement to the right made me turn and Grim landed another shot at the third guard who didn't even have time to aim.

"Is it really necessary to take out all of my guards?" he asked in a bored voice, eyeing me up and down.

"They're not *your* guards," I bit out. "They were my father's and he's dead."

"By your hand. Traitorous bitch!"

Grim raised his rifle, aiming it at Marcus' chest. "Watch your mouth, asshole."

"Maybe if you'd ever treated me like an equal instead of a worthless little girl, we wouldn't be in this position," I said. "Or maybe, if Albert ever listened to me instead of being a greedy, self-serving, tyrant, then he would still be alive."

Marcus glared at me, his right hand lifted and I gasped at what he held. He chuckled darkly. "Looks like they didn't retrieve *all* the weapons."

He inspected the grenade in his hand, running his finger along the rough bulb of it.

"What are you going to do? Blow us all to smithereens?" I asked.

He shrugged. "It's me or you, and if it's me, I'm taking you along, sweetheart. Don Roman's nephew may have gotten away, but you three are nothing to him but collateral damage. This entire warehouse goes up in flames and all that's left are the ashes."

I pointed my gun toward his head. "I'll kill you before you pull that pin."

"What are you going to do when this is over, Aida? Do you honestly think you'll be welcomed with open arms to the Mafia? They don't care about you."

"Neither did my father," I said. "Why do you care what I do?"

"Because you're the last living heir to the Ricci throne and you'll taint your father's legacy if you don't continue his pursuits."

I scoffed. "He's the one that tainted his legacy. If he'd gone to Don Roman instead of collaborating with the Gallos and trying to take over the city, maybe things could have been mended. Better yet, he should have accepted defeat a long time ago and not killed my mother."

"Even if you kill me," Marcus shifted his gaze to Grim who was ready to put a bullet in him, "there are others who want to see the Mafia burn. Gallo will come back to the city, he'll take over."

"Gallo chickened out and is currently being deported," Grim said. "Once he realized that you were planning to ice them out and use their weapons, he caved faster than a soufflé."

"Thompson's partner is—"

"Dead," I growled. "He was executed earlier today and his club was burned down to nothing. You're the only one left."

I watched as realization sunk into his features; his throat rolled in a swallow and his brow crumpled. This ended with Marcus and once he was gone, it would all be over. I'd finally have the freedom I so desperately craved the last twenty-two years. I'd be able to move on, wherever that may be.

All I ever wanted was to live a normal life and experience the world around me without the fear of enemies and my father's overbearing rules. I was finally on the brink of a whole new life and nothing was going to stop me.

"Any last words?" I asked, cocking back the hammer of my gun.

A slow wicked grin spread across his face and he raised his hands in front of him. "Yeah, see you in hell." He pulled the pin from the grenade as I squeezed the trigger. It fell to his feet and rolled toward us.

"RUN!" Grim yelled, grabbing my forearm and yanking me backward toward the exit.

I stumbled as I turned and bolted for the door, tugging it open just as the explosion erupted, instantly heating my back. I made the mistake of looking behind me. I should have just kept running, but my stupid curiosity got the better of me. I watched as the Mafia soldier fell to his knees, vibrant orange surrounding him in seconds as he screamed out for help.

"Come on!" Grim urged, pulling me further from the building, toward the edge of the parking lot.

We didn't stop running until we were yards away, near an old, abandoned cannery. I bent at the waist, clutching my knees as I gasped for air. Tears were streaming from my eyes beyond control and my body trembled.

Grim strapped his rifle behind him and pulled out a cell phone. I didn't hear who he was calling because the explosion made my ears ring. The gun I had slipped from my hands to the ground and I sunk down to my knees heaving as sobs rocked my body.

We were alive. However, there was no elation, no feeling of peace rushing through me at this newfound liberation. I murdered my father tonight. Yes, we took out several of his men, but not all of them. I had to live with his blood on my hands the rest of my life and worse than that, once his gang found out, I'd be targeted.

I couldn't gain control of my emotions and as my hearing slowly came back to me, I heard the screams of that soldier echoing in my mind. Fabiano was wrong about me. I may be capable of taking out the bad guys, no matter the cost, but I wasn't strong. I couldn't endure a life like this forever. It would break me.

I sat in my uncle's office, fidgeting with the cast around my wrist. I had a splint and a sling to keep it elevated for the next several weeks thanks to that bastard, Marcus Pelossi. Because the bone had protruded through my skin, I had to be prepped and given emergency surgery, lying to the medical staff about a wicked fall. I also had to get stiches in my chest where Albert had carved an X over my tattoo. He hadn't done a very precise job, so I was able to attribute that to the fall, too.

It had been one week since the night Aida rescued me. I hadn't seen her since then due to all the chaos that unfolds when taking out a group. Even though I had my own injuries to attend to, I was growing more and more worried about her. I knew she was close, staying in a room at my uncle's house where she would be safe for the time being. However, that didn't ease my mind. I'd grown so used to seeing her nearly every day that being apart from her had me feeling empty.

I'd been living back at my old apartment since I'd been released from the hospital two days ago. Uncle Roman wanted me to meet him at his house today to discuss all of the new developments since Ricci's territory was now gone. Thankfully, I didn't have to be as involved in the cleanup like out West. It wasn't typically in my nature to be sedentary too long, but this time was different.

Not only was I injured pretty badly, but for the first time in my life, I was interested in something more than work. My priorities had shifted considerably in the last month and all that mattered to me was ensuring that Aida would be okay after everything went down.

Ricci had men that ran away, scared that they'd be offed after our attack. Others came out to reveal they were glad he'd been killed, and some were even willing to give up his secrets in order to gain favor with the Don. One person in particular, Gio's main contact was a person I hadn't expected. Patrick. He'd been undercover the entire time, and damn did he do a good job of staying silent about his loyalties.

I just wanted to take some fucking time off and see Aida.

"It's been discovered that Ricci was involved in an underground gambling outfit throughout the Tri-state area that we hadn't been made aware of," Uncle Roman said from behind his large, mahogany desk.

"Damn, who runs that?" I asked. My wrist itched like crazy so I slid my finger in the opening, trying to get relief.

"Quit fucking with that," Gio snapped and I glanced up at him.

"It itches," I said. "Don't treat me like a fucking child."

"Boys …" Uncle Roman said in warning. "Fabiano, pay attention." I rolled my eyes, fisting my free hand against my thigh. "It's some Irish gang running the gambling. They aren't really hurting anyone, so I'm not worried about it. However, I'd like someone to go talk to them, figure out if they respected Ricci. The last thing I want is some other gang coming out of the woodwork trying to take us on."

I scoffed. "*Trying* being the operative word."

"Yes," he said. "Gio, can you make a call and pay them a visit?"

"Sure. I need to get out of this fucking city for a bit anyway." He scratched at the stubble on his jaw.

"That detective giving you hell again?"

"Detective?" I asked.

"This woman who's trying to solve some cold case from a few years back. She's barely seasoned on the job and thinks she has new leads."

"Why are you involved?" I ran a hand through my hair, trying to distract myself from the itching sensation. Fuck this cast and fuck Marcus for breaking my wrist. I hoped he was burning in hell.

"I'm the murderer, she just doesn't know that yet," he said with a shrug and I raised a brow at him.

"No more questions, Fabiano," Uncle Roman said.

I knew Gio had offed some people throughout the years but wasn't aware he'd been targeted by the police for any of them. Most of the people the Mafia killed were wastes of life. Whoever he'd killed must have been important.

"We should be able to tie up any other loose ends with the Ricci issue before summer. However, there is still one important factor we need to discuss. My uncle looked at me. "What are we doing with the girl?"

"How is she?" I asked.

"She's adapting for the time being. Celeste is enjoying her company here at the house."

With everything going on because of Albert Ricci, my sister was also staying at my uncle's house until further notice. Knowing both her and Aida, I had no doubt they'd get along. They were equally tough as hell with an eye for fashion. I hoped Aida was happy, that she was coping with what she'd been through and all that she did for me.

"I say we ask her what she wants to do," I said. "Let her walk if she wants to, give her a job if she doesn't."

"What would be her occupation?" Gio asked. "She doesn't want to be a soldier. She made that perfectly clear the other night."

"You saw her?" I was on my feet instantly. "You spoke with her?" Rage bubbled to the surface when I recalled yesterday morning and a phone conversation we'd shared. I'd specifically asked him if he'd seen or heard from her and he'd said no.

"Relax, Fab. I didn't say anything because she told me not to. She doesn't want you to worry about her right now."

My heart plummeted to my stomach. It felt like I'd been punched in the chest. There was no way I wouldn't worry about her. Did she really think I'd sit back and do nothing if she was hurting?

"Aida needs time to heal, to move on from what she's done. She killed her own father, Fabiano," Uncle Roman added.

"I can help her through it," I growled. "She needs me."

"She has Celeste and Betty to talk to. Lord knows both of them have plenty of experience in grieving loss," Gio said.

I glared at him. "I don't care. I'm going to see her." I grabbed my coat from the back of the chair.

"You're too attached to her." My uncle's voice halted my exit. I turned to look at him. "Fabiano, your job was to investigate Albert Ricci. Nothing good comes from mixing business with pleasure."

"Yeah, you should let her go," Gio piped up. "If you're not careful, you'll fall in love with her and that won't be good for either of you. She needs time to herself and you … well, I think you do, too."

Uncle Roman nodded. "Which brings me to our next topic. I want you to take some time off. Maybe a few months. You jumped right into a new job after coming back from the West Coast."

My jaw muscle worked as I stared between the two of them. Time off would be nice and they were right; I probably did need it. As far as Aida Ricci went though, I didn't want to let her go. Not at all.

"I'll take a break for a while," I said. "Not from Aida though."

Gio frowned. "Fab …"

I shook my head. "No!" I refused to negotiate with them when it came to her. "You're worried I'll fall in love with her? I already have."

I didn't stick around for a reaction from either of them. Instead, I marched down the hall and up the stairs into the main part of the house. I didn't care what my uncle or the capo thought was best for either of us right now. I knew Aida more than them. I understood her.

I could hear voices coming from the kitchen and followed the sound. Aida was sitting at the center island, drinking what looked like a margarita. There was a large bowl of tortilla chips and some salsa laid out on the counter in front of her. Celeste was sitting next to her, talking animatedly about something.

I approached the island, standing on the opposite side, across from Aida. Celeste stopped talking, furrowing her brow at me. I narrowed my eyes at her, fully prepared to argue if she didn't make herself scarce.

"You want to give us a minute?" I asked, nodding my head toward the living room.

She glanced between me and Aida, sliding off her stool. "I'll catch you later," she said before disappearing.

Aida stared up at me, lowering her glass to the counter. She looked every bit as beautiful as the last time I saw her. Her hair was straight, falling over her shoulders. She was wearing an oversized gray sweater that contrasted with her eyes. I wanted to kiss her, but now wasn't the time. We needed to talk first, so I stayed on my side of the island.

"How are you doing?" I asked, hating the way her eyes refused to focus on me.

Her throat rolled in a swallow. "I'm … good."

I raised a brow. "Really? Because Gio told me you don't want to see me."

"Fab—"

"No," I growled. She finally met my eyes. "You don't get to do this."

That spark I'd missed flared for the briefest moment as she glared at me. "What exactly am I doing?"

I leaned forward over the counter. "Don't lie to me. You're not good, you probably won't be for a long time."

Her shoulders slumped and she shook her head. "Fine. I'm not good, okay?"

"You want to talk about it?"

"I didn't even hesitate. Twenty-two years of my life— gone." There was anger and disappointment in her voice.

I bit down on my bottom lip, studying her. She was hurting for sure and feeling remorse for what she'd done to Albert, regardless of just how evil he was. I understood what that felt like. It was one of the multitude of reasons I had nightmares. She needed to understand that she wasn't alone. I could help her through this as long as she didn't shut me out.

"Do you want to know why I don't sleep well?" I asked, moving to the side of the island, a little closer to her but not too much. I didn't want her to bolt on me.

She frowned. "Your nightmares?"

I gave her brief smile. "Yeah, those damn memories that continue to haunt me over and over again," I said. "We blew up his house, Randall Hawks.' The whole thing erupted thanks to some C-4 laid by a couple of men I now consider friends."

Her eyes widened slightly. "Were you near the explosion?"

"I was just pushing off the last stair on the front porch when everything blew up. Sometimes in my nightmares, I can still hear what it sounded like. Almost like a freight train slamming straight into a brick wall at hundreds of miles an hour."

She winced and I realized she could relate. I'd heard about the grenade going off as she shot Marcus. One of our soldiers had died in the explosion. There were so many dark sides to this business that she hadn't been aware of until now.

"Do your ears ring when you wake up?" she asked.

My heart ached for her and I risked a few steps closer. She didn't seem to mind. "Yeah. The worst is waking up and thinking your body is engulfed in flames. I can't tell you the number of times I've been startled awake because of that."

"That's terrible," she said.

"I can still smell it, too, sometimes. It's almost like motor oil and for a few weeks after everything went down, I'd wake up and vomit."

"Fab ..."

I didn't want her to feel sorry for me. That's not what this conversation was about. I wanted her to realize she wasn't alone. That I'd do anything and everything in my power to help her move on.

"Do you remember that night when you rescued me?" I asked.

She snorted, muttering sarcastically, "How could I forget?"

I grimaced. "I'm talking about the good parts of it. Not the ones that haunt your dreams."

Her lips tipped up slightly. "It's difficult to remember everything." She gazed down at the granite countertop.

I moved to stand beside her, reaching my good arm out and lifting her chin with my index finger. Her eyes met mine. "You made me a promise."

Her eyes pooled with tears, a few sliding down her cheeks. "I'm right here," she whispered. I shook my head.

"You're a million miles away in your memories, the bad ones." I leaned toward her, placing my lips against the shell of her ear. "Come back to me, Aida. Please, stay with me."

I straightened, lowering my hand to the countertop in front of her. She closed her eyes, her breath hitching as she began crying more. My beautiful, spirited queen was broken. Not in the way she was used to, but in an entirely new way. The kind that you never really healed from but eventually pushed down deep enough to forget for a while.

I stared at her hand near the base of the margarita glass. Her purple nail polish was chipped as usual, her skin looking so soft, delicate. That's what she was despite her tough exterior and upbringing. Regardless of the fact that she'd killed several men in less than an hour. Aida was delicate, like the roses she smelled of.

As I admired her hand, I noticed it slowly slide toward mine. Her index finger traced the outline of the heart tattoo near the base of my thumb. I shivered from the touch as longing filled me.

"Why did you get this tattoo?" she asked.

I smiled down at the faded black ink before meeting her curious gaze again. "When I first started working for my uncle, before I ever took the vow to become a spy, I'd learned that vengeance and hatred could only destroy your soul. It turns everything a dull gray, crushes your spirit, and leaves you empty." I shrugged. "I got this tattoo as a reminder."

"A reminder of what?" she asked.

I slid my thumb along the back of her hand, holding her gaze. "Well now, it reminds me of you. Before that, it was just a word." I swallowed the lump that formed in my throat as she raised a brow.

"What?"

"Love, Aida," I replied. "It's a reminder of love and it helps pull me back."

She smiled up at me and my heart felt like it was going to beat right out of my chest. That smile, I'd do anything to see it. Unable to stop myself, I bent again, lowering my lips toward hers. She trembled when I cupped her cheek.

"I love you," I said, pressing my lips against hers.

It was a quick kiss, not nearly as long as I would have liked, but that was my intention. I wasn't trying to make out with her in my uncle's kitchen right now. Okay, I would totally be down for that if she was, but that wasn't the point.

No, the point was to tell her that I loved her because I did, with everything I had. I loved her more than I ever thought was possible for a guy like me. She was the sun and stars, the beauty in the ugliness of the world, the only person who ever challenged me and won.

Aida Ricci was mine, but not as an object or a trophy. She was so much more than any earthly thing. She was *everything* and she owned my heart completely.

She still had the smile on her face as she looked into my eyes. "I love you, Fabiano Cuccione."

I grinned at her, tucking her hair behind her ear. "I know you do, babe."

In that moment, I had her back with me. It would take time for her to grieve over the man she killed and the others who were no longer with us. Loss wasn't easy, no matter what the circumstances.

She'd have nightmares, like me. Probably for years to come. But as long as I could pull her out of her own head and

remind her to keep going, she'd be okay. I knew that because
Aida Ricci, the enemy's daughter, had been doing that for me
since the first time I'd gotten lost in those ocean eyes.

THE END

K. MORGAN

www.melissakmorgan.com
Instagram: @melissa_k_morgan
Email: authormelissakmorgan@gmail.com

ACKNOWLEDGEMENTS

First and foremost I want to thank you, the reader for taking the time to read this story. I hope that you were entertained and that you'll leave a review on Amazon and/or Goodreads. It's because of people like you that I am able to continue doing what I love, which is sharing stories with the world. Thank you. Second, I want to thank my incredible husband who is always supportive and encourages me to keep going even when I struggle with that dreaded imposter syndrome and doubt. Thank you for always listening to me when I'm plotting, when I ask weird questions for book research purposes, and for allowing me the opportunity to get work done. I'd be lost without your wise words and funny jokes.

I'd also like to thank my amazing team at Aurora Publicity for keeping me motivated! Cam, I love that you love Steven (because you refuse to call him Fabiano) and that you help me in making my stories better than I ever could on my own. I'd be lost without you. Seriously. You're stuck with me. To Melody, cover designer extraordinaire! You take my jumbled up descriptions of what I want and create absolute beauty. I am so grateful for your ability and brilliance. I'm so excited to continue authoring more books and sharing them with you all.

<u>**Silver Series**</u>

Something to Believe In, Book #1
*She's nothing he expected. He's nothing she wanted.
Mackaela Stone is damaged. Haunted by her past, she's
worked hard to wall herself off from ever repeating the
mistakes that left her feeling too filthy for love. But meeting
Simon Silver might be enough to crack those fortifications—if
he can overcome his own turbulent history.
Trusting one another is hard enough, but finding faith, hope
and love may be more than they can manage. Is their
connection enough to give them something to believe in? Or is
the damage done too great to overcome?*

Something to Hold Onto, Book #2
*She was supposed to be the key to everything he ever wanted.
He was the shadow of a past she swore she'd leave behind.
Claire Evan's is risking it all. She knew her new job—working
for the golden boy of Seattle, Mickey Silver—might be too good
to be true. But the perks of playing his game were more than
she could resist, even if the price included being dragged
deeper into his cruel, dark world. Now his game of revenge
may take them both down a path of mutual destruction.
Can working together finally open their eyes to what matters
most? Or will the cost of cold ambition leave them both broken
and alone?*

<u>Standalone Contemporary Romances</u>

Always Beautiful

Sometimes fate doesn't just throw you a curve ball, it hits you in the face. Breaking your nose, blackening your eyes, and making you second guess everything you've spent your entire life working toward. Do you ignore that ball and continue in the direction of security and stability? Or do you throw caution to the wind, follow your heart, and potentially become so damaged that you'll never recover?

Experiencing an intensity she's never known, a passion she's never felt, and a way to escape the mundane has Lucky changing her once solid foundation. But seasons change and so do people. When she discovers Zeppelin is hiding something from her, those walls she let fall so easily begin to build back up. Zeppelin finally reveals his devastating secret and Lucky is left with two choices. Walk away and forget him entirely or take his hand and follow him into the darkness and sorrow.

Self-Inflicted

I'm the queen of self-sabotage.

A messy, chaotic downer with a heart buried so deep in the dark depths of my body, I'm not sure it can ever be found. Then I meet Remington Paulson - my new stepbrother.

He makes me glow despite the rusted patina of trauma coating my soul and forces me to consider taking a stand for the first time in my life. So why do I want to break his heart?

I swear I didn't know she was my stepsister when I pursued the most beautiful, scowling creature I'd ever seen.

The moment I tasted those cherry lips and experienced an unguarded version of her, I fell hard.

Nothing in life is easy, but that hasn't stopped me from barreling head-first into making my dreams come true. Layla Barlow will be mine. I don't care if the entire world knows it.